"I understand the Enterprise *is ready to get under way. . . .*

I hope you were able to enjoy some of the brief leave time you had while here on Earth?"

"Yes, Madam President, thank you," Picard answered, wondering.

"And you're wondering why I'm bothering to call you, while you're waiting to receive your next orders," the president said, interrupting his thoughts.

Picard allowed himself a small smile. "I admit, the question did occur to me, ma'am."

"Captain," Admiral Akaar interjected, *"this isn't being shared outside of Command, but the fleet is in far worse shape than is being publicized. We have possibly billions of homeless refugees to resettle; catastrophic damages suffered on Vulcan, Andor, and Tellar; not to mention the help the Klingons are going to need from us, with Qo'noS now barely habitable."*

Intellectually speaking, none of this was particularly shocking to Picard. But hearing it so bluntly, he felt his heart fall in his chest. "I see."

President Bacco leaned forward, elbows on her desk, and looked directly at Picard. *"The debt the Federation owes you can never be adequately repaid, Jean-Luc. And I wanted to be certain you understood that this assignment is in no way meant to diminish that."*

Picard nodded, and waited.

OTHER BOOKS FEATURING
STAR TREK: THE NEXT GENERATION

STAR TREK

THE NEXT GENERATION®

LOSING THE PEACE

WILLIAM LEISNER

Based on
Star Trek® and
Star Trek: The Next Generation
created by Gene Roddenberry

POCKET BOOKS
New York   London   Toronto   Sydney

Pocket Books
A Division of Simon & Schuster, Inc.
1230 Avenue of the Americas
New York, NY 10020

This book is a work of fiction. Names, characters, places, and incidents either are products of the author's imagination or are used fictitiously. Any resemblance to actual events or locales or persons, living or dead, is entirely coincidental.

First Pocket Books paperback edition July 2009

POCKET and colophon are registered trademarks of Simon & Schuster, Inc.

For information about special discounts for bulk purchases, please contact Simon & Schuster Special Sales at 1-866-506-1949 or business@simonandschuster.com.

The Simon & Schuster Speakers Bureau can bring authors to your live event. For more information or to book an event, contact the Simon & Schuster Speakers Bureau at 1-866-248-3049 or visit our website at www.simonspeakers.com.

Cover art by John Blackford; cover design by Alan Dingman

Manufactured in the United States of America

10 9 8 7 6 5 4 3 2 1

ISBN 978-1-4391-0786-7
ISBN 978-1-4391-2341-6 (ebook)

To those who survive
and who persevere

HISTORIAN'S NOTE

The main events in this book take place in late February to early March of 2361 (ACE). This is just after the Borg Invasion and the Caeliar's resolution of the crisis (*Star Trek: Destiny—Book III: Lost Souls*) and prior to the Federation's discovery of a new force at work in the galaxy (*Star Trek: A Singular Destiny*).

But to my mind, it is of vast importance that our people reach some general understanding of what the complications really are, rather than react from a passion or a prejudice or an emotion of the moment. As I said more formally a moment ago, we are remote from the scene of these troubles. It is virtually impossible at this distance merely by reading, or listening, or even seeing photographs or motion pictures, to grasp at all the real significance of the situation. And yet the whole world of the future hangs on a proper judgment.

—George C. Marshall,
U.S. Secretary of State
June 5, 1947

PROLOGUE

"Here's to the Borg: may they all rot and burn in hell!"

A new wave of cheers filled the transport ship's Latinum Lounge, as various glasses of alcohol—the genuine article; replicated or syntheholic drinks wouldn't do for such an occasion—were raised aloft to celebrate the greatest feat in Federation history since the defeat of the Dominion, perhaps since the very founding of the Federation itself.

Arandis raised her glass also, though hers was filled only with quinine water. She had never actually left Risa before—like most Risians, she never felt any desire to do so—and had been fighting space-sickness since leaving orbit. But she never let anyone else see her discomfort; a good hostess, after all, always put her guests' needs above her own. Even though they were all light-years away from Risa, these people were still technically guests of the Temtibi Lagoon Resort, making their contentment her responsibility.

Keeping them content hadn't been easy, either, at least not at first. The order to evacuate the planet had gone out earlier that morning, "just as a precaution," as the Minister of Safety had put it in his broadcast. Arandis knew that there had been a series of sneak attacks on other Federation worlds over the past several weeks, and in response, Starfleet had assigned a fleet of six starships to defend her homeworld. But then today, just as she was getting the weekly beach hoverball tournament under way, reports had started coming in of a massive armada of Borg cubes breaking a combined Starfleet, Klingon, and Romulan blockade at the Azure Nebula, and fanning out all across the Alpha and Beta quadrants. All events were canceled, and the guests were all ushered out of the resort, as quickly and calmly as possible, and taken to the nearby spaceport.

There had been only minimal panic, thank the Givers. The simple mention of the Borg was enough to inspire horror in the hearts of most citizens of the Federation. This was particularly true of her human guests; all the Borg incursions into the Alpha quadrant had been targeted against their homeworld, Earth, the most recent one having come less than a year earlier. But Arandis made it a point to take those worried souls aside, place a comforting hand on their shoulders, and remind them that, in all those past incidents, Starfleet had been successful in ultimately defeating the cybernetic invaders. And she let them know that she had complete faith that Starfleet would ultimately save them all once again.

And her faith had been rewarded. The Borg had been defeated—not just this invasion force, but the entire race, having been transformed in some way that she did not understand. When the transport's pilots relayed the news they were learning through official channels, the entire passenger cabin—which until then had seemed to be holding its collective breath—erupted into a near-deafening victory roar. When Arandis later learned that one of the three ships most instrumental in Starfleet's triumph was commanded by Captain Ezri Dax, the current host of her dear, sweet friend Curzon's Trill symbiont, she felt a particular surge of pride in Starfleet's accomplishment fill her chest.

Arandis moved through the crowded lounge in the direction of the bar, making certain everyone's glasses were filled and none of her guests wanted for anything. As she signaled to one of her assistants to bring a drink tray around to the far corner of the room, she was intercepted by the man who had made the latest toast—a young human with tousled sandy blond hair, wearing multicolored beachwear and still sporting a striped hotel beach towel around his neck. "Hey, sweetheart!" he said, flashing her a broad, inebriated smile. "Izza great day, izinit?" he said, raising his wineglass to her.

She had to fight back a new wave of space-sickness, triggered by the overpowering scent of alcohol on his breath. Her young guest—Donald Wheeler, she remembered, was his name—had been drinking fairly heavily during the news blackout in the first hours after the evacuation, and he had continued to do so following the victory announcement. "Yes, it is, Donald," Arandis said with a smile, giving his arm a grazing touch as she turned to move along.

Wheeler caught hold of her wrist, not tightly, but firmly enough to force her to turn back to him. "So, I was thinkin', we oughta celebrate this momon . . . mo . . . momentous moment in history," he told her, struggling mightily to make his lips and tongue do what he wanted them to. "I forgot my *horga'hn* on Risa, so's it okay to just out and out say, I want me some *jamaharon* with you, darling?"

Arandis gave him a perfect, practiced smile. "Of course; all that is ours is yours," she told him, "but it would be impossible, with so many others on so small a vessel, to establish the proper ambience."

"Hey, I'm on vacation." Wheeler gave her what he no doubt thought was a charming wink and loosened his hold on her wrist, running his fingers up her arm. "I don't need to be proper."

Without letting her smile waver, Arandis removed the man's hand and pressed it gently between both of hers. "You may seek *jamaharon*," she said, looking him in his brown, bleary eyes, "but you will not find it with this outlook. It is not merely a physical experience, but an emotional and spiritual one." As long as Arandis had worked in the guest service industry, it never ceased to amaze her how many visitors came to Risa claiming to seek *jamaharon,* thinking it was nothing but an exotic form of copulation, as if her people had no deeper philosophies than simple hedonism. "But I promise you, once we have returned to Risa, that I will show you how all these aspects, properly combined, can become something greater and unexpected."

Wheeler gazed back into her eyes for a moment, as if he had momentarily seen something within them beyond the superficial. Then the moment was over. "I need me a *horga'hn,*" he shouted as he turned away from her, nearly sloshing his glass of red wine down the back of the Bolian man behind him. "C'mon! Who's got a *horga'hn* I can borrow?" he called, moving away as he scanned the lounge for someone who wasn't pointedly ignoring him.

As relieved as she was to have him move away, Arandis regretted that she couldn't meet his desires. That was, after all, the nature of the Risian people. She resolved, once they'd returned to Risa (and Wheeler had hopefully sobered up somewhat), to seek him out and offer to rectify the situation. Arandis glanced at the ornate old clock that hung behind the lounge's bar, noting that it was getting close to first sunset back home—time for the evening banquet. A grand seafood feast had been planned for this evening, with over two dozen different dishes harvested fresh from Risa's crystal blue oceans, to be followed by a choice of . . .

Arandis looked again at the bejeweled clock,

and it struck her that they'd been aboard this vessel for almost eight hours. News of the Borg's defeat had come about three and a half hours after they left Risa. Shouldn't they have turned around at that point? And if they had, shouldn't they have made it back to Risa an hour ago? Thinking back now, Arandis didn't recall the ship slowing from its high-warp speed away from the Borg, nor did she feel it executing any kind of course change. Of course, as unfamiliar with space travel as she was, she wouldn't be expected to. And maybe there was a very good engineering reason why the second leg of their flight was taking longer than the first—subspace eddies and anomalies, all sorts of things her Starfleet friends would often talk about.

When another hour went by, Arandis realized it wasn't subspace anomalies, and she noticed more and more guests, like herself, regularly glancing at the antique timepiece with confused expressions playing across their faces. Arandis instructed the other members of the Temtibi Lagoon staff to start offering more hors d'oeuvres along with the drinks, while she slipped out of the lounge and moved forward through the restricted areas of the vessel to the cockpit.

She made her way down an unfamiliar corridor, and after a moment's hesitation, pressed the signal chime at the sealed forward hatch. Once she identified herself as director of the resort where the passengers had been staying, the door opened, and a tall, perfectly muscled and toned Risian male, wearing the uniform of the Risian Safety Ministry, stepped out. "Is something wrong?" he asked her, his brow furrowing around the gold-hued *ja'risia* on his forehead. "What is the mood amongst our guests?"

"They are generally content," Arandis answered, confused. "What's happening? Why have we not yet returned to Risa?"

The man's placid blue eyes started to fill with tears as he first looked over Arandis's shoulder for eavesdroppers, then fixed his sad gaze on her. "Because . . . there is no more Risa."

Arandis simply stared for a moment. Then a mirthless laugh escaped her tightening throat. "What do you mean, 'no more Risa'?"

"I mean, the Borg razed the planet," he answered, his tone harsh and rough. "They killed every living thing. There's nothing . . ." His voice cracked, and he covered his mouth with his hand.

"No," Arandis said in disbelief. "The Borg were beaten. Starfleet . . . the reports said . . ."

"The Borg weren't beaten until after they had reached Risa," the officer said. "We kept those reports from being piped back to the passengers; it would only have upset . . . the images they were showing . . ."

Arandis stopped listening as every other conscious thought fled her mind, as if washed away with the tide, with only the maddening roar of waves filling her head.

No more Risa.

It was too enormous, too unimaginable. How could Starfleet have failed them? There had been six ships, with hundreds of crew on each. Had they all been killed too? And Risa itself . . . Catona Bluff was gone. The Tolari Tower, from now on, existed only in her memory. There was no longer any such thing as a Risian Grand Delight. Arandis felt her knees begin to buckle underneath her . . .

"We can't tell the guests, not yet," the officer said, pulling Arandis back from the edge of madness. "Our first responsibility is to them."

"Yes, of course," she agreed in a forced whisper. *All that is ours is yours,* she intoned in her thoughts.

All that is ours is gone.

"But it won't be long until they start to realize something is wrong," she added aloud.

The officer gave her what was supposed to be an encouraging smile. "This is like all moments: only temporary. We shall endure it, and then forget it in the better ones to follow."

Arandis returned his smile and nodded as he spoke the old proverb. But when he withdrew back into the cockpit and closed the hatch, her smile quickly fell away. *This is more than a single moment,* she said to herself as she started back down the short enclosed corridor to the main passenger cabin. *Risa is gone. My whole world . . . my whole race. . . . How could something like this be simply forgotten?*

She reached the hatch to the cabin, then stopped and doubled over as she purged the contents of her stomach, for reasons that had nothing to do with space-sickness.

1

———

The boy lay on the grassy hillside, the back of his head cradled in the roots of the old poplar tree, staring up into the infinite nighttime sky. Below him, the entire valley seemed asleep, with only a few scattered lights coming from the windows of its farmhouses and villages. The near perfect darkness made even the dimmest stars of the Milky Way shine like lighthouse beacons, guiding ship captains on their long journeys across the sea of space.

"Jean-Luc!"

The boy did not hear the voice coming from the direction of the house at first—or rather, he chose not to hear it. He didn't want to have to give up this place, this memory frozen in time. He kept his eyes and his imagination fixed on the stars above.

"Jean-Luc!" a second, younger voice called from much closer by, accompanied by the rustling of grass and snap of twigs. The boy's thoughts now fell away from the sky and down to earth. Specifically, he wished for the ground underneath to open up and swallow him, hiding him from the pair looking for him.

But to no avail. "Here you are!" the boy crowed triumphantly, leaping from out of nowhere and landing his heavy work boots on either side of Jean-Luc's waist. "Dreaming again, are you, *mon petit frère*?" Robert grinned down at him, long dark hair flopping over his eyes. He had always been the bigger of the two brothers, and in the summer of his twelfth year, he had gained a full ten centimeters. "Don't you know what monsters lurk in the dark?"

Robert then let out a roar and fell atop his younger brother. The boy put his arms up to ward off the attack, catching the other in the chest and easily deflecting him. He then rolled in the same direction, seating himself on the bigger boy's stomach and pinning his shoulders to the ground with both hands—though only momentarily, before their positions reversed again. Arms and legs flailed as they wrestled wildly, his brother laughing as he grabbed his wrists and pinned them to the ground. The boy was surprised to find himself laughing as well, finding the roughhouse play strangely liberating, and he laughed even louder.

"Enough fighting," came the first voice again from just overhead. "There will be no more fighting."

Robert jumped off his brother and went to stand beside his father. "What are you doing out here in the dark, *mon garçon*?" Maurice Picard asked in a deep, authoritative voice. Despite his bald pate and deeply lined face, prematurely aged by a lifetime tending to the vineyard, his sharp eyes and hawk-like nose marked him as a man one did not lightly cross. "Dreaming again?"

"No, Papa," the boy fibbed. "I was just . . . I couldn't fall asleep, and I . . ." He hesitated, knowing there was no point in trying to lie; his father knew full well that his younger son did not share his feelings of obligation to tradition, and had no desire to remain forever bound to the place in which he had happened, by chance, to be born. And he knew there was no avoiding his father's disappointment in that regard.

But strangely, his father's scowl fell away, and a broad smile flashed across his weathered face. He lowered himself onto one knee and put a large, calloused hand on the young boy's shoulder. "You need to be true to yourself, Jean-Luc," the older man told him. "What I've given you—our name, our land, our traditions—was only a foundation, not a limitation. And no matter where else you go and what else you do, it will always be yours."

The boy smiled, and then threw his arms around his father's neck, hugging him with an entire life-time of unexpressed emotion. Papa returned the embrace, and after an indeterminable time, they let go and fell back, along with Robert, onto their backs in the grass. The stars looked close enough now that Jean-Luc thought he could reach out and touch them.

"All we're seeing now is old light," Maurice said. "The stars we see are how they appeared years and years ago."

"The past is the past," Robert added. "To know what is now, you have to go out and explore on your own, eh?"

That sounded like a grand idea, Jean-Luc thought as he closed his eyes and continued to dream. *A grand idea, indeed . . .*

"Jean-Luc?"

Picard opened his eyes again, and was surprised to find that the starlit vista above Château Picard had been replaced by a sky of brilliant blue. He was further surprised to realize the figure before him calling his name was not his father or brother, but his wife. Beverly Crusher smiled down at him, standing so that her shadow fell over him, shading his eyes from the brightness of midday. With the sun at her back, she appeared as a classical angel, surrounded by an ephemeral light, her long red tresses like flames as loose strands flew in the breeze. She had no wings, of course, and her rounded, pregnant stomach was also at odds with the traditional depiction of asexual divine messengers, but as far as Jean-Luc Picard was concerned, she was most definitely a heavenly being. "What are you doing out here?" she asked him, amusement in her tone.

"Not napping, certainly," Picard said, grinning

up at her as he pushed up into a sitting position. "Only old men doze off in the middle of the day."

"Old men, and exhausted ship's captains," Crusher retorted, smiling back sweetly at him. "You're supposed to be on rest leave, and you need all you can get," she told him.

Picard refrained from contradicting the doctor. They were at his ancestral home in Labarre while the *Enterprise* was in drydock at McKinley Station, undergoing repairs to the widespread damage it had suffered during the most recent conflict with the Borg. He'd slept little during the crisis, of course, and had operated almost exclusively on adrenaline and sheer willpower when awake.

Despite all that, he did not feel exhausted. What he experienced at the end of the war—witnessing the dismantling of the Borg collective by the Caeliar, and sharing, in a limited way, the absorption of billions of former drones into the Caeliar gestalt— relieved him of his fatigue, instead filling him with pure joy as he was finally emancipated from his lingering, fifteen-year link to the Borg.

Beverly lowered herself onto the grass beside her husband. Spring was officially still a few weeks away, but already the world around them was coming back to life in a riot of green. "Though, if you are going to nap," she said as she settled in and leaned backwards against his chest, "you might pick a more comfortable spot for it."

Picard chuckled as he slipped his arms around her and laid his cheek on the top of her head. "This actually has always been my favorite spot on the entire estate," he said. "I would sit or lie here for hours, watching the Paris-bound shuttles by day and the stars by night. Of course, part of that was the fact that, if I lay in just the right position, I couldn't be spotted from the house." He looked back over his shoulder at that house now—or rather, the house his sister-in-law, Marie, had rebuilt on the original's foundation following the tragic fire that had claimed the lives of Robert and his son, René. It was a near-perfect re-creation; if not for the loss of the roof-high shade trees closest to the house, he would have no trouble imagining himself over a half century back in time. "I had a most curious dream," he mentioned as the nostalgia washed over him again.

"Oh?"

Picard nodded. "I was a boy again, lying here, staring up at the stars. My father and brother came looking for me, and when they found me . . ." Picard paused significantly before continuing, "Father gave me his blessing to leave home, to follow my dreams." He smiled at the marvel of it. "Robert and I were able to reconcile before he died. But Father . . ." His voice broke momentarily. Beverly shifted her position so that she could look at him directly once he was able to continue. "I was away, on the *Stargazer,* when he died, and I'd always assumed that, to the end, he stayed as stubborn as he ever was in life." So certain of this was he that, when Q had presented him with a vision of his father during his own near-death experience, Jean-Luc had no trouble accepting bitter, disappointed old man as an accurate representation.

That negative image fell away now. "I feel now, though, that I've finally been given his absolution," Picard told Beverly, smiling again. "That all those old wounds have at long last been healed."

"That's wonderful, Jean-Luc," Beverly said, smiling back. "I know your relationship was troubled for a long time, and I'm glad you've finally found peace with your father's memory." She took one of Picard's hands and placed it on her swollen abdomen. "And I know your experience is going to make you an even better father to our son."

He answered by leaning forward to kiss her mouth. Jean-Luc Picard could not remember another time in his life when he had felt such peace and contentment.

"You know," Beverly said once their lips had parted again, "when you told me just now that you had a curious dream, I thought for a moment you were going to tell me . . ."

"What?" Picard prompted.

Hesitantly, as if afraid of bringing on a curse, she continued, ". . . that you dreamed about the Borg again."

Picard blinked in surprise. "Why . . . ?" he began, then stopped. "No, Beverly," he assured her. "The Borg are gone, forever, from here and everywhere."

Crusher nodded, though she clearly did not feel

Picard's confidence. "Yes. But . . . we've thought they were gone before."

Picard sighed. He wished that he could share with her the absolute certainty that had been conveyed to him by the Caeliar—or whatever they and their newly liberated brethren had now become. All he could do was to look deep into his loved one's eyes and tell her, with all the conviction he could muster, "Beverly, believe me when I tell you: There are no more Borg. They are never coming back. We are all free."

Beverly stared back, and then allowed herself a small smile of relief. "Of course I believe you, Jean-Luc. Always."

Geordi La Forge turned his face up to the equatorial sun high overhead, letting its warmth wash over him. There were still a few weeks left until the rainy season came to this part of the African Confederation, and it was significantly warmer than he was used to on the *Enterprise*. But he couldn't very well complain about that.

Because, after all . . . he was home.

From his vantage point atop the metal bleachers bordering the Zefram Cochrane High School athletic field, he could see the Mogadishu skyline to the southeast and—by virtue of his cybernetic optical implants—the Indian Ocean beyond. Old-fashioned sailboats drifted lazily on the blue waters that lapped against the pristine white beaches along the Somalian coast. It was hard to believe the city had been largely destroyed in the years between the second and third world wars, and abandoned to rival militias. The ancient port city experienced a renaissance in the late twenty-second century, and was rebuilt in a manner that reflected its long history as a major trade center, using the most modern architectural techniques. It may not have been Paris or San Francisco, but it was as pristine and perfect a city as any other on the paradisiacal world called Earth.

And on the field, he was watching the Cochrane Flyers face off against their crosstown rivals, the Mogadishu Central High Scorpions. The school band played as, all around him, the other spectators shouted encouragement to the players or chatted among themselves about nothing in particular. All of a sudden, the entire crowd jumped to its feet and exploded in a mighty roaring cheer. Geordi stood up a second later and saw the Flyers celebrating what must have been an impressive goal.

"So help me, Geordi, if that was my kid scoring a goal you made me miss . . ."

La Forge turned and saw his sister, Ariana, climbing the bleacher steps toward him, carrying a disposable cup in each hand and wearing a disappointed frown. His eyes flicked fleetingly to the playing field, and he noticed that his niece, Nadifa, seemed to be at the middle of the celebratory circle. She beamed and waved as she spotted her mother and uncle in the stands.

Geordi waved back meekly as he relieved his sister of one of the cups. Where the hell had his mind been during her score? "Sorry, 'Riana," he said.

Ariana gave him a look that eerily mirrored the ones their mother would use any time her young children tested her patience. With her now-free hand, she swatted her brother on the back of the head—playfully, but still with a touch more force than necessary. "Next time, *you* get the drinks."

"Hey, I offered," he said as he sat and took a sip. "Ugh . . . I should have insisted," Geordi continued, his face twisted in reaction to the tart concoction.

"What? I thought you loved *isbarmuunto,*" she said.

"Is that what it is? I thought it was straight lemon juice on ice."

"Starfleet has spoiled you. Made you—"

Ariana stopped suddenly, and her teasing smile disappeared at just the same moment Geordi snapped his head in her direction, jaw set tight. They stared at each other like that for several seconds, while play resumed on the field.

"I should rephrase that," Ariana eventually noted.

Without acknowledging her words, Geordi said, "I'm going to go stretch my legs a bit."

"I'll come with you."

"No, stay." Already on his feet, he made his way down the bleacher steps. "There might be another goal, or something else just as important." He started walking aimlessly away from the field.

"Geordi!"

Ignoring his sister, La Forge continued idly in the direction of the school building, sipping his drink. A group of teenagers congregated on the library steps, talking and giggling and carrying on the same way Geordi had done over half a lifetime ago.

"Geordi!"

He knew he was probably making more than he ought to of what was just a thoughtless comment. On the other hand, Ariana had been unapologetically disdainful of Starfleet since she'd been Nadifa's age. She hated that their parents spent so little time living together while their kids were growing up, with one or the other usually off on some mission at any given time during their childhoods. She hated that, once she had turned eighteen and headed off to college, Mom decided to switch back to the command track and pursue her own starship command—a decision that eventually led to her disappearance over ten years ago. She hated that their father was three hundred light-years beyond Federation space aboard the *U.S.S. Amalthea,* one of the new *Luna*-class explorers (although she admitted to being grateful that his ship had been too far off to be called back during the recent threat).

Geordi, for his part, hated how much she looked down on the life he'd chosen, though he normally kept it to himself. Now just wasn't a very normal time.

"Geordi!" Ariana shouted again as she caught up

with her big brother, one hand holding her head-dress atop her head. "Hey, I'm sorry, you know I didn't mean it."

Geordi stopped, but did not look at her. Instead, he slowly turned in a half circle, taking in the whole of the school grounds. "It all looks the same as always, doesn't it?" he asked, gesturing to the field, the students, the trees and the sky. "So normal, like nothing happened. You would have no idea, seeing all this, how close we all came to losing it all."

"Well, that's not fair," Ariana countered. "You weren't here when things were looking their worst. There wasn't much normality then."

Geordi was sure that was true, but still . . . "But it didn't take you long to go right back to soccer games and picnic lunches, did it."

"And what are we supposed to do?" Ariana asked. "Cover ourselves in ashes and sackcloth and beg the universe for mercy? Life goes on, Geordi."

"For *you*," Geordi snapped. "Never mind the billions of people who weren't so lucky!"

Then it was as if time just stopped. Ariana stared with her expression frozen, stunned by his bitter words. And Geordi felt just as stunned, mortified that such vitriol could have come from him. "Oh, my God," he said in a strangled whisper. "'Riana, I'm sorry. I don't know what . . ."

His sister shook her head. "Don't be sorry, Geordi."

"I didn't mean it," he insisted. "I just . . . I don't know . . ."

"I know you didn't. You gotta stop beating yourself up, Geordi."

"But that was a horrible thing to say!" Geordi nearly shouted. "I have no right blaming you for what happened!"

Ariana reached out and put a gentle hand on her brother's arm. "And you have no right to blame yourself, either."

Geordi felt as if all his insides were contracting. "Wh-what?"

"You lived, Geordi." His sister looked him directly in his cybernetic eyes. "You can't let yourself feel guilty for that."

His mouth moved up and down a few seconds before he was able to form sound again. "I . . . what? That's . . . that's ridiculous. I don't feel guilty . . ."

"I know you better than that, Geordi La Forge. You survived the Borg when billions died. This after surviving them about a half dozen times before, and surviving the Dominion, and the Tezwans, and the Remans. You've outlived Mom. You've outlived Data . . ."

He almost felt like he was going to double over. "That's stupid," he insisted, as tears welled up around his implants. Yes, it had been a hard few years, and yes, all these deaths had hit him hard, especially Data's, who had been his best friend for years and who was supposed to live for centuries, but . . . "I shouldn't feel guilty for living . . ."

"No," Ariana told him. "You shouldn't."

La Forge clamped his eyes shut, but that

couldn't keep the tears from starting to pour. He felt Ariana pull him into a hard embrace, and he returned it, wrapping his arms tight around her and burying his face in her shoulder. He felt like an idiot, letting his little sister see him like this. "I'm very proud of you, big brother," Ariana told him softly, "for putting on that uniform and going out there so that we *can* all live here safely and have picnics and play soccer and all that. But I'm also very, very grateful that you get to come back every once in a while and share it with us."

Brother and sister stood like that for a long time, as the game and the world went on around them.

The suborbital shuttle caught up with and passed the sun minutes after leaving Paris, on its way to San Francisco. Picard watched the clouds below as he replayed his earlier conversation with Beverly in his mind. If this meeting turned out to be anything like the others he'd taken part in over the past week—and he had no reason to think it wouldn't—he would need to cling to the assurance that there was at least one person in the universe who had complete faith in him.

It had been eight days now since his return to Earth, and half of those days had been spent in stuffy conference rooms, briefing Starfleet Command, then President Bacco and the Federation Security Council, then representatives of the governments of Earth, Luna, Mars, and other Sol system colonies, repeating over and over his account of the end of the Borg collective. And in each of those meetings, one question would inevitably be asked, repeatedly, in a number of different ways, couched in hypotheticals and vague expressions of distrust, but all boiling down to one simple concern: *How can you be so completely certain the Borg are really gone forever?*

To which, Picard could really only give one answer: "I just *know*."

He had felt the cataclysmic metamorphosis as it happened. He'd sensed the severing of every single drone from the collective, and then felt the embrace of the Caeliar gestalt, taking in all those lost souls and making them a part of themselves. It was the single most remarkable experience of his life . . . and there was no one else in the universe who could truly understand it.

The shuttle landed on the grounds of Starfleet Command, and Picard was met on the tarmac by a young female human in security gold. "Captain Picard?"

"Yes."

"I'm here to escort you to your appointment," she said, her spine perfectly stiff, a sure sign that she had been wearing the pip on her collar for only a very short time. Picard had heard that most of this year's Academy seniors were granted their commissions early, so they would be ready to deploy on short notice, just in case. With the estimates of Starfleet losses during the Borg assault at over forty percent, there would still have to be a major recruitment effort to bring forces anywhere close to what would be considered secure levels.

They rode the lift in silence to the Headquarters building's uppermost floor—the sanctum sanctorum of the admiralty—and then the ensign led him through the dimly lit corridor lined with portraits of Starfleet's past leaders, arranged in no discernible order; a white-haired human in the dark jacket and necktie of the pre-Federation era hung beside an Andorian in the gold-green silken dress tunic of the following century.

Presently, they reached a set of solid double doors, and the ensign gestured to Picard to place his hand on the security panel beside it. The captain did so, and the doors parted with a slight mechanical moan to reveal what appeared to be an oversized holosuite.

Today's briefing would be for the benefit of the members of Starfleet's admiralty stationed off-Earth, who would be attending via holocom. A long table was positioned at one end of the room, facing the open space that would soon be filled with holographic images of those flag officers who would be participating from afar. A small handful of HQ-based admirals were also here: Leonard James Akaar and Marta Batanides stood talking at the near end of the table, while Admirals Masc, Batiste, and Montgomery were huddled in the far corner, engaged in what appeared to be a rather animated discussion. Picard was approached by the sixth admiral present, Alynna Nechayev. "Good morning, Captain Picard."

"Good morning, Admiral," he echoed automatically, even though his body was telling him it was early evening. "I take it we're just waiting now for Admiral Jellico?"

Nechayev frowned slightly. "No, I'm afraid not," she said. "The admiral last night tendered his resignation to President Bacco."

Picard's head snapped back at that. "He what? Why?"

"Don't be obtuse, Picard," Nechayev said, scowling at him. "The man was the commander of Starfleet during the greatest debacle in all of recorded history. Whatever else you may think of Edward Jellico, he is a man of honor who has always taken responsibility for his actions and decisions. And that's what he's done now."

"I have never questioned Admiral Jellico's honor," Picard quickly asserted. He'd questioned many of the senior officer's decisions over the years, as well as his tendency to turn a deaf ear to contrary viewpoints once he'd made up his mind on a given matter. "But still, he shouldn't have felt obligated to fall on his sword because of this," Picard continued. "What happened was beyond the power of any mortal being to control."

Nechayev sighed and nodded. "I essentially told him the same thing. I suspect it was the lack of control that finally pushed him to his decision."

Picard didn't know what more to say. He'd butted heads with Jellico more than a few times, and he had not thought much of the decision, following Admiral William Ross's well-earned retirement last autumn, to promote Jellico to fleet commander. All things being equal, he couldn't honestly say he was sorry to see Jellico step down.

But "things" were not equal anymore. Starfleet had suffered devastating losses, and the loss of the man at the top of the chain of command could only serve as one more complicating factor in getting the organization back on track.

His thoughts were interrupted by the sound of the doors opening again. Picard turned, and for a split second failed to recognize the tall blond woman who entered. Part of that was due to her face, which now lacked the metallic Borg implants that had encircled her left eye and pierced her neck just below her right ear. But the more striking difference was the way in which she carried herself. Seven of Nine, the former Borg drone who had been liberated by the crew of the *U.S.S. Voyager* seven years earlier, had always struck Picard as one of the most self-confident people he'd ever encountered—a trait made all the more impressive by the fact that she had been stripped of her individuality at the age of eight.

However, that quality was now gone. Though she put on a good show of fearlessness, the woman who entered the conference room clearly wished to be any place else.

"Captain?" Picard turned again, and then looked up to meet the gaze of Admiral Akaar. "If you'll take your seat; we're just about ready to begin," the imposing Capellan said.

Picard moved behind the table and took the chair indicated, which happened to be right beside the late arrival. She sat, hands folded in her lap, clearly straining to keep the perfect posture that had always seemed to come naturally to her. "Hello, Annika," Picard said to her, with a small, friendly grin.

The woman flinched in response and jerked her head to the left. "Captain Picard," she said, and quickly turned to face forward again.

Realizing he'd committed a faux pas, Picard added, "I'm sorry, Professor . . . I assumed you no longer favor your Borg designation." In earlier encounters, the woman had objected to the use of her human name, Annika Hansen, insisting for whatever personal reasons on retaining her Borg designation. Given recent events, the captain had thought she would understandably feel different about it now.

"It is irrelevant," she said, without looking back at him.

Picard stared quizzically at her profile for a moment longer, noting the tightness of her jaw and neck. What he had felt during the Caeliar's merging with the Borg—what he had felt in concert with the entire Collective—was so positive, so uplifting, it was difficult for him to believe that this fellow former drone could have come away from the experience in such a clearly haunted state.

But before he could question her any further, the holo-emitter grids surrounding them shimmered out of existence, replaced by a brightly lit conference room. The table at which he and Seven sat became part of a long wooden oval, around which some fifty or sixty admirals from across the Federation were seated. Picard immediately noticed Admiral Elizabeth Shelby, commanding officer of Bravo Station, who earlier in her career had established herself as one of Starfleet's first experts on the Borg. There were several other familiar faces, some of whom he had not seen for years and was surprised to learn had been promoted above him. As they realized the hololink had been activated, they all looked expectantly to the head of the table.

The physically present admirals took seats on either side of Picard and Seven, except for Admiral Akaar, who remained on his feet. "Good day, friends," he greeted the assemblage. "Thank you for your time today. As I'm sure I needn't tell you, the past two months have been the most catastrophic in the history of any of our worlds. Beginning on stardate 58011, the Borg launched a new, intensive offensive against the Federation. You all are aware of the horrific results: over sixty-three billion deaths on over a hundred worlds, ships, and starbases. Approximately forty percent of our fleet destroyed, most of those at the Azure Nebula, when the Borg armada invaded the Federation en masse. Vulcan, Tellar, and Andor were hit by crippling attacks, along with our allies on Qo'noS, and several other independent worlds.

"However, in all this tragedy, there is reason for optimism. Not only because the Federation has survived this most recent onslaught, but because the evidence leads us to believe that the Borg threat has been eradicated forever.

"At this point, I yield the floor to Captain Jean-Luc Picard of the *U.S.S. Enterprise,* who witnessed the ultimate fate of the Borg."

Akaar took his seat. Picard remained seated as he repeated his piece of the narrative: the tale of how a starship captain from the old Earth Starfleet, thought dead for over two hundred years, had instead lived in a loop of time for the last eight hundred and fifty years among a race called the Caeliar. And of how that captain was able to bridge what was apparently a very narrow gap between Caeliar and Borg, enabling the Caeliar gestalt to dissolve the Borg collective, to silence the queen, and to transform the Borg into something new.

"What do you mean, 'something new'?" interrupted Admiral Nyllis, the short, compactly built Pentamian commanding Starbase 120.

"What we witnessed was a physical metamorphosis," Picard said, as he pressed a control button on the flat panel before him. In the well at the center of the circular table, the classified sensor log recording from the *Enterprise* played back, showing Axion, the Caeliar's spaceborne city, surrounded by the thousands of Borg cubes it had drawn back from their onslaught against the Alpha and Beta quadrants. The Caeliar city began to glow, and in a flash, seemed to become a mass of pure light. Its radiance expanded, washing over the surrounding armada, overcoming the ability of their black hulls to absorb visible light. And then, those nigh-impenetrable metallic hulls cracked like eggshells, spilling out even greater brilliance as they hatched what looked like giant spiked spheres of pure silver. "According to Captain Hernandez," Picard continued, "the Borg—*all* the Borg, all across the galaxy—had become part of the Caeliar gestalt, and were now dedicated to the cause of peace throughout the universe."

"Captain Picard . . ." Unsurprisingly, it was Shelby who now spoke. "Please forgive my cynicism, but that sounds to me like a very tidy, pat resolution: the Borg are taught the error of their ways, and decide to dedicate themselves to good instead of evil from now on. It's a bit hard to swallow, isn't it?"

Picard grinned. "When you characterize it that way, yes, of course it is. But not when you understand that the entire nature of the Borg has been altered—"

"The last time the nature of the Borg was allegedly altered, it was by the android Lore," said a Saurian admiral Picard did not recognize. "And they weren't altered for the better."

Picard could have pointed out that Lore had not altered the Borg, but had rather taken advantage of an alteration effected by himself. Explaining this, however, would not have helped his argument in the least. "But what Captain Hernandez and the Caeliar have done to the Borg is fundamentally different—"

"Captain, I'm sorry," interrupted Admiral Rollman, C.O. of Starbase 401, "but it seems to me that a lot of what you're telling us hinges on the acceptance of the claim that this Erika Hernandez was in fact the same person who disappeared with the *Columbia* two centuries ago."

"Yes. Didn't you once have an alien claiming to be Captain Bryce Shumar try to take over the *Enterprise*?" Admiral Toddman added skeptically.

"The *Titan*'s medical staff did perform a DNA test," Picard replied, "and confirmed Captain Hernandez indeed was who she said she was."

"And have we already forgotten how easily the Founders managed to get around our blood screenings during the Dominion War?" asked Admiral ch'Evram, who had been captain of the *Bellingham* during that conflict. "I don't think an alien power that could do what we just watched in that playback would have much trouble creating fake DNA."

Picard sighed. He could spend another half hour vouching for Hernandez, or countering every question about every niggling little detail, but he couldn't see the point, other than to drag this meeting out as long as possible. So, he simply pulled himself upright in his seat, tugged his uniform in place, and, making certain to meet the eyes of everyone appearing to be in the room, said, "Sirs, I understand your doubts and your concerns. The Borg have been like a specter hanging over us for a decade and a half, and it's difficult to believe, after fearing them for so long and after witnessing the worst that they could do, that the threat could be over so suddenly, and so finally.

"Yet, it is."

The room was suddenly silent. Picard let that simple declaration sink in for a moment, and just as the buzz of contradictory disbelief started to build again, he continued, in his authoritative tone, "I was assimilated by the Borg. And in the years since then, the Borg maintained a low-level psionic connection with me. I was not even aware of it at first, thinking my nightmares following the Battle of Wolf 359 were the product only of my own subconscious mind. But four years later, just before the Battle of Sector 001, I realized that the dreams were not created by my mind alone. I was forced to recognize that a part of me was still Locutus, and that this shade of the Borg would haunt the darkest part of my mind for the rest of my life.

"That was, until Hernandez insinuated herself into the Collective, and the Caeliar sundered the link. I felt that break. I felt . . . millions of souls suddenly liberated, as well as my own liberation. And then . . . Locutus was gone. Along with the

Borg. Along with the weight that had been on my soul for so long, I could hardly remember when it hadn't been there.

"I realize this is not the testimony you expected here today, sirs. But I have never been so confident of anything in my entire life as I am of the fact that the Borg are gone, forever."

Again, a hush fell over the room, as the gathered admirals processed Picard's words. Being admirals, however, they could not go without hearing the sounds of their own voices for too long. Several spoke at once, but it was Admiral Batiste who made himself heard above the rest. "And what about you, Professor Hansen?"

Picard noticed her flinch again at the use of her human name. "What about me?" she snapped.

"What do you have to add to Captain Picard's testimony?"

"I have nothing to add," she said. "I have no insights into the captain's feelings or beliefs whatsoever."

"But he talks about what he perceived through his residual link to the Borg," Batiste persisted. "You also have maintained some connection to the Collective since your liberation seven years ago, isn't that correct?"

"It is," she said. "Do note, however, that our experiences with the Borg are quite disparate, as are the specifics of our links. For instance, Captain Picard failed to note that Admiral Janeway and the *U.S.S. Einstein* had been assimilated by a supposedly dead Borg cube, leading to the near destruction of Earth nine months ago."

Picard turned toward the former drone, surprised by her words. He knew that she and the admiral had forged a strong bond following her liberation from the Borg and through her early reintroduction to humanity. He had no doubt Janeway's death had had a profound effect on her. But he'd never thought that she might somehow resent him for not anticipating or preventing the admiral's death.

Picard's old friend Marien Zimbata spoke up then. "It was right at the time that the *Enterprise* was witnessing this metamorphosis of the Borg that you had a breakdown at the Palais de la Concorde, and that your remaining Borg implants mysteriously disintegrated."

Seven shot a harsh look across the head table at Akaar and Batanides. They both had also been in the presidential offices with her at the height of the crisis, Picard knew, and the younger woman seemed to feel one or both of them had betrayed some kind of confidence. "Yes," she answered.

"Can you tell us what you were experiencing at that time?"

"Clearly, I was experiencing the metamorphosis," she shot back. "I could not have told you that then, as I did not learn what the *Enterprise* witnessed until a later time. And, I cannot tell you more than that now."

Admiral Batiste folded his hands and tapped

his knuckles against his bottom lip. "So you don't share Captain Picard's certainty that the Borg are gone, and the Borg threat is over forever?"

Picard caught the former drone sneaking a furtive glance his way from the corners of her eyes before stating, "Admiral, at this point in time . . . I have no certainty about anything."

Though he had no idea what this woman had gone through to make her sound so lost and forlorn, Picard considered her with great sympathy. At the same time, though, he was dismayed to look around the virtual conference room and see that her uncertainty had been transmitted, like a virus, throughout the Federation.

2

———◆———

Worf fell back onto the hard deck of the shuttle, naked and breathing hoarsely. His pulse roared in his ears, and he tasted blood on his tongue—both his own and the thinner, saltier tang of his companion's.

He opened his eyes and turned his head to Jasminder Choudhury, the *Enterprise*'s chief of security, lying beside him. Her eyes were closed, and her chest rose and fell slowly with each of her long, measured breaths. Her dark brown skin was covered with a sheen of perspiration, and as Worf slowed his breathing, he took in the distinctively human scent of her sweat, mixed with his own in the confines of the small cabin.

Those scents, however, did not cover the acrid smell of smoke and ash that had infused the clothing they'd shed earlier and left scattered on the deck around them. They had just left Deneva, Choudhury's home planet—or rather, what was left of it—after paying their respects to those who had been killed there in the recent Borg attack. Deneva had often been cited as one of the most beautiful planets in the Federation, but the Borg attack had devastated it. What had once been the Choudhury family's land, in the township of Mallarashtra, had been turned into an empty, gray alien landscape without a single familiar landmark or bit of scenery. Even the Sibiran Mountains on the eastern horizon, denuded of their snowcaps and evergreen-covered slopes, had been unrecognizable.

Jasminder opened her eyes and turned then to Worf, giving him a small, joyless smile before turning away. Worf did not know what to say to her. He knew what it was to lose loved ones: his parents had been slain by the Romulans on Khitomer when he was a child, and both K'Ehleyr and Jadzia had died at the hands of honorless foes. But there were no words that could lessen the pain he knew she felt over the loss of her family.

Jasminder sat up, grunting softly in pain as she reached behind her neck and pulled her long loose black hair into a ponytail. As Worf's eyes wandered over her bare back, he wondered, not for the first time, how they had come to such a point in their relationship. Although he had felt an attraction to Jasminder from the start (there was something about tall, dark-haired, sharp-witted women . . .), her pacifistic beliefs and ideals seemed on the surface to be in direct conflict with the Klingon ethos. Where they had found a common bond, remarkably, was in their respective spiritual natures. Following a firefight with a Borg-assimilated Starfleet vessel, he found himself in a fascinating discussion with Jasminder about the necessity of violence, drawing parallels between the teachings of the *Bhagavad Gita* and the code of honor Kahless implemented in order to rein in the worst of the Klingon people's savagery in war. This conversation had led to many others over the past several months, ranging from Choudhury's lifelong fascination with the myriad of belief systems that permeated the galaxy, to Worf's varied experiences in Starfleet, the Klingon Defense Force, the Federation Diplomatic Corps, and the Boreth Monastery.

Still, their relationship had been completely professional and platonic, until these last couple of weeks. After another mindlessly destructive confrontation with three Borg cubes, it was becoming clear that matters with the Borg were going to get worse—much, much worse—before anyone could even hope things might get better. While the crew was effecting repairs to the ship, he and Jasminder had used the brief lull to visit the holodeck and continue her beginning *mok'bara* lessons. Both had been tense and frustrated, concerned about the pressure being put on Captain Picard and the entire crew, and fully cognizant of what their failure to stop the Borg could mean to the galaxy as they knew it.

This shared frustration came through in their vigorous workout. Although his lessons were still at the very basic stage, Jasminder was already familiar with tai chi, anbo-jyutsu, and *Suus Mahna,* and had proven an extremely quick study. Worf had decided to test her limits, and started throwing unexpected new moves at her. She managed to block or evade almost all of them, intuitively determining the most effective countermoves and then throwing the same attacks right back at him. "Is that all you've got?" she'd taunted.

"Hardly," he'd assured her, launching into a combination of moves that succeeded in knocking her feet out from under her. However, Jasminder managed, as she fell, to twist and grab hold of his wraparound exercise *gi,* taking him down with her. For a moment they were frozen, one atop the other, their noses centimeters apart. Then her fingers were in his hair, his mouth was on hers, and the *mok'bara* lesson was ended.

This time had been no less impulsive, but now, as they both dressed in silence, there was a palpable sense of awkwardness. Again, Worf glanced at his companion's turned back before moving forward through the shuttle and taking the pilot's seat. After a moment, Choudhury joined him, taking the seat to his right. Neither spoke a word for several minutes, as they both watched the stars warp past.

Finally, still without looking his way, Jasminder said, "We should talk."

Worf also kept his eyes straight ahead. "Yes. We should." Following their initial liaison, both had agreed (after hobbling into sickbay, one a minute after the other in a futile attempt to hide the mutual cause of their respective injuries) to put such a conversation on hold and concentrate on the impending battle with the Borg. Neither had found the courage to broach the subject again, until now.

"I . . ." Jasminder said, then stopped herself, pulling her swollen lip between her teeth. She turned in her seat to face him and started again: "I . . . what we did just now . . . it's just . . . after seeing what happened to my home . . . my family . . . I just needed to . . . do . . . feel something . . . else. Something that wasn't so . . ."

"I understand," Worf told her in what he hoped would be a soothing tone of voice.

"It's not that I regret it . . . well, not much," she said, trying again to smile as she rubbed her sore left shoulder. "But . . . this isn't the kind of person I am, Worf. I don't normally . . ."

"Jasminder," Worf interrupted, "you do not need to explain. The circumstances of the last several days have been . . . singular." He turned away and quietly sighed. "In fact, I should apologize to you. As your superior officer, I should have been more prudent in my behavior and exercised greater restraint."

Jasminder gave him an unreadable stare at that. "Oh."

Realizing he had committed a gaffe of some sort, he quickly amended, "And of course, I speak not only as your superior, but also as a friend."

Jasminder's expression shifted to a small, sad smile. "Thank you, Worf. That means so much to me right now. It's good to know that I still have that, at least . . ." Her smile faded as her eyes grew distant and began to fill again with tears.

Worf reached out and laid a hand on her shoulder. "Jasminder, do not give up hope yet of finding your family," he told her. "It will be some time before there's a complete accounting of all ships and evacuees who managed to escape prior to the Borg's arrival."

"One chance in a million," she whispered bitterly.

Worf knew that the odds were, indeed, somewhere in that range. Deneva was a world of over two billion inhabitants, and had had only a few hours' warning before the Borg armada reached their system. But what he said to Choudhury was, "Even so, you cannot dismiss that one chance. Your mother and your father are a part of you, always. No matter what has happened to them, you must not stop trying to find them." He reached across to put a hand on Jasminder's shoulder and looked her in the eye. "I will help you in your search, if you like."

Choudhury placed her hand on top of his. "Thank you, Worf," she said, and again tried to smile.

Her eyes, though, remained inconsolable.

• • •

For most of her life, Beverly Crusher had felt that she'd never had a real home.

She'd lost both her parents as a small child, and one of her earliest memories was being told to get all her toys and clothes together because she was leaving her house and never coming back. She was taken in by her grandmother on Arvada III, and though Beverly loved the old woman dearly, she had always felt that Arvada was someplace to get away from. (In fact, almost as soon as she entered Starfleet Academy, her grandmother decided to pull up roots on Arvada and move to Caldos, so she must have felt somewhat the same way.) During the course of her own career, she had never stayed in any one place long enough to form that kind of connection. The *Enterprise*-D came close to feeling like a home, but she had no difficulty leaving after her first year to head Starfleet Medical, and the crash on Veridian III drove home the fact that starships were impermanent, a poor substitute for a true hearth and home.

But from the moment she first set foot in the Picard ancestral home, she had a feeling of finally arriving at the place where she belonged. Marie, Jean-Luc's sister-in-law, immediately opened her arms wide and took Crusher into a tight, familiar hug. "Beverly! I can't tell you how happy I am to finally properly welcome you after all this time!"

"And it's wonderful to meet you at last, Marie," she replied, squeezing back. Shortly after her and Jean-Luc's hastily arranged wedding last year,

Marie's was the first congratulatory message she received. And just as she had done for Jean-Luc during his extended time away from Labarre, Marie continued a steady stream of correspondence, making sure that Crusher felt like a member of the family. Meeting her was like being reunited with a long-lost sister.

Marie eventually released her grip and lowered her eyes to the other woman's stomach. "And how are you coming along?" she asked, lightly placing a hand on the bulge there.

"Just fine," Crusher said, beaming. "He's doing just fine."

Marie's eyes started misting then. "A darling baby boy," she whispered, and Crusher could feel in her soft voice the soul-deep sorrow she still felt over René's loss, and her heart went out to her. Jean-Luc's nephew was only a few years younger than Wesley, and even though she knew he was alive and well, Beverly still missed him terribly, and could only imagine what it would be like to lose him permanently.

After a moment, Marie blinked her tears away and smiled. "I can't tell you how happy I am . . . that Jean-Luc finally decided to stop being alone, and that you and he—our whole family—has been blessed like this." Marie kissed her on both cheeks, and Beverly, overtaken by the emotion of the moment, kissed both her new sister's cheeks in return.

Being accepted as a full-fledged member of the

Picard clan did not make her feel any less uncomfortable, though, as she sat and watched Marie rush back and forth from kitchen to dining room, carrying dishes and bowls and platters of food. "No, you sit!" she told her and Jean-Luc both. "Let me enjoy cooking for others again." Marie had had a replicator installed in her kitchen when the house was rebuilt—a change Jean-Luc had noticed immediately—and had fallen out of the habit of cooking "real" food. Given her new responsibilities in tending the vineyard, it made little sense to plan and create elaborate meals when she had only herself to feed. But, if this past week was any indication, she had not lost any of her gastronomic talents.

As Marie circled the table and disappeared again into the kitchen, Picard poured a small bit from the wine bottle he'd opened into his glass. Silently, he went through the rituals that he'd been taught from an early age as the son of a vintner—color, swirl, smell, taste, and savor—before nodding his approval. As he filled his glass, then Marie's, Crusher said, "You haven't said anything about your debriefing today."

Picard looked up at her, then shrugged. "There isn't much to tell. Other than the news of Admiral Jellico's resignation, it was fairly standard."

"Jean-Luc," Beverly said, tilting her head, "you think, after all these years, I don't know when you're holding something back?"

"This is what I get for putting things off for so long," he sighed. "Not even a year since the wedding, and already you read me like we're an old married couple."

"I know, it must be terrible, not being able to keep your secrets," Crusher teased, then asked seriously, "What is it that's bothering you?"

Picard sighed again. "Seven of Nine was at the debriefing as well. She, apparently, has been affected differently by the eradication of the Borg than I have."

"Well, that's to be expected, isn't it?" Crusher asked. "After all, from all I've heard about her, there are only superficial similarities between your experiences after being liberated."

"Yes, but . . . for me, there was an absolute finality in what the Caeliar did."

"But not for Seven? Then, you think the Borg are still—"

"No!" Picard said in a tone that made it clear he would brook no argument. "The Borg *are gone!*" He paused to regain his composure, then continued, "I have no way of knowing what's happening inside Seven's mind—nor, understandably, did she seem willing to open up her soul before a gathering of the admiralty." A look of empathy for the young woman washed over Picard's face. Then he shook his head as his frustration returned. "Starfleet cannot afford to dwell on a threat that no longer exists. But, what little she did say was enough to sow mountains of doubt."

As Picard finished his thought, a knock came from the front door. "Now, who can that be, at dinnertime?" Marie wondered as she emerged again from the kitchen, a bowl of steaming *haricots verts* in her hands.

"I'll get it," Picard said, putting his wineglass down and moving to the door. Beverly leaned back in her chair, where she had a straight line of sight to the front of the house.

"Captain Picard!" the visitor said in a high, warbling voice as the door opened. Picard was momentarily taken aback. Although the seat of the Federation government was in France, one rarely saw nonhumanoids outside of the metropolitan Paris area. So it was a bit surprising to have found a two-meter-tall insectoid, dressed in civilian human garb, standing on the front stoop. "Hello, how are you?" the alien asked, its small mouth curled into a semblance of a smile.

"I'm fine, thank you," Picard answered in a tone of uncertainty. Crusher could not immediately place the species of the visitor, though she got the sense that she had encountered its kind before. After a moment, during which her husband also apparently failed to recognize the visitor, Picard said, "Forgive me, but, do I . . ."

"Oh, I beg your pardon, Captain," the insectoid said. "Of course, I shouldn't have expected you to recognize me from such a long time ago. I am Barash."

The name didn't seem to help the captain, but it immediately registered in Beverly's memory. "Barash!" she exclaimed, getting up from her chair and going to greet their visitor. "Of course, Barash!" She took the alien's long-fingered hand and squeezed it gently, careful not to fracture his delicate exoskeleton. She then turned from his large, multifaceted eyes to Picard's. "You remember little Jean-Luc Riker, don't you?" she said with a teasing grin.

"Ah," Picard said, the light of recognition turning on behind his eyes. Fourteen years earlier, the *Enterprise* crew had rescued the young alien from a solitary exile on Alpha Onias III. He had been hidden there by his mother after fleeing an enemy attack on their homeworld, along with an advanced holographic generator programmed to create whatever environment or companions he wanted. He was found by Will Riker—or, more accurately, Riker was found by Barash, after the commander beamed down to the planet to investigate anomalous energy readings. The lonely young alien then created a complex holographic scenario by which he convinced Riker that they were father and son, the alien child presenting himself as a human teenaged boy. Riker eventually saw through the ruse, and when Barash finally revealed his true nature, the commander offered to rescue him and bring him back to civilization.

Although the captain was not particularly amused by Riker's continuing to call their new passenger Jean-Luc, he did become rather fond of Barash during his brief stay aboard. The rest of the senior staff felt much the same, as did Wesley, who spent much of the trip to Starbase 718 teaching Barash to play parrises squares. At the starbase, they all said their good-byes, and Barash was given over to the care of a kindly Andorian *zhen* working in the Displaced Persons Agency office.

"I spent a month on Seven-One-Eight," Barash told them as he, Picard, Crusher, and Marie all gathered in the parlor, "while Admiral Sternberg and her crew tried to determine what had become of the rest of my people."

"And were they able to learn anything?" Crusher asked.

Barash shook his head as he masticated a small piece of cheese. He had politely declined Marie's invitation to stay for dinner, but relented when she insisted on serving him some simple hors d'oeuvres and wine. "No," he said aloud after swallowing. "They examined the technology my mother had left with me on Alpha Onias III, but that only ended up raising more questions than answers. And I was a mere larva when we first fled, so I couldn't offer much help. We think my people are possibly from a planet somewhere in Romulan space. Maybe, if détente with the factions there holds, there might be a chance to find out."

Crusher half smiled as she nodded. While she of course hoped for the best, relations between the Romulan Star Empire, the newly formed Imperial Romulan State, and the Federation were extremely tenuous, and bound to remain so for years to come.

"At any rate," Barash continued, "I eventually ended up in a youth community home on Earth, in Ho Chi Minh City. Myself and a hundred other orphans and lost children."

"So you grew up in an orphanage?" Marie asked, then clucked her tongue. "Oh, you poor thing."

"It wasn't so terrible," Barash assured her. "Oh, it wasn't easy, particularly for someone like me, the only one of his kind. But I preferred by far being among other people, a part of a larger community." He took a sip of wine and continued, "As I grew older, I began mentoring the younger children, and by the time I reached full maturity, I was offered a formal position. This was right after the establishment of the Cardassian DMZ, so there were plenty of new arrivals."

"I can imagine," Picard said soberly. A number of planets in that border region had been ceded to the Cardassians by the treaty with the Federation, necessitating the abandonment of several Federation colonies—some by violent means. "And then the Dominion War after that."

"With the war with the Klingons in between," Barash added, dipping his head. "They were busy years for the agency, but I fear all that's come before will pale in comparison to the situation we face now."

The three humans all nodded somberly. The Borg had damaged more worlds than all the Federation's previous conflicts combined, and far more thoroughly. Hundreds of millions of refugees had been created by the war, none of whom would be able to return to their homes anytime soon, if ever.

"That brings me to the reason for my visit," Barash then said. "I need your help, Doctor Crusher."

Beverly was visibly surprised when he addressed her rather than Jean-Luc. "What can I do?"

"I've received a series of dispatches from Pacifica. It was a primary destination for many of the refugee ships fleeing the Borg invasion, being one of the most distant Federation worlds from Earth. We're hearing reports now that the planet is being overwhelmed by the numbers arriving there."

"That wouldn't take long, given their limited amount of available land space," Crusher said. Pacifica was an oceanic world, populated primarily by an aquatic race, the Selkies. In all, Pacifica's land area amounted to about a third of Earth's, the bulk of it divided among several hundred islands, the biggest of them just a little larger than Greenland. And while the Selkies had long welcomed off-worlders who came to enjoy the planet's vast oceans and the pristine beaches of the smaller islands, most of the larger land masses were restricted, being the habitat of younger Selkies still in the amphibious stage of their life cycles.

"No, not long at all," Barash agreed. "We need to send a team to Pacifica to report on the current conditions there, and to render whatever immediate aid is needed. Unfortunately, the current situation is stretching the agency to its limits. We have a runabout available, but we need Starfleet assistance, and—"

"—Starfleet is also stretched dangerously thin at the moment," Picard finished for him.

"Yes." Barash dipped his head and for a moment said nothing. They all observed the moment of silence for the dead before Barash looked up again. "That's why I knew it would be pointless to ask that the *Enterprise* undertake the mission." He turned to face Crusher again. "But Doctor Crusher, as both a medical doctor and a command-level officer, you could lead the small investigative team I've assembled for this task."

"Oh?" Beverly responded, surprised and, truthfully, proud to be considered for such an undertaking.

"The *Enterprise* is scheduled to depart within the next thirty-six hours," Picard said, looking a bit uncomfortable in his seat.

"But your crew should be able to get along without her for a short while, shouldn't they?" Barash asked. He then looked from the captain to the doctor. "I know this is a terrible imposition, but every day we wait to send a team to Pacifica is another day they go without the help they need."

Hearing that, Crusher had no hesitation in saying, "Then by all means, I'll do it."

"Well, now, hold on a moment," Picard interjected. "Beverly, you cannot—"

Crusher snapped her head in Picard's direction, fixing him with a sharp stare, one eyebrow arched toward her hairline. Picard paused, reconsidered, then turned to Barash. "May we contact you later with an answer?"

"Of course," he said, setting his glass down and unfolding his giant frame from his seat. "I still have to find an environmental sciences specialist for the team. Please contact me via the DPA in Paris once you've decided."

Marie walked Barash to the door, and then somehow disappeared into another part of the house, leaving the newlyweds alone. "Beverly . . ."

"Jean-Luc, you heard what he said," Crusher barreled right over him. "There's a humanitarian crisis in progress, and it's escalating as we speak."

Picard shook his head, not yet willing to admit this concern trumped all others. "There must be someone else Barash can find. Someone—"

"Another physician with command experience? Who's presently on Earth and available?"

"The *Enterprise* needs—"

"The *Enterprise* does not need," Crusher countered immediately. "The *Enterprise* will be just fine for a few days with Doctor Tropp in charge of sickbay. The people on Pacifica need me, and the others Barash is sending."

Picard opened his mouth, but there was nothing that could reasonably be said to counter that bottom-line assessment. And so, to his apparent chagrin, he voiced his concern: "Beverly, you're pregnant."

Crusher just smiled sweetly at him, saying nothing, letting him reflect privately on what a stupid thing that was to say. "What I mean is that, in your condition . . ."

"Pregnancy is not a debilitating disease, Jean-Luc," Crusher told him. "And may I remind you that, when you officially approved Miranda Kadohata's promotion to second officer, she was in her eighth month?"

"I did, didn't I?" Picard replied, smiling ruefully. "Would you believe I had never noticed her condition until she raised the subject of her maternity leave?"

Beverly almost laughed aloud. "Actually, yes, I would." The captain had rarely shared the bridge with the relief ops officer, and when he did, she was sitting behind a large console, with her back to the command chair. "I'd believe it because I know that you know it's not supposed to be relevant."

"No, it's not," Picard said simply, leaving unsaid the plain reality that Beverly's pregnancy *was* relevant to him, whether it was supposed to be or not.

Beverly understood, of course, that he was genuinely, if illogically, expressing his love and concern for her, and for their son. "Would it make you feel better if I were to have someone like Miranda with me on the mission? Barash said he still needed a science officer." Kadohata had become, in the time since joining the senior staff, one of the captain's most trusted and respected officers. Even following the incident last summer, when Miranda, under orders from Admiral Nechayev, briefly took command of the ship from Jean-Luc, she had been able to regain his regard. And, having just recently been through her own second pregnancy, she would be more likely than most other officers to be sensitive to Beverly's condition, without being overly protective.

Picard considered the idea, then nodded. "Yes. I believe it perhaps would. If you can convince her, of course."

Beverly smiled at her husband. "I'll contact her right now." Kadohata was still on liberty with her family on Cestus III, but it would take only a slight detour for the DPA's runabout to pick her up there en route to Pacifica. And by saving her the need to meet the *Enterprise* at Earth, Miranda would have an extra twelve hours to spend with her husband and children. "And then I'll let Barash know."

Picard nodded again, and a corner of his mouth twitched slightly upward. "Make it so."

Beverly kissed him on the cheek, and then made her way to the small guest bedroom she and Jean-Luc had been using during their stay. As she keyed in her request for a subspace connection to Cestus, Marie appeared in the doorway, drying her hands with a dishcloth. "That was quite nicely done," she said, with a glint in her eye.

"Thank you," Beverly said, returning the bemused expression. "Jack was away on the *Stargazer* for almost the entire time I was carrying Wesley. I've never had to deal directly with the stereotypical overprotective father-to-be before."

She and Marie shared a knowing chuckle. Then the humor faded from Marie's eyes, and she turned her gaze away, saying, "Just don't dismiss his worries completely, Beverly." Her attention was seemingly drawn to the door frame, and she ran one hand over the slightly dulled, nine-year-old varnish covering the flawless, unburnt wooden molding. "No matter how safe our loved ones are, you never really know . . ."

Beverly nodded. "I promise to be careful, *ma soeur.*"

"See that you are," Marie replied, flashing a grin and waving a mock-warning finger at her. "And don't spend long chitchatting," she added, heading back for the kitchen. "Dinner's already starting to get cold . . ."

3

———◆———

Lieutenant T'Ryssa Chen stood in front of the full-length mirror in her quarters, turning first one way and then the other. She grabbed at the material of her white dress uniform jacket just below the armpits and tugged. There was a brief moment of relief before the fabric snapped back, pinching hard on a very sensitive part of her chest. "Gahh!" she shouted in a most typical but un-Vulcan manner as she fought against the accursed uniform in order to free her tender skin.

After several minutes of yanking and jerking and wriggling, she finally found an arrangement that almost approached a degree of comfort, but gave the uniform more wrinkles than a raisin. After another tug at the two gold-trimmed points at her waist, she regarded her reflection once more, tossing her hair back over her delicately pointed ears, and decided she'd achieved an acceptable balance between looks and comfort. *Of course, looks started out with the advantage,* she thought, giving her reflection a wink.

Her door chime sounded, and after one last visual check, she crossed the cabin to the doors. With a touch of a button, they slid open, revealing Lieutenant Dina Elfiki waiting in the corridor. "Ready, Trys?" she asked.

Chen's face fell. Not because Elfiki, with her huge brown eyes and dark Egyptian facial features, banished almost all confidence in her own good looks, but because the woman stood there, waiting to escort her to the shuttlebay to greet the captain back aboard, dressed in her standard-duty black, gray, and blue uniform. "What the hell?" Chen sputtered. "Dina, you told me this was full-dress!"

"Did I?" Elfiki said, her eyes growing even wider as she feigned surprise. "Oops. Well, no time to change," she added, grabbing Chen's elbow as she tried to turn back into her cabin. "The captain's shuttle is already on its way."

"You are so going to pay for this, Elfiki," Chen snarled as she half stumbled into the corridor and grudgingly let herself be guided to the turbolift.

"Oh, please," the science officer replied. "After that prank with the alternating gravity plates in stellar cartography? Or reprogramming the food replicator in my quarters with the menu for Commander Worf's cat?"

"You still have no proof that was me," Chen argued, though she failed to keep the "Yes, I am guilty" grin from splitting her face.

"If I really wanted to pay you back," Elfiki continued, "I would have . . . oh, I don't know . . . tapped into the clothing replication systems and tweaked the body measurements on file for you."

It took a moment for Chen to see through Elfiki's perfectly deadpan expression and register what she was telling her. "You mean, *you* . . . ?" she started to ask, then trailed off when the science officer answered her with a tiny smirk. "I'm starting to think I liked you better before I got to like you," she said, pulling at her collar.

Elfiki giggled out loud then, and Chen let her annoyance wane enough to laugh along with her. Before this past week, neither had made much effort to get to know the other very well; Chen was more interested, frankly, in getting to know the male members of the crew (though she had maintained an exclusive relationship with security officer Rennan Konya for a lot longer than she would have expected when it had started), while Elfiki seemed just as happy to spend her off-duty time alone in her quarters. But they had been the only members of the senior bridge crew to volunteer to stay aboard the *Enterprise* during her stay at McKinley, and with Rennan spending his liberty at home on Betazed, Elfiki found herself the target of a full-bore assault by a bored contact specialist. As it turned out, the two found they had quite a bit in common, from strained family relations (though Elfiki refused to elaborate on the specifics) to troubles with men (about which she had absolutely no trouble elaborating) to—most surprising to Chen—a wickedly sharp sense of humor.

Chen was about to describe how she would take her revenge on Elfiki for this most recent prank, stressing to her the amount of intricate planning she would use and the exquisite attention to detail that would keep Elfiki from recognizing the trap until it was too late. However, before she had the opportunity, the turbolift arrived, already carrying Lieutenant Taurik, the ship's Vulcan assistant chief engineer. He nodded to Elfiki as she entered the car and then raised one eyebrow in a typically condescending Vulcan manner as he considered Chen and her choice of apparel. "What, a girl can't try to look nice for her captain?" she demanded.

Taurik pointedly shifted his gaze to a spot just above the car doors. "I made no comment about your appearance one way or another, Lieutenant. Resume to main shuttlebay."

The lift bleeped in acknowledgment and started to ascend. "Seriously, Dina," Chen said in mock-serious tones, ignoring the car's other occupant, "when you least expect it . . . expect it!"

"I do hope," Taurik said, still without turning his gaze from the front of the lift, "that with the rest of the crew and senior staff back aboard, the recent rash of practical jokes plaguing the ship will now come to an end."

Chen smiled behind his back. She'd learned early on that she tended to make full-blooded Vulcans uneasy with her humanlike behavior. For all their talk of Infinite Diversity in Infinite Combinations, they somehow never seemed to make peace with the idea of *V'tosh ka'tur*—Vulcans without logic—or anyone who too closely resembled them.

Which made it all the more fun to flaunt her un-Vulcan-ness around other Vulcans at any given opportunity. "Aw, lighten up, Taurik," she said. "I was going to recalibrate graviton generators on Deck Eight. Really."

"Nevertheless," the lieutenant said, turning around to face them both, "you are officers aboard the *U.S.S. Enterprise,* one of the most celebrated ships in Starfleet. It is not unreasonable to expect that, as such, you display a certain degree of decorum." He sounded so much like Commander Semkal, the supercilious Vulcan first officer on Chen's previous ship, the *Rhea,* that she had to bite back another chuckle.

"Aye, sir," Elfiki said softly, as if she were in fact being dressed down by a superior officer instead of one of equal rank.

Chen, of course, would have none of that. "Come on, we were just blowing off steam. We've been through a rough couple of weeks, you know. Well, maybe *you* don't know," she corrected herself, "but for those of us who feel emotions like fear, anxiety, empathy . . ."

Chen stopped as Taurik's subtle look of irritation suddenly took on a harder edge. He glowered at her silently for several seconds before saying, "Computer, halt," still in his regular cool, flat tone.

The sound of the turbolift's magnetic drive fell still, and Taurik took a slow breath before telling Chen, "You are unaware, I take it, that I had a mate and a daughter in ShiKahr."

Chen found herself frozen in place. ShiKahr was the largest city on the planet Vulcan, home to over five million living beings, including tens of thousands of off-worlders. As such, it had been the Borg's primary target when their genocidal rampage had reached that planet. The attacking cube was eventually destroyed by the Starfleet ships defending the 40 Eridani system, but not before it had succeeded in turning the ancient metropolis into just another piece of flat wasteland extending out from Vulcan's Forge.

"'Had'?" Elfiki asked, in a dry whisper.

"Yes, Lieutenant," Taurik said. "My use of the past tense was intentional, and accurate." His voice still betrayed nothing, though in his dark eyes, riveted on her own, Chen thought she could see the struggle between the older man's Vulcan emotions and his ability to control them.

Then, thankfully, he looked away. "Resume." The turbolift started rising again, then stopped seconds later outside the main shuttlebay. Taurik marched straight out, while Chen was momentarily frozen in place.

T'Ryssa Chen knew that Vulcan emotions were more volatile than human emotions. At least, that was what she had always heard, and that was her favorite excuse whenever she let her own feelings get the better of her—"Sorry, that was my Vulcan half"—but in reality, she had no idea how one actually measured emotional strength, or whether she would fall closer to human or Vulcan on that theoretical scale. But now, she did know that she never wanted to see the full power of a full-blooded Vulcan's unleashed emotions.

"Trys?" Elfiki tapped lightly on her shoulder. "Hey, Trys, you okay?"

Chen jerked as if caught daydreaming. "Yeah. Fine," she said, giving her friend an exaggerated devil-may-care shrug. "Let's hurry, I don't wanna get on Worf's bad side before we even leave dock," she said, her face turned away, and then darted out of the turbolift car so Elfiki only saw the back of her head.

Early on in his Starfleet career, Ensign Geordi La Forge of the *U.S.S. Victory* had been assigned to pilot a shuttle for a senior officer conducting an inspection tour of his ship. That officer—one Captain Jean-Luc Picard—had commented about a minor variance in the shuttle's engines, and Geordi had spent the rest of the following shift running diagnostics and chasing down faulty components, trying to get the craft's performance up to spec.

Nearly twenty years later, La Forge was again at the controls of a shuttle, conducting Captain Picard on a slow survey around the *Enterprise*-E in drydock, reviewing the repair job that had been done, and all that had yet to be completed. "She looks better than she did," Picard said, in a far more diplomatic tone than he had used during that long-ago inspection.

La Forge couldn't argue with the captain's assessment, but that was only because the ship had been so badly damaged when they first returned to Earth. The *Enterprise* had suffered more than a dozen hull breaches, ranging from a three-meter fissure near main engineering (to which he had lost five of his engineers in the blink of an eye) to an unholy gash across the top of the saucer section, where the ship had collided with a Hirogen attack craft at the far end of a trans-galactic subspace tunnel discovered just prior to the Borg invasion. The ugly blackened scar was gone now, as were all the others, the ruptures mended by the molecular refusion of the ship's duranium composite skin. There was still, however, some slight color variation that stood out to La Forge's cybernetic eyes.

The chief engineer wasn't going to get upset at the McKinley team for not touching up minor cosmetic flaws, though. Given how thinly their staff was stretched in the wake of the Azure Nebula incursion, La Forge considered himself lucky that they had completed all the most vital work, as well as all that required extravehicular activity. Unfortunately, that meant a lot of crawling through Jefferies tubes for him and his team, finishing the less critical tasks and running diagnostics, once they were released from drydock and set off on their next mission.

La Forge was reviewing the list of those remaining repairs on a padd as he guided the shuttle in one more circuit around the ship. As they passed the end of the starboard nacelle and looped around to run parallel to the port, Picard cleared his throat and said, "Geordi . . . I never did personally apologize to you for my . . . lapse in judgment at the peak of the conflict."

La Forge raised his eyes from his padd, looked at Picard, then turned his eyes away. "It's all right, sir," he said, almost under his breath. "You weren't yourself." Given the captain's history with the Borg, it wasn't too surprising that the recent war had affected him so drastically.

"No, Geordi, it is not 'all right,'" Picard insisted, in that characteristic, commanding tone of his. "I issued what amounted to an illegal order. I put you in an untenable position, and I owe you a debt of gratitude for standing up to me as you did and refusing to re-create Shinzon's thalaron weapon."

La Forge hesitated before saying anything in reply. Shinzon, a Romulan-created, Reman-raised clone of the captain, had used the thalaron radiation generating device just over a year ago to assassinate the entire Romulan Senate, destroying every molecule of organic matter in their bodies and turning them, literally, to dust. Data had sacrificed his own life to stop him, destroying Shinzon's weapon, his ship, and the madman himself. Then just over a week ago, as it was starting to look as if the Federation was in its death throes, Picard had issued the order to reconstruct the immoral device for use against the Borg. Geordi had refused, flatly, to Picard's face.

"That was probably the hardest thing I've ever done in my career," La Forge finally replied. Privately, he wondered what would have happened if the Caeliar had not ended the Borg threat when they did, and if Earth would have been lost, too, because of his refusal. "I've served under you for a lot of years, sir. And with the exception of my father, I respect you more than any other man alive."

"I appreciate that," Picard said, smiling.

"But I have to tell you, though, sir . . ." La Forge continued, and then faltered momentarily.

"Go on," the captain prompted him.

La Forge looked the other man directly in the eyes and told him, "To be blunt, sir . . . at that point, it was becoming very difficult to continue respecting you."

Picard's smile fell. "No, I suppose, the way I had been behaving, it must have been quite difficult, indeed," he said, dipping his head. La Forge watched as a shadow of self-disappointment washed across the older man's expression. "I also have a great deal of respect for you, Mister La Forge, and I have always found you to be a most keen judge of character." He paused, then said, "I sincerely hope that, in the future, I do not present such challenges to your regard for me. But if I do, I hope you will show the same strength and ability to call me out for it."

La Forge gave the captain a small, sympathetic smile. "I'll do my best, Captain," he promised, before turning back to the controls and guiding the shuttle toward the starship's massive shuttlebay.

"Commanding officer, *Enterprise,* arriving!"

The assembled officers snapped to attention as a bosun's whistle sounded, and Picard stepped through the shuttle's open portal and grinned like a schoolboy. The shuttlebay was not particularly remarkable—a cavernous and largely featureless space, broken up only by the narrow catwalk that ran along its perimeter and a few no-nonsense warning signs. But as he stepped off the shuttle and his boot hit the deck, he felt himself become a part of it again. As much as he had enjoyed the week in Labarre, for most of that time he had itched to get back, and the anticipation had served to make this moment all the sweeter. This was his ship—his place in the universe.

Then the captain's focus moved from the shuttlebay to the people gathered there. *My crew,* he thought with pride. He stepped a few paces closer to the review lines, then addressed the assemblage. "This sort of ceremony is usually reserved for welcoming a new captain aboard when she or he takes command of a vessel for the first time. Some of you here were present at just such a ceremony in this same place nine years ago." Scanning the lines, Picard was slightly surprised to realize how few of those present actually fit that bill. "And some of you, I believe, are yourselves brand-new to this vessel," he added, noting a young Payav ensign and a tall, orange-haired human woman in sciences blue he was sure he'd never seen before.

"However, while my command of this ship is not new, it is a new universe that we shall be dealing with together. We stood fast against the most perilous threat to the Federation, and we have prevailed. Our long galactic nightmare is over; today, we mark the start of a new era. I look forward to exploring it with all of you."

A brief round of applause punctuated the captain's address. Worf stepped forward from the line and extended his hand. "Welcome back, sir."

"Thank you, Number One," Picard said, grasping his hand. "It's good to be back."

Worf nodded and gave him one of his narrow Klingon smiles. It was hard to see even a trace of the rash young lieutenant who had joined his crew with the launch of the *Enterprise*-D in this matured, seasoned man before him anymore. Worf released his hand, fell in beside Picard, and marched beside him as Picard stepped forward to review and greet the rest of the crew.

At the head of the line was his chief of security. "Lieutenant Choudhury," Picard said, extending his right hand. "How are you? Have you heard anything yet about your family?" he asked in a quiet, sympathetic tone.

The Denevan woman looked past the side of his

head, avoiding direct eye contact with both him and Worf. "No, sir," she said through her tightened jaw.

Picard put his left hand over the back of Choudhury's right, and gave it an extra squeeze. "If there is anything I can do, any way I can help . . ."

The security chief managed a small smile. "Thank you, sir. But I'll be fine, and I'm eager to resume my duties."

Picard simply nodded, not wanting to prod her any further. He moved to her left then, to Counselor Hegol Den. The middle-aged Bajoran man was the second person to fill the post long held by Deanna Troi, and seeing him at this moment, Picard wondered if he'd have to start looking for a third. Hegol had not taken leave at Earth, but had remained on ship and on duty, offering what help he could to an understandably shaken crew. From the look in his sunken brown eyes and carelessly shaved face, they had kept his schedule full, perhaps even around the clock. "Counselor. How are you bearing up?"

"*I'm* fine, thank you, sir," Hegol answered, letting whatever else he might have added remain unsaid. Picard understood, and nodded, letting him know that they would talk further later.

Next to Hegol stood the assistant chief medical officer, whose position in line only served to remind Picard of the chief medical officer's absence. "Doctor Tropp," he said, forcing Beverly out of his thoughts for the moment.

The Denobulan physician did not help. "Captain. I'm pleased to report that, despite Doctor Crusher's absence, the medical staff is at full preparedness, and ready—though not especially eager—to handle whatever situation may arise."

"I have every confidence," Picard assured him, as well as the other medical staffers standing in the rows behind him. The captain continued down the front row, greeting and shaking hands with Lieutenants Taurik and Dina Elfiki, finally reaching the end, where Lieutenant T'Ryssa Chen stood, conspicuous in her dress whites.

"I take it you were the victim of someone's prank, Lieutenant?" he asked, favoring the young woman with a tiny smile.

Giving him a tiny chagrined smile of her own, Chen answered, "I was going to tell you that this was a demonstration of how much more I respect you than the rest of the crew."

"Indeed?"

"Yes, sir," she said, and then grabbed at the bottom of her jacket and gave it a sharp downward tug.

Picard's smile faded. He arched one eyebrow at her, and he could have sworn he heard, from behind, a quiet chuckle from Worf.

"Hmph," Picard said, before looking away to address the rest of the assemblage. "Thank you all. Be prepared for an imminent departure. Dismissed."

As the assembly dispersed, Worf fell in step with

the captain. "How imminent do you anticipate our departure to be?" he asked as the two made their way out of the shuttlebay.

"Just as soon as Command lets us know where it is they'd like us to go," Picard answered, at the same time tapping his combadge. "Picard to bridge."

"Bridge. Rosado here, sir," replied the voice of the beta-shift operations officer currently manning the conn.

"Have we received any communiqués from Starfleet Command, Ensign?"

"We have not, sir."

Picard frowned. "Very well. Please alert me as soon as we do. Picard out."

"Sir," Worf said as soon as Picard had finished his conversation with the bridge, "I regret to tell you that the *Enterprise* is not prepared to leave orbit."

Picard sighed. "Yes, Number One. I've discussed the state of repairs with Mister La Forge on the way here. But there are too many other ships that require McKinley Station's particular services, so—"

"Sir," Worf interrupted, "that was not what I was referring to."

"Oh?" Picard said. "This isn't about our armaments, is it?"

The Klingon looked mildly offended. "No, sir. While I still believe we should continue to arm the ship with the best available weapons, we are still more than able to defend ourselves against any current enemies without transphasic torpedoes."

Picard nodded. Transphasic torpedoes had, for a brief time, been Starfleet's most effective defense against the Borg. Picard was gratified to know that Worf, unlike some others in the fleet, accepted and acknowledged the Borg's defeat.

Worf continued, "The problem, sir, is that we do not yet have a full crew complement. Starfleet has yet to assign personnel to replace our recent casualties."

"What?" Picard asked, stunned. He'd been told, in his many meetings with the admiralty, that thousands of ground- and station-based officers on Earth and around the Sol system would be reassigned to ships, and that the entire senior class at the Academy had been granted early commissions in order to deal with the staggering casualties Starfleet had suffered in the recent war. "We've had no new transfers whatsoever?"

"Ten, sir."

Picard stopped in mid-stride, just short of the turbolift doors, and put a hand out to halt Worf as well. "Ten. Starfleet has sent us *ten* crew members to replace our thirty-nine casualties?"

"It is my understanding that the *Enterprise* is not the only ship facing this problem," Worf reported. "Given the losses Starfleet has suffered . . ."

"Yes," Picard sighed. He supposed, all things considered, he should have simply been grateful for the ten new personnel he was getting. "Well, we can make do for the time being with twenty-nine open billets," he said. Presumably, as things became more settled around the Federation, more reassignments would come.

"That's not all, sir," Worf continued.

Picard almost considered not asking the question. "What else?"

Worf hesitated, then told him, "Twenty-six crew members have requested extensions to their loaves—"

"Denied," Picard said quickly, and started for the turbolift again.

"—for reasons related to their mental fitness," Worf finished, following the captain into the open car. "These requests did come with the proper supporting reports from examining counselors." Worf scowled as he added, "If these individuals are in fact psychologically unfit for service . . ."

"Do they forget we have counselors aboard?" Picard snapped. He instantly regretted his harshness—not for any fear that Worf might be offended, of course, but because he knew his crew would not be asking for extended leaves lightly. Picard could still vividly recall the pain he'd felt when he first learned of Robert's and René's deaths, and he knew many of them had suffered losses that, in comparison, dwarfed his.

On the other hand, he hadn't had the luxury of turning the ship over to Riker in order to mourn his brother and nephew. For all the sympathy he felt for these people, they were Starfleet officers, and they were sworn to perform their duties selflessly. "These are all requests, correct, rather than notices that these men and women are certified as unfit for duty?"

Worf nodded. "Yes, sir."

"Then have them all called back," Picard said, as the lift slowed to a stop at the top of the ship. "And forward the psychiatric reports to Doctor Hegol." Picard recalled the deeply wearied expression he'd just witnessed on Hegol Den's face. He regretted the additional burden he was putting on the man, but it was unavoidable.

"Captain on the bridge," Ensign Rosado announced when the turbolift doors swept open and Picard stepped out onto the bridge. The rest of the bridge crew, who had arrived moments earlier via the secondary turbolift from the welcoming ceremony, snapped to attention. "Welcome back, sir," Rosado said, giving him a broad smile that crinkled the corners of her eyes.

"Thank you, Ensign," he replied, though it felt odd addressing a woman his own age as such. Jill Rosado had come to Starfleet as her second career, and brought with her a wealth of life and practical experience the typical Academy graduate simply did not possess.

"McKinley Station has cleared us to leave dry-dock," she reported.

"Excellent," Picard said. "I relieve you, Ensign."

"I stand relieved, sir."

Rosado returned to her ops seat, but Picard remained standing. "Number One," he said, turning to Worf, "would you do the honors of taking us out?"

Worf nodded. "Aye, sir."

Picard returned his nod. "Very good. I shall be . . . in my ready room." And with not a small amount of trepidation, the captain turned toward the private entryway at the starboard side of the viewscreen.

During their investigation of the series of subspace tunnels terminating in the Azure Nebula, the *Enterprise* had ended up in the Delta quadrant, facing a pack of ten Hirogen hunter ships. A hit to Deck 1 had sparked a series of overloads and fires, one of which engulfed the captain's ready room. He'd lost many of his most valued possessions, including the Mintakan tapestry given to him during an accidental first contact mission, a rare twentieth-century printing of *The Globe Illustrated Shakespeare,* the small flute that had once belonged to a man named Kamin on a long-extinct world, and other mementos of his fifty-plus–year career.

The doors opened ahead of him, releasing a faintly antiseptic scent of new carpeting and other materials that gave the duranium cubicle the semblance of a livable space. Entering his restored sanctuary, he discovered the space had not only been repaired and refurbished, but redecorated. The centerpiece was a large, antique wooden desk which, upon closer inspection, Picard was surprised to recognize as his father's. It had been built by his great-great-grandfather, its top made from the face of an old wine cask. For as long as Jean-Luc could remember, it had sat in the corner of the winery warehouse, where Father kept his shipping records and weather logs. Picard ran his fingertips along its smooth, newly refinished and revarnished surface, and the intricately carved grape leaf and vine design that adorned its edges. So few Picard family heirlooms had survived the house fire, and Picard felt tremendous gratitude to Marie for parting with this one.

The next new addition to catch his eye was a framed painting that was hung above the new couch, depicting a flock of black birds in flight. It took a moment for him to understand the significance of this gift, until he noted the artist's mark: Data.

Picard recalled then that this particular work had been done at his own urging, shortly after Data had first discovered his "dream program." The birds, Data explained following his second vision, symbolized his newly discovered ability to break through his limitations and to explore the greater aspects of his being. Picard nodded at Geordi's choice from the myriad of Data's collected artworks; he couldn't think of a better symbol for what he foresaw in this new post-Borg era.

On a stand to the left of the sofa sat what was clearly an ancient piece: a Klingon Second Dynasty bloodwine vessel, painted with a depiction of Kortar and Lunob's slaying of the gods. Very few Second Dynasty pieces had survived the Dark Time, and Picard marveled at the surprising artistry of the ancient warrior responsible for this piece.

And at the right end of the couch, under a white card with the words "To my husband, with love, Beverly," sat a new Shakespeare volume—or rather, an old one: a first edition of *The New Britannia Complete Shakespeare,* published in 2054. Picard caressed the brittle but intact binding gently, reflecting on the fact that, in the year following the end of the Third World War, even at the height of the Post-Atomic Horror and in the face of Colonel Green's genocidal purges, there were those who saw the preservation of this bit of human culture as a priority. A red ribbon bookmark stuck out of the bottom; Picard opened the book, and laughed as he read the title of the play that began on the marked page: *All's Well That Ends Well.*

Just as he was about to settle onto his new couch with the Bard, the comm chimed and Worf's voice announced, *"Captain, there is an incoming message for you, sir. From the presidential office at the Palais de la Concorde."*

Picard's eyebrows snapped upward. "Thank you, Number One," he said, wondering for what possible reason the president would be contacting him. He set the open book carefully onto the stand that had accompanied it, then crossed the room to his desk and activated the anachronistic-looking computer monitor sitting on the far corner. After a few moments, as the Palais communications system initiated its extra security protocols, the image of Nanietta Bacco appeared, seated at her own desk before the wide, panoramic window of her office overlooking the Champs-Élysées. Standing just behind and to the right of the president (and blocking the view of the Tour Eiffel) was Admiral Leonard James Akaar. At nearly two and a half meters' height, the new head of Starfleet Command was almost as impressive as Gustave Eiffel's famed monument, and towered over the petite white-haired woman. "Madam President. Admiral," Picard said in greeting.

"Captain Picard," the president said, giving him a small, personable smile. She looked far more at ease than she had a week earlier, when he had last met with her, but there was still clear evidence of the weight of her office pressing down on her shoulders. *"I understand you and the* Enterprise *are ready to get under way again. I hope you were able to enjoy some of the brief leave time you had while here on Earth?"*

"Yes, ma'am, thank you," Picard answered, wondering.

"And you're wondering now why I'm bothering to call you, while you're waiting to receive your next orders," the president said, interrupting his thoughts.

Picard allowed himself a small smile. "I admit, the question did occur to me, Madam President."

Bacco glanced briefly over her shoulder at Akaar, who remained perfectly still and silent behind her. Then she turned back to the captain. *"I assume you've heard the address I gave following the Borg's . . . disappearance."*

Picard nodded. "Yes, ma'am."

"And you'll recall, in that speech, I made a special point of saying, despite the blow we've been dealt, that Starfleet would continue its commitment to peaceful exploration."

"Indeed," Picard answered. "It was quite inspiring, ma'am."

The right corner of the president's mouth twitched upward in a sardonic-looking half-grin. *"Perhaps too inspiring,"* she said.

"Captain," Akaar interjected, *"this isn't being shared with a lot of people outside of Command, but the fleet is in far worse shape than is being publicized. We have possibly billions of homeless refugees to resettle; catastrophic damages suffered on Vulcan, Andor, and Tellar; not to mention the help the Klingons are going to need from us, with Qo'noS now barely habitable. Widespread exploration solely for exploration's sake? It's simply not feasible."*

Intellectually speaking, none of this was particularly shocking to Picard. But hearing it so bluntly put by the president and Starfleet's ranking admiral, he felt his heart fall in his chest.

"What of the *Titan*, though?" he asked after a silent moment. Will Riker's ship had been specifically named in Bacco's speech as one that would continue Starfleet's exploratory mission.

"The Titan *will be an exception,"* Akaar said. *"The rest of the* Luna-*class ships are still out there, as it's important to keep up the image we've presented. The* Titan *will be at Utopia Planitia for another month or so; we're planning to formally relaunch her and get her back under way on First Contact Day—make it a bit of a morale booster for the Federation."*

"I see," Picard answered flatly. He dared not tell either of his superiors what he thought of using a Starfleet ship as part of some sort of public relations stunt.

President Bacco leaned forward, elbows on her desk, and looked directly at Picard. *"The reason we're telling you all this, Captain . . . the reason I personally wanted to be part of telling you . . . is because I believe you deserve to see the decision-making process behind your new assignment. The debt the Federation owes you can never be adequately repaid, Jean-Luc. And I wanted to be certain that you understood this assignment is in no way meant to diminish that."*

Picard nodded, and waited.

"Captain Picard, where the Enterprise *is most needed,"* the president finally said, in an almost frighteningly disheartened tone of voice, *"is here, as close to home as possible."*

And Picard's heart dropped even further.

4

———

Donald Wheeler woke up with a dead hairy rat in his mouth.

That's what it tasted like, at any rate. He lifted his head off his pillow and immediately regretted it, as bolts of pain ricocheted around the inside of his head like spiked tennis balls. Then, against his better judgment, he opened his eyes. Wheeler had no idea where he was; only that it was too goddamned bright. He blinked and squinted until either his eyes or the light adjusted, and he could see he was in a narrow bed in a small, white compartment.

The infirmary? No, the infirmary was larger than this. He'd been to the Gerrold University Medical Center more than a few times during his matriculation—while feeling much the way he did now, come to think of it. G.U. was surrounded by some of the best wineries and distilleries on Sherman's Planet, and Wheeler had taken full advantage of their proximity to campus. But the G.U. Med Center had a lot more beds, a lot more equipment, a lot more space . . .

It then occurred to him that no, he wasn't at G.U. anymore. He'd finally, after six years and a couple of false starts, finished his studies and earned his degree in pre-Federation Tellarite literature. Then, with diploma firmly in hand, he set off from G.U. and Sherman's Planet, and headed for Risa to celebrate his accomplishment. He'd been celebrating nonstop for three months now, because were he to stop, he'd be forced to figure out exactly what he could do with a degree in pre-Federation Tellarite literature, other than teaching *The Shallash Epics* to a new generation of aimless students. And that was a fate just too horrible to contemplate.

Except, this wasn't Risa, either. He remembered . . .

Well, he couldn't remember much of anything, not with this hangover. *This is a pretty lousy infirmary,* Wheeler thought, *if that's what it is, if they haven't shot me up with an alcohol inhibitor. How long have I been here unconscious, anyhow?* Well, he would just have to check out and cure himself— a little hair of the dog that bit him should do wonders in that regard.

After a few deep breaths and an enormous effort, he pushed himself up, swung his legs over the side of the bed, and somehow managed to get himself upright. The room was small enough that he could put his hands out to the walls on either side, and in that manner he moved to the door.

Once his eyes had adjusted again to the full-intensity lights on the other side, he remembered: he was on a Risian transport, ordered to temporarily evacuate . . .

Another bolt struck him right between the eyes, and Wheeler opted to put thinking on hold for a moment. He staggered past clusters of his fellow passengers, all of whom seemed strangely subdued, toward the nearest courtesy bar, and powered up the replicator. "Wine. Red—a Pinot Noir. And not synthehol, either."

The computer sounded an off-key tone, and answered, *"Unable to comply under current restrictions."*

It took several seconds for that to penetrate the haze that had enveloped his brain. "Restrictions?" he said. "On a Risian transport?"

"Per emergency protocols," the machine explained, *"this unit can only fill requests for essential foodstuffs."*

Emergency? The word reverberated in his mind, along with the thunderclaps of pain. "Listen, this *is* essential. My head'll split open if I don't get a little something to take the edge off." Normally, Wheeler knew better than to try to plead with a computer, but that didn't quite matter to him at the moment.

Which was only fair, since his condition didn't matter to the replicator, either. It just gave him that same discordant chime and stubbornly refused to give him his wine. Frustrated, Wheeler punched the wall. "Come on, I'm sick! Give me something!"

Finally, the dispenser slot lit up. Surprised but pleased, Wheeler watched as a small storm of energized particles glowed bright and then dimmed. For some reason, instead of a glass, it had given him his request in a wide-lipped ceramic cup. The scent hit him at about the same moment his hand wrapped around the cup and registered the fact that it was heated, and that the replicator, responding to his claim of being ill, had given him chicken soup. Growling, he flipped the cup over, spilling broth all over the inside of the replicator and down its front surface. *"Phinda!"* he cursed loudly as the hot liquid scalded him.

"Hey, hey!" Someone was suddenly behind him, one hand on his shoulder, the other on his soup-splattered forearm. He turned—or was turned—and was pleased to see it was the gorgeous chief facilitator from the Temtibi Lagoon Resort. "What are you doing?" she demanded, in a very stress-filled, un-Risian tone of voice.

"I was just trying to get a drink," Wheeler answered. He noticed that the smile that seemed permanently plastered onto the hostess's face—just as it was on every Risian's—had disappeared; she spoke to him now through tightly clenched teeth that seemed nowhere near as bright as they used to be.

"The bar is closed," she told him, making it sound very final. "Let's get you back to the dispensary."

The Risian woman started to guide him back through the subdued lounge to the small white room. If he were thinking clearly, he would have let her do so, and then after allowing her to lay him on the dispensary's bed, he could have convinced her to lie beside him and show him some of that famous Risian hospitality. Instead, he shook her hands off him and said, "What the hell is going on? Why can't I get a simple stinking drink, for crying out loud?"

"Oh, shut up," said one of his fellow passengers, a disheveled, unshaven Ktarian, sitting with a hand draped over his eyes. "You'll get your precious wine when we get to Pacifica."

"Pacifica? What happened to Risa?" No one answered him, and for some reason, everyone turned away. But it hardly mattered; Pacifica, he knew, was an ocean world, with lots of beautiful beaches . . . and beautiful, four-breasted females. "When'll we get there?" he asked, suddenly impatient.

"Soon," the Risian woman said. She still wasn't smiling at him.

"Fine," he said, thinking now that it would definitely be better to find him some gorgeous, quadruply-endowed sea maiden, rather than this cold fish. He stumbled back to the dispensary on his own and fell into the bed, where he could dream of the warm beaches and cool drinks waiting for him on Pacifica.

But somehow, those pleasant dreams did not come, and he instead lay awake, recalling the strangely haunted looks on the faces of the other passengers.

Yesterday, Miranda Kadohata considered herself the happiest woman on the face of Cestus III.

She had been scheduled to leave Lakeside at midday, in order to travel to Earth and report back aboard the *Enterprise*. However, now that she was going to Pacifica with Doctor Crusher, her stay on Cestus had been extended by an extra half a day. She and her family—husband Vicenzo Farrenga, five-year-old daughter Aoki, and twin one-year-olds Colin and Sylvana—took advantage of this temporary reprieve by taking an all-day outing to April Beach. They spent the entire, perfectly sunny day playing in the crystal blue waters, building sand castles, and chasing an oversized beach ball up and down the shore. Aoki ran along the water's edge, turning fearless cartwheels, while the twins primarily sat under the umbrellas, fascinated by the way they could grab handfuls of sand, and how it would then slip away between their fingers. The family stayed until Cestus began its descent beyond the water's western shore, turning the surface shimmering shades of orange and red. At home, as Miranda tucked Aoki into her bed, her daughter told her, "Mummy, this was the best day *ever!*" Miranda told her she agreed as she gave her a good-night kiss and turned out the light.

Today, all that changed.

Today, Miranda appeared at the family breakfast table in her gold Starfleet uniform shirt and gray uniform slacks, with the matching gray jacket, with its freshly shined Starfleet arrowhead emblem pinned to the breast, draped over her forearm. Even the babies seemed to realize the significance of her wardrobe choice this morning: Mummy was going away today.

Miranda forced herself to smile through her feelings. "Good morning, loves," she said, circling the table to give Aoki a peck on the cheek. The little girl pouted and tried to squirm away, but her mother still managed to get her lips to their target. She then moved over to where Colin and Sylvana, side-by-side in their tandem highchair, looked back and forth between their mother and the porridge bowl from which their father had been feeding them. Miranda kissed each of their foreheads, at the same time grabbing a nearby towel and wiping wayward lumps of cereal from their cheeks and chins.

Then she turned to her husband. Vicenzo smiled back at her as they shared a quick peck, though she could plainly see his smile was just as forced as her own. "Good morning, sweetheart," he said. "You sleep okay?"

"Oh, just fine," she said as she draped her jacket over the back of her chair. Colin had been up once during the night, wanting a bottle and a clean nappy. Even though Vicenzo had been taking care of the midnight cries all by himself, Miranda had trained all her career to wake quickly in case of an emergency, and had beaten him out of bed and into the nursery. And at any rate, this was a far more pleasant type of emergency than she'd had to deal with for the past several months on *Enterprise.*

She took her seat and reached for the jam jar at the center of the table. As she spooned a dab on her toast, Aoki asked in a small voice, "How long till you gotta go, Mummy?"

"Just about an hour now, sweetie," Miranda told her.

"Will you be home for my birfday?"

Miranda lightly bit her bottom lip. "I don't know, love," she answered, in complete honesty. The *Enterprise,* as far as she knew, still hadn't gotten its new assignment, and with so much uncertain in the wake of the Borg attack, heaven only knew where she might be three weeks from now, when her firstborn turned six years old. "But I promise to try."

"Okay," Aoki mumbled into her breakfast bowl. At five years and eleven months, she was well aware that "I'll try" was a far lesser promise than "Yes, I will." The rest of the morning meal passed in relative silence, with Aoki poking at her cold and clumpy porridge for several minutes before asking to be excused.

Aoki played quietly in her bedroom until the *Runabout Genesee,* Miranda's assignment for the next several days, hailed to let her know they were coming out of warp and entering the Cestus system. She had to call twice before her daughter emerged with a sullen expression on her face. "Come here, my love," Miranda said softly, getting down to Aoki's height on one knee. She wrapped her arms tightly around her daughter and whispered in her ear, "I'm going to miss you so much, my big girl." Aoki did not hug back right away, withholding her affection as a way of protesting her mother's departure, as Counselor Troi had explained to Miranda after the first time it happened a couple years ago. But her resistance wore down, and her tiny arms went around Miranda's neck. "I'll miss you too, Mummy," she said in a half sob.

After a long minute they disengaged, and Miranda turned to grace Colin and Sylvana, standing up in their walkers, with their own kisses and murmurs of endearment. She stood then to face her husband, but before she could say anything, he turned and looked past her. "Aoki, look after your brother and sister while I say good-bye to Mummy outside."

The girl nodded, and Vicenzo opened the front door onto the porch. Miranda grabbed her duffel bag and followed him out, wondering what this was about; Vicenzo had never been shy about showing affection in front of the children.

As the door closed behind them, Vicenzo turned back to his wife, looking deep into her dark, almond-shaped eyes. He reached out to run his fingertips across her finely sculpted cheek and brush her dark hair back. "This is never going to get any easier," he told her.

Miranda smiled sadly and put her arms around his waist. "No, I'm afraid it isn't," she whispered into his chest as she laid her head on his shoulder.

"So don't go."

Miranda shook her head back and forth in answer to his routine plea. "You know I don't want to. You—"

She cut herself off when Vicenzo broke their embrace and took a step backwards. She looked up at him, surprised by the intensity with which he stared back at her. "Then don't," he said, his tone almost desperately urgent. "Stay here, with us."

"Vicenzo? Why are you trying to make this harder than it already is?"

"We spent six days on that transport, Miranda," he said. "Six days completely cut off from the entire galaxy, having absolutely no idea what was going on. All I knew was, the Borg had already destroyed a dozen other planets in sneak attacks, and that my wife, up on the front lines of the war, had told me to grab the kids and run, get off Cestus III as fast as we could."

Miranda said nothing. She had contacted Vicenzo shortly before the *Enterprise* made its first excursion through the subspace tunnel network the Borg had been using to violate Federation space, worried that she might not make it back. Regulations forbade her to tell him how dire the Federation's tactical situation had been at that point, but she was able to get her point across, urging him to take the children to visit the farming colony on

Kennovere, and quickly, before the growing season ended. A transparent cover, but it had gotten the message through.

"I knew Cestus was lost," he continued. "The world where I grew up, home to everything I ever knew or loved—gone. But that didn't matter. Because all of this," he said, swinging his arm around to take in the entire planet around them, "paled in comparison to the thought that I had lost you." Tears started to stream down his craggily lined cheeks. "It wasn't until I saw you in the front door when we got back that I could let go of that feeling. But now you're leaving again . . . and I just can't bear the thought of ever going through anything remotely like that again."

Miranda was speechless. She and Vicenzo had been married for close to ten years now, and she'd never seen him so distraught at the end of a leave. Before she could form any kind of appropriate response to him, her combadge chirped, then spoke in Beverly Crusher's voice: *"Runabout Genesee to Commander Kadohata."*

Miranda lifted a hand to tap the device on her chest, but Vicenzo caught her wrist. "Don't go," he said plaintively. "Tell Doctor Crusher . . . something."

They looked deep into each other's eyes for several long seconds, then Miranda pulled her hand free. "Kadohata here."

"We're in orbit and ready to beam you up, Miranda."

"Stand by, please, Doctor." She cut the comm channel, and looked back to her husband. "Tell her what?"

"I don't care. Anything. I . . . I know I'm being selfish and inconsiderate and not respecting your choice to live this life, but the thought of you flying off into danger again—"

"We're going to *Pacifica,* love . . ."

"And then from there?" her husband asked. "Will you only be assigned safe missions from now on?"

"Vicenzo, I have a duty—"

"You have a *family*!"

Miranda was knocked back a mental step by the vehemence of that last outburst, and all that was implied by it. "You've known I was a Starfleet officer from the day you met me," she almost shouted back. "It's hardly fair for you to stand here now and tell me you're unhappy with my career choice."

"And what part of this is fair to the children?" Vicenzo demanded. "Is it fair they hardly know their mother? Is it fair that every time she leaves home, it might be for the last time?"

Miranda was spared the need to answer that question by an insistent beep from her combadge. *"Crusher to Kadohata. I'm sorry to interrupt your good-byes, Miranda, but we really—"*

"It's okay, Doctor," she interrupted. "One to beam up."

"Miranda, no . . ." Vicenzo protested. He tried to reach out for her, almost as if he thought he might physically restrain her, but the transporter effect happened far too quickly.

And yet, even as the runabout's transporter alcove took shape around her, the image of Vicenzo's face, and the look of hurt he wore as he watched her beam away, stayed with her.

People never realized how good they had things until they were deprived of the small comforts they took for granted.

For instance, after serving for so many years aboard Starfleet's biggest top-of-the-line vessels, sharing the limited living space of a *Danube*-class runabout with four others felt incredibly confining and claustrophobic. After trying to catch a few hours of sleep on the narrow little shelf that passed for a bunk, constantly shifting position in an effort to make herself comfortable (which would have been a futile exercise, she suspected, even if she wasn't pregnant), Crusher gave up, sat up, and padded in her stockinged feet to the door of the tiny cabin.

"Good morning, Doctor-Commander," said Doctor Meron Byxthar, the Betazoid sociologist Barash had recruited for this mission, as Beverly emerged into the communal living area. Byxthar was an unassuming-looking woman Beverly's age, about half a head shorter, with medium-length hair dyed a nondescript shade of brown. She did not turn to face Beverly, but kept her attention on the man across the table from her.

The man, Paul Dillingham, looked up briefly, greeted Beverly with a half-muttered "Doctor Crusher," and immediately turned his attention back to the table. An array of tiles, not unlike dominos, were arranged between the two, forming some sort of pattern that only an aficionado of the Betazoid game Rivers could discern. Dillingham, an individuals' rights attorney—also in the employ of the Federation government—was clearly less than an aficionado, and chewed on his salt-and-pepper mustache as he pondered which of his tiles to place where.

Crusher returned the greetings as she headed for the replicator. "Croissant with icoberry jam and . . . cold milk," she told the computer, pausing to reflect on just how good a cup of coffee would taste just now.

"Most physicians say caffeine, in moderate amounts, is acceptable for pregnant humanoids," Byxthar said while still watching Dillingham. Then she turned and said, "Sorry, Doctor-Commander," in response to Beverly's unspoken irritation at having her thoughts read.

Crusher said nothing as she took a long, unsatisfying sip. As much as Doctor Byxthar had tried to maintain an inconspicuous appearance, in order to better blend in with refugee communities and make her observations, she'd made little effort thus far to similarly tone down her personality. As a noted and respected expert on the issues concerning dislocated persons and cultures, she had balked when

Crusher first requested that she also be addressed as Doctor, rather than Commander. "Or 'Beverly' works, too," she had added with a smile. Byxthar rejected that idea, and on her own came up with the compromise title Doctor-Commander. Beverly finally just shrugged and resolved to put up with it for the few days they had to work together.

She took a seat at the table and tore into her flaky pastry while watching the game unfold before her. Though Beverly only understood the game in the most general sense (she had tried to learn it once during a stay at a Lake Cataria resort on Betazed), she knew enough to tell that Dillingham was playing out of his depth. Each of the tiles represented either a piece of land or a body of water. The goal of each player was to shape the contours of the land between them, so as to direct the flow of water, to moderately irrigate their own territory, or to cause either flooding or drought to their opponent's.

Dillingham maintained a cool, serious demeanor and gave no hint of acknowledgment that his land was as dry as Tyree. After a long moment of consideration, he selected one of the tiles from the hand in front of him and placed it near the center of those already laid out.

Whatever he had done, it apparently was not good for Byxthar, who had been poised to place a tile of her own down immediately following Dillingham's turn, and now paused to reconsider. Beverly wondered, as she spooned a daub of preserves on her croissant, how the Betazoid could have been so surprised by the shift in the game.

"Because reading an opponent's thoughts would be unsporting," Byxthar said as she studied the game tiles.

Crusher furrowed her brow. "But reading everyone else's isn't a problem."

"You wanted to know, Doctor-Commander," Byxthar answered, still not looking up.

Crusher stopped herself before making a retort, and shoved a large chunk of croissant in her mouth to make the temptation to say anything easier to resist. She reminded herself that once they got to Pacifica, both would be doing their own work, without much need to interact with one another.

The comm then came to life, and a voice from the runabout's cockpit said, *"Gliv to Crusher. We're approaching the Cestus system and dropping out of warp."*

"Acknowledged," she answered, brushing the crumbs from the front of her uniform. After returning her empty plate and half-full glass to the replicator, Crusher wended her way toward the front of the ship.

In the cockpit, Ensign Thur chim Gliv, a young Tellarite with a coat of short rust-brown fur, turned in his seat as he sensed another person enter. "Sir."

"Ensign," Crusher said. Through the forward portals, over the pilot's shoulder, she saw the bright green-blue globe growing closer. "Have you hailed Commander Kadohata yet?"

"Not just yet, sir," Gliv answered. "Cestus Orbital Control has us holding just beyond standard orbital distance at the moment."

Crusher was about to ask why that was, but then shifted her attention to the short-range sensor readout, and saw the answer for herself: at least six dozen other ships, ranging from shuttlecraft to class-V transports, were in immediate range, all identified with civilian registries. The largest share originated from Regulus, one of the first planets obliterated following the Borg invasion. That planet had had barely two hours' warning before the devastating armada swept across their system. At first, Crusher found herself happily surprised by how many Regulans had managed to escape before it fully dawned on her what a small percentage of that world's total population even this volume of ships represented.

"Cestus Control to Runabout Genesee,*"* the voice over the comm interrupted her thoughts. *"You are cleared to enter standard orbit. Coordinates are being transmitted now. Please* do not *deviate from these coordinates!"*

Gliv bristled at the sharp tone of the controller. What Beverly perceived as stress in the man's voice—no doubt he had rarely, if ever, had to deal with so many vessels at once—the Tellarite apparently interpreted as a suggestion that the pilot would refuse to follow instructions. But all he said in response to the perceived insult was, "Acknowledged. And I hope you have a nice day, too."

The comm channel bleeped and went quiet without any response from the planet. Gliv ran his cloven hands over his control panel, and Crusher watched as he maneuvered expertly around the satellites and other vessels currently circling Cestus III. After a minute, he powered down the main impulse engines and announced, "We are now in standard orbit directly above the city of Lakeside, the most unimaginatively named settlement in the sector," he added while flashing a row of small, stubby teeth.

Crusher suppressed a desire to wince. "Ensign, that line wasn't all that funny the first dozen times you used it."

The Tellarite's smile disappeared. "It wasn't?"

"I'm afraid not," she told him with a sympathetic smile. The young ensign had been trying his best to ingratiate himself to her and the rest of the team, but so far all his attempts at humor and camaraderie had come across as clumsy and forced.

As Gliv reflected on Crusher's critique of his comedic performance, the doctor slipped into the chair beside him and tapped into the comm system. "*Runabout Genesee* to Commander Kadohata."

"*Kadohata here,*" came the response.

"We're in orbit and ready to beam you up, Miranda."

"*Stand by, please, Doctor.*"

"Of course," Crusher said, just as she heard the audio channel being closed on the other end, and smiled bittersweetly. She and Jack had gone through such good-byes too many times (and, at the same time, far too few times), and she was willing to give Kadohata the time she needed with her husband and small children.

"I don't believe I made my observation about Lakeside's name as many as a dozen times," Gliv said, interrupting Crusher's thoughts.

Crusher turned and gave the Tellarite a deadpan stare. "I was using hyperbole, for comic effect."

Gliv pondered that a moment, then his lips parted to display both rows of teeth. "Aahh! Very good, sir!" Whether his amusement was real or just an effort to humor a senior officer, Crusher could not say. The engineer was the one team member who showed genuine enthusiasm for this mission; he'd freely admitted that he hoped it would serve as a step toward a more prestigious posting than the one he'd held at Lunar Colony One for the last year. And he seemed to have no issue with flattering the team leader during this brief mission if that meant getting a good report in his file.

After what she thought was a generous extra amount of time, Crusher keyed the comm panel again. "Crusher to Kadohata. I'm sorry to interrupt your good-byes, Miranda, but we really—"

"It's okay, Doctor," Kadohata answered. *"One to beam up."*

Crusher turned to Gliv, who had already turned to the console at his left-hand side, awaiting the order. "Ensign, energize."

In the narrow alcove at the rear of the cockpit, a

column of swirling matter and energy illuminated and faded, leaving a human woman with dark hair and mixed European and Asian facial features. She stepped forward, hitching the strap of her duffel bag up over her shoulder, and stood at attention as she faced Crusher. "Permission to come aboard?" she asked, with a British-sounding accent.

"Granted," Crusher said, smiling. "How was your leave?"

"Good, quite good," she answered as she turned to the Tellarite now stepping toward her.

"Commander Miranda Kadohata," Crusher said while gesturing, "Ensign Thur chim Gliv, our engineering specialist."

Kadohata put out her right hand. "How do you do?"

Gliv smiled as he wrapped his thick fingers around the human woman's. "That's for me to know, and you to find out!" he said, then waited for the gales of laughter he'd been sure would result.

Miranda stared at him, and then at Beverly, bewildered. "Never mind," the doctor said. "Ensign Gliv's sense of humor is still a work in progress."

Gliv let out a bark of a laugh. "A work in progress! I like that!"

Crusher sighed. "Take us out of orbit, Ensign, and resume course to Pacifica, maximum warp."

As Gliv returned to the pilot's seat, Crusher escorted Kadohata to the aft of the runabout, where she introduced her to Byxthar and Dillingham, and showed her where to stow her gear. The Rivers game had apparently been fought to a kind of stalemate, though neither competitor seemed anywhere near willing to concede.

The two *Enterprise* officers then moved forward into the cockpit. "We've cleared the Cestus system," Gliv reported. "ETA to Pacifica is eight and a half hours."

"Very good," Crusher answered, then asked, "Are you ready to be relieved, Ensign?" Gliv had been at the helm since coming aboard at Luna.

He grinned. "Do Terran bears defecate in wooded—?" He quickly stopped himself after reading the reactions of the two senior officers, dropped his smile, and said, "I mean, yes, sir. Thank you, sir."

"I bet he's a blast at parties," Kadohata said once Gliv had left the cockpit and she had assumed the pilot's seat.

"Only when he leaves," Crusher replied, then added, "Damn, now he's got me doing it." She sighed and fell back into the copilot's chair. "So . . . leave was good?" she asked, folding one leg underneath herself.

"Yes," Miranda said, shooting the doctor a quick sideways glance, and then forcing a smile for her. "The twins have grown so much, I couldn't believe it. And Aoki . . . she's fearless, that one. You should have seen her the other day at the beach."

Crusher nodded indulgently. "And Vicenzo?"

"Well . . . Vicenzo . . . he's . . ." Kadohata trailed

off, and then broke a long pause with a shoulder-slumping sigh. "Well, we had a bit of a row just now as I was leaving."

"I see," Crusher said neutrally, then waited to see if the other woman would elaborate.

"He asked me to go AWOL!" She shook her head in disbelief, even though she was the one telling the story. "To just leave you high and dry on this mission."

"Really?" Crusher said, raising an eyebrow.

"I know he frets when I'm away," Kadohata said. "I fret, too, wondering what might happen to him or the little ones. But he knew from the first that I was in Starfleet. Good heavens, the only reason we met in the first place is because a ship got blown up out from under me!"

Crusher nodded, recalling the story of how Kadohata had returned to Cestus after the destruction of the *Enterprise*-D at Veridian III, and met her future husband while attending a baseball game. "This is my life, my career," Kadohata continued. "And I've finally reached this position, after almost twenty years: second officer of the *Enterprise*! Two steps away from having my own command! But all he cares about is . . ."

". . . is you."

Kadohata turned toward Crusher at that, and suddenly, every bit of anger drained from her face. "And then I just walked out on him—well, beamed out—right in the middle of our tiff. The last words we had . . ." She trailed off and put a hand over her face. "Bleeding hell. I'm just a self-ish git, aren't I?"

"No more so than the millions of other Starfleet officers in your situation," Crusher said. "Not to mention every other sailor and explorer since the dawn of time."

Kadohata shook her head, unconvinced. "It just keeps getting harder. When it was just the two of us, oh, we'd cry and kiss and have truly epic good-bye sex." She shared a sly smile with Beverly on that point. "But there was never a question that I wouldn't be shipping out. After Aoki came along, though . . ."

Crusher nodded. "A baby changes the whole dynamic," she said, reflecting on Jean-Luc's initial reaction to her heading up this mission. Once upon a time, he had trusted her to take command of an entire starship; but now that she was carrying his child . . .

"Same with you and the captain?" Kadohata asked, and for a moment, Crusher thought she was dealing with her Betazoid team member again.

"No," she quickly lied. All other things being equal, she would have had no problem commiser-ating with Kadohata about her husband. But as her husband was also the other woman's commanding officer, a certain amount of discretion had to be maintained. "I was actually thinking about me and Jack, right after Wesley was born," she covered.

"Oh?"

Crusher nodded, even as she wondered why

those decades-old, long-buried memories had suddenly jumped into her conscious mind. "It wasn't quite the same situation, of course, since we were both Starfleet—I'd earned my commission after my four years pre-med. I was in my second year of medical school, and Jack was on the *Stargazer*. They took off on a year-long deep-space exploration mission as soon as we got back from our honeymoon, which was hard enough for us to deal with. Then I found out, four weeks later, that I was pregnant." The memories started to flood back, the fear and the joy and the panic of being twenty-four years old and expecting, with her new husband hundreds of light-years away.

"A whole year?" Kadohata asked, eyes widening.

"That was actually one of the *Stargazer*'s shorter missions," Crusher answered. It was a bit strange to realize how foreign the idea of such lengthy missions had become in recent decades, at least until the launch of the *Luna*-class. "And Jean-Luc, bless him, found a reason to get back to a starbase halfway through, and let Jack take his paternity leave." Beverly had actually cursed Picard's name at the time, as Jack had not made it to Earth until five days after Wesley was born. By the time he did make it, though, she had forgotten all her anger— forgotten everything, in fact, except for how much she loved this man, how happy she was to have him with her and their child.

The weeks that followed were among the fondest of Beverly's memories. Jack and Wesley bonded instantly, to the new father's surprise. He would sit for hours by the baby's crib, staring in undisguised wonder. During his waking hours, Wesley would stare right back, seeming to display a degree of cognition well beyond that of an average newborn.

Theirs was the very picture of domestic bliss, until the day Starfleet showed up at the door to the Crushers' San Francisco apartment. "Beverly Crusher?" said the tall, grim-faced man in an immaculately pressed maroon uniform jacket.

"Yes?" she said, rocking from one foot to the other as the baby started to drift off in her arms.

The officer glanced at the baby briefly, and then met Beverly's eyes again. "I'm looking for your husband."

She felt her chest tighten as she stepped back away from the door, allowing the security officer in. She led him into the apartment's small kitchen, where Jack was fixing sandwiches for their lunch. "Hello?" he said as the stranger entered, looking a bit less surprised than Beverly might have expected.

"Lieutenant Crusher. I'm glad to have found you here. Commander David Gold." He offered his right hand, which Jack reluctantly shook. "Your C.O. is going to be relieved to learn you're alive—though you may not be after he gets his hands on you."

"What?" Beverly moved around the kitchen table to Jack's side. "What do you mean, relieved he's alive?"

Gold raised one thick dark eyebrow up his high forehead. "Well, he doesn't report back to his ship at the end of his leave time, there's no message, no excuses . . ."

Beverly's mouth fell open. "End of his leave?" Her head snapped right and she looked up at her husband. "Jack?"

Jack gave both her and Gold a sheepish grin. "Umm . . . what day is today?"

The superior officer crossed his arms over his chest and said, "Five days after your captain expected you back aboard the *Stargazer*."

Jack winced, just as Beverly did. "Commander . . . sir, I know that I'm technically absent without official leave, but . . . Please, this is my first leave since my first son was born. I missed his birth already, so I wanted to make the most of what time I did have, and . . . I guess I just didn't want to think about leaving him, and . . . well, I guess I lost track of the days. I know that's a piss-poor excuse, but if there's any way we could . . ."

"Overlook your oversight, and make this go away without formal charges?" Gold asked, giving him a stern, unyielding glare. Then a small grin cracked his façade. "I'm not Shore Patrol, Lieutenant. I'm just an old friend of your captain's, from way back. He knew I was on Earth, and asked me to check up on you, your wife and son, make sure nothing had happened."

Beverly studied Gold's face. "Then . . . Jack's not . . . ?"

The older man gave her a kindly smile. "I have six kids of my own. Not so much kids anymore, though," he added, and for a moment a look of melancholy crossed his face. Then he turned to Jack. "My ship, the *Schiaparelli,* is leaving orbit within an hour. You get your *tuchus* on board, we can take you as far as the Denobulan sector. And I'll see what I can do to smooth things over with Jean-Luc for you."

"I'd appreciate that, Commander. Thank you, sir."

Gold nodded to both Jack and Beverly, then reached out to gently brush his fingertips across the downy-haired top of Wesley's head before turning and letting himself out.

"That was a close one, huh?" Jack said as he collapsed back into his chair and picked up his sandwich.

"Jack! I can't believe you just lied like that to a superior officer—and a friend of Captain Picard's!"

"Lied?" Jack asked, perfectly innocent.

"You *forgot* when your leave ended?" Beverly shook her head at the ludicrousness of that claim. "You know the captain is never going to believe that."

"Don't worry about it," Jack told her in a reassuring tone. "Jean-Luc will bark a little, put a mild reprimand in my file, and that'll be that. You know what they say: it's easier to ask for forgiveness than for permission."

" 'Don't worry about it,' " she repeated in disbelief. "You've technically deserted, you're taking terrible advantage of your friendship with Captain Picard . . . and you're not even going to make your ride to Denobula if you keep sitting there!"

"Yeah," Jack said, staring down at the half-eaten sandwich sitting in front of him, drumming on the tabletop lightly with his fingertips.

Beverly sensed the sudden, uncharacteristic swing in Jack's mood. Shifting the drowsing baby in her arms, she pulled out another chair and sat at the table beside him. "Jack?"

"How can I leave, Beverly?" he whispered, still not looking up. "I'm a father now. How can I?"

"You have to. You have your duty, your career."

He shook his head slowly. "My father was almost never around. He didn't want to be; he made it real clear to me, for as long as I've been old enough to understand, that he thought getting married and having a kid was a big mistake." He turned and looked at his wife and child then. "I don't want Wesley to ever feel like that."

"He won't," Beverly answered automatically.

"But if I leave . . ." He looked into the boy's face, and the boy looked back.

"He'll know you left for a reason," Beverly told him, putting one hand out and resting it on the back of Jack's. "Because you're an honorable man, a man who keeps his promises and lives up to his responsibilities."

"How can he know that?"

"Because he's going to grow up the son of two Starfleet officers," she promised him. "And we'll have our entire lives to let him know how much we care for him."

"Bev . . . if this all is supposed to make me feel better . . ."

Crusher blinked and stared at Kadohata. How long had she been talking, lost in her own reminiscences? And what had been the point she had been trying to make to the other woman when she started out? "I'm sorry, I think I got a little off track there. But the thing is, you have to be true to yourself. You're a wife, a mother, and a Starfleet officer. If you put limits on yourself—any one of those facets—you're not only denying yourself, but denying Vicenzo and the children of the person you really are."

"I suppose," Kadohata said as she pondered that. "Thank you, Bev."

"You're welcome," she said. They sat for a moment longer, in companionable silence, as the stars streaked past through the forward viewports.

"I should really call Vicenzo . . ." Miranda said.

"I'll give you some privacy," Beverly answered with a smile, already halfway out the cockpit door.

5

———

"It should have been me."

Doctor Hegol Den said nothing, but just continued to stare placidly at the young Betazoid man sitting on the couch opposite him. Lieutenant Rennan Konya in turn stared at his own lap, fidgeting with his hands. After a moment, the counselor prompted him: "Why do you say that?"

"I'm the assistant chief of security," Konya snapped back. "I was the one telling them what to do, and now they're dead! These are guys who were fighting Jem'Hadar when I was still going through basic training; what the hell am I doing, giving them orders, getting them killed?"

The Bajoran counselor continued to listen with one ear as he jotted notes on his padd. He'd been hearing many cases of survivor guilt since the end of the Borg's assault; he was sure he'd be dealing with plenty more such cases for months, if not years, to come. He continued to listen to Konya pour out his guilt and grief and shame, only occasionally prodding him. At the end of the session, Den urged the lieutenant to try and take an objective look at himself and reconsider the harsher judgments he had made.

Once Konya left, Hegol heaved a mighty sigh. It had been another full day of appointments, and, as his rumbling stomach was reminding him, he had worked straight through lunch. The muscles of his back and legs protested as he pushed himself up out of his chair for the first time in hours, and crossed the room to the replicator.

Just as he was retrieving his *veklava* and *jumja* iced tea, his door chime sounded. His shoulders sagged, and just for a moment, he considered simply pretending he wasn't there. His sense of responsibility to those who needed him—plus the realization that the ship's computer would give away his location, anyhow—won out, and he called, "Who is it?"

"It's Commander Worf, Doctor," replied the first officer through the comm.

Of course. "Come in," Hegol said, trying to keep the weariness from his voice.

The Klingon officer entered and stopped just inside the door when he saw Hegol getting ready to eat. "Doctor. I apologize for disturbing you during your off-duty time."

"It's all right, Commander," Hegol said, gesturing for him to come inside. "The price I pay for having no interruptions while I'm on duty. Have a seat. Can I get you anything?"

"No. Thank you." Worf hesitated before taking the seat opposite the counselor at his desk, giving Hegol the opportunity to take a large bite, happily silencing his stomach. "I was hoping you had completed your evaluation of those crew members who'd requested psychiatric leave," Worf then said.

Hegol nodded as he took a sip of tea. "I just saw the last of them. Ensigns Bulthaus and H'Mupal, I would recommend be transferred out of the security section, at least temporarily."

Worf scowled as he considered that. "Commander La Forge has been asking for additional assistance in engineering to deal with our still-pending repairs."

"Good," Hegol said, swallowing another bite of *veklava*. "Let them be part of fixing things for a while. That should be just the kind of therapy they need, after being part of so much destruction."

"And what of the others?"

"The others . . ." Hegol sighed, his fork hovering above his plate. "They're all suffering from post-traumatic stress to one degree or another, but they at least recognize they need help working through their issues. With continued regular counseling, I don't see that any of them would be unable to carry out their duties."

Worf nodded, seemingly satisfied with this report. Hegol hesitated a moment before broaching another subject, but then said, "Actually, Commander, I'm far more concerned about the ones who refuse to face their emotional issues and try to behave as if nothing is wrong. Lieutenant Choudhury, for example."

The commander stiffened in his seat. "Lieutenant Choudhury?"

"Yes. Our chief of security has seen her entire planet obliterated by the Borg and most likely lost her entire family. Yet, to see her on the ship here these past couple of days, you would never know anything had happened."

Worf narrowed his eyes at him. "Perhaps you just don't know the lieutenant well enough to see how she is coping with her losses."

Hegol shrugged slightly. "I suppose that could be so. I haven't actually talked with her at any length since her return. Although, that's another cause for concern."

"What is?"

"That she hasn't come to me," Hegol said. "Or to any counselor since her loss. In point of fact, according to her records, Lieutenant Choudhury has not voluntarily sought or received any counseling since her first year at Starfleet Academy."

"Is that so unusual?" the first officer challenged him. "Not every Starfleet officer needs to undergo counseling."

"Commander, I know that Klingon culture doesn't put much credence in what I do—"

Worf gave him a frown that verged on being a snarl. "You must also know that I was close friends with one of your predecessors, Deanna Troi, and that I often welcomed her counsel."

Hegol held his tongue. He indeed did know about Worf's past relationship with Deanna Troi, but chose not to express any opinion on that particular topic. "Commander, when I was in the Resistance, I had a colleague named Tafka. He was a deeply religious man who believed in peace, yet just as devoted a fighter as any of us, knowing if we were ever going to get our planet back, we could give the Cardies no quarter. But each night he prayed to the Prophets and promised to walk Their path. Well, the Occupation ended, and Tafka entered the monastery. Two months later, he had killed himself, leaving a note saying the Prophets could never forgive him for all he'd done."

"And you believe Lieutenant Choudhury is capable of such a thing?" Worf asked, almost sounding personally offended.

Hegol kept himself perfectly calm and still as he answered, "Lieutenant Choudhury, too, is a devout adherent of a belief system that puts great importance on pacifism and peaceful behavior. She is also a security officer who, over the course of her career, has participated in three major interstellar wars, plus dozens of isolated armed conflicts, and has just recently suffered a loss most of us would consider inconceivable. Yet through all of this, she has maintained this image of . . . I think the humans' word for it is 'unflappability.'

"As I admitted, I do not know her as . . . intimately as you do." Hegol noted the way Worf flinched at his choice of terms, and quietly filed it away in his mind. "But at the same time, I have to be somewhat concerned that beneath her serene exterior, she's bottling up all of this emotion, letting it build up. And without adequate outlet, all that pressure . . ." With his hands and fingers, he silently mimed a small explosion.

Worf glowered and stood up from his chair, looking as if he was making a significant effort not to fling it across the room. "Doctor . . . do you wish me to order Lieutenant Choudhury to see you?"

Hegol would have liked to have answered yes to that, but the fact was, he didn't have a solid basis to do so. Still, he couldn't simply ignore the concerns he felt. Finally, he looked up and answered Worf by asking, "Do you believe you would need to order her?"

Worf stared at him for a moment, then said, "Thank you for your report, Doctor. Enjoy your meal," after which he turned and left.

Hegol continued to stare after him for a few seconds after he'd gone, wondering what precisely was triggering the Klingon's apparent protectiveness.

As if you don't already have enough on your platter, he chided himself, then put all thoughts of work aside as he turned his attention back to his dinner.

The moment Arandis felt the transporter effect fade away, there were a pair of cold, webbed hands on her back and bare shoulder, pushing her roughly. "Move! Out of the way; there are more still coming!" the owner of those clammy hands barked. She and the three others she beamed down with were "escorted" down off a transporter platform that sat off to the side of a large, elegant hotel lobby. They were steered away from the check-in desk, though, into a line that led out the exit doors.

"Wait, where are we going?" Arandis asked the Selkie male doing the steering. He wore a loose, dark-blue tunic and matching pants, which looked casual enough, but when added to the phaser rifle he wielded, was clearly a law enforcer's uniform. "We've come here seeking sanctuary for those under our care. Why—"

"This isn't a sanctuary," the guard said, and accentuated that point by motioning with his weapon for her to keep moving. "The Eden Beach Hotel is merely allowing use of its lobby and transporters as a favor to the government—that's all. Its rooms are already full to the gill crests."

"Then where . . . ?" Arandis managed to ask before the guard turned his attention to others further back in line, ordering them to keep moving. They were funneled, single file, toward a dead-eyed Zakdorn woman sitting at a small table at one end of the lobby. "Handonthescanner," she said in a lifeless mumble. Despite everything she'd been through, Arandis still had enough of her Risian empathy to wonder how many survivors of the Borg this worn woman had had to deal with. As the device hummed under Arandis's palm, the Zakdorn asked for her full legal name, planet of birth, and most recent residence. "Thankyounext," the Zakdorn woman concluded, and before Arandis could ask any questions of her own, another armed Selkie reached for her arm and maneuvered her back into the queue leading out the doors.

"I thought the war was over. What's with all the soldiers?" Arandis turned her glare away from the guard and found herself standing directly behind Donald Wheeler in line. He was looking far more sober than he had earlier aboard the transport, thanks to a second round of anti-inebriants and a few more hours of rest. Given their present circumstances, however, she didn't think a little dulling of the senses would be terribly unwelcome.

Arandis turned to survey the faces of the Selkies populating the hotel lobby, as they in turn watched the new arrivals shuffling for the doors. After more than fifty years as a hospitality hostess, she'd learned to read others quite well and to determine at a glance what their troubles were, in order to relieve them. "They're frightened," she said.

"Frightened? Of what?" Wheeler blanched slightly then as a thought occurred to him. "The war *is* over, right? The Borg *are* really gone?"

"Yes," Arandis said. "It's *us* they're frightened of. To them, *we're* invaders."

"*Khrught,*" he said, turning the Tellarite profanity into a derisive laugh. "Yeah, after all the Borg have done, *we're* scary." He gave her a sideways glance and another of his inexpert leering smiles. "I mean, you . . . If you were to tell me resistance was futile, I'd have no reason to want to resist."

Arandis ignored the inept and inapt compliment as they reached the Eden Beach Hotel's front entrance and stepped out into the brilliant tropical sunlight. For a moment, as the sun's warmth fell on her face (coming from only a single star, but just as strong as Risa's binary pair), she closed her eyes and let the sounds and smells of the nearby ocean tickle her senses. For just a fleeting moment, she allowed herself to believe she was back home.

Then, she lowered her face and opened her eyes.

The street—a broad thoroughfare that led up from the ocean between rows of hotels, restaurants, and entertainment parlors—had become an ocean itself, swollen and surging with humanoid life. Most of the beings, it seemed, wore expressions similar to Wheeler's—confusion and disbelief, in some verging on severe illness.

"Inland!" shouted another of the Selkie soldiers. "Head inland! We have food, shelter, and medical facilities prepared for you."

"No wine, though, huh?" Wheeler said under his breath as he jostled his way into the moving mob.

"No, probably not," Arandis said, in a sarcastic tone she never before would have dreamed using with a guest. But he wasn't a guest anymore—not of hers, anyhow. Arandis had always heard that the Pacificans' hospitality ran a close second to that of Risa. She had to say, from her time here so far, she couldn't agree.

After a few minutes of silence, Wheeler muttered something else. "What?" Arandis asked him.

"Sherman's Planet had a lot of great wines," Wheeler repeated himself quietly. "Nothing like Earth wines; the hybrid grapes they grow—*grew* there won't grow anywhere else. I went to this one winery in New Sonoma a couple years ago, where they had a tasting of this very rare vintage, this '45 cabernet sauvignon. This was an incredible wine. Full-bodied, dark, complex . . . it exploded on the palate . . . and the finish . . ." He sighed rapturously at the memory; then his expression turned bittersweet. "But I guess all Sherman's wines are rare vintages now, huh?" Arandis, having no idea what to say, simply shrugged and nodded at her fellow refugee.

More people joined the throng from the hotels and resorts that lined the main boulevard of this seaside village. At the edge of town, the boulevard narrowed and became a path winding through a forest. The canopy of leaves overhead cast them into shadow, and Arandis, in the light, silky sundress and diaphanous wrap she'd had on when the call to evacuate Risa went out, began to shiver slightly. She was more than a little surprised when she felt Wheeler drape his beach towel over her shoulders. She looked at him, but he'd turned away, feigning interest in the endless range of trees off to the other side of their trail.

Arandis had lost all sense of how long they'd been walking. From the occasional glimpses she caught of Pacifica's one sun through the trees, she thought they must have been walking for hours—but then, she had no idea how long a day on Pacifica was. Truth be told, she wasn't even sure how long it had been since they left Risa—she thought it had to have been at least a full week, but at the same time, that just seemed incredible. She trudged on, her feet aching, and her stomach starting to gurgle audibly.

Finally, the parade of refugees came to a stop, still in the middle of the woods. "So, where is this food and shelter they were talking about?" Wheeler asked, sparking similar rumblings from the others around them.

As the question of what was holding them up traveled from person to person moving forward, an answer was passed back from those at the site of the logjam: "We're at a river," an exhausted-looking Efrosian woman announced from several meters ahead, "and they won't let us cross."

"They *are* letting us cross," the equally tired-looking Efrosian man standing beside her contradicted. "It's just a very narrow bridge."

"A rickety, makeshift piece of *pyurb* is what it is," another voice in the crowd said.

"Well, what do the Selkies know from building bridges?" asked one of the refugees pressing up from behind Arandis. "They can just swim across."

"Hell, I can swim . . ." a Caitian man growled.

"Oh, but they don't want us contaminating their precious waters," a disheveled Yridian man sneered.

"Well, in your case . . ." Wheeler said under his breath while rolling his eyes. Arandis, though, took a critical look at herself and her disheveled and bedraggled traveling companions, and wondered if, in their current conditions, that wasn't a legitimate concern.

"Off-worlders!" The sound of the electronically amplified voice instantly silenced the entire crowd. *"We are trying to make this resettlement as orderly and nondisruptive as possible. We ask that you please remain patient and calm. We are all doing our best to deal with extraordinary circumstances."*

The address by the anonymous Selkie peacekeeper did its job. The crowd continued to move, slowly, at times almost imperceptibly. When Arandis reached the now fabled bridge, she saw it was indeed only wide enough for a single file of people to cross at once, and she also noted that the gently flowing river it traversed was only a few meters wide at this spot.

Looking upstream, she saw a small group of Selkies barely hidden by a dipping tree branch, submerged almost to their eyes, observing her and the others. They must have noticed her direct stare, and quickly dropped below the water's surface, but not before Arandis could see the apprehension in those eyes. On the opposite bank, once she'd made it across, she paused to glance upriver again. The eyes were gone, but before she turned away, she saw a tiny bluish-green face emerge from the water's surface. A pair of oversized eyes blinked, and the mouth opened, emitting a high-pitched gurgle that, despite the immeasurable differences between species, was unmistakably that of a baby.

"Idiot Selkie," more than a few refugees muttered as they set foot on the soil on the other side of the bridge. Arandis moved away from the water and rejoined the crowd continuing up a gentle slope, away from the riverbank.

As a kid, Trys Chen used to love exploring the Jefferies tubes of the ships her mother and she had been assigned to. Even on the smallest vessels, there were literally kilometers of the service tunnels for an angry young half-breed pissed off at the universe to crawl into and get away from all the drama of shipboard life. She particularly liked the ones that ran over the reduced-gravity areas of the ship, like the shuttlebay, where she could stretch out and almost float, as if in a tub of dry water. She would camp out for hours there, just letting her eyes trace the lines of the conduits and opti-cable lines, listening to the soothing murmur of the ship's mechanical operational systems.

Of course, the Jefferies tubes quickly lost their appeal once she joined Starfleet herself, and got the occasional assignment to repair this system or conduct a physical inspection of that piece of equipment. And, after crawling through the *Enterprise*'s access tunnels for almost half her regular duty shift, she came to utterly despise the cramped, uncomfortable, overheated spaces.

"It's something to keep you off the streets, at least," she muttered to nobody as she crawled along, echoing her mother's usual response whenever she would complain about a boring chore or school assignment. Given the *Enterprise*'s current mission, there was no call for her services as contact specialist, so Commander Worf "suggested" that she "volunteer" to help out Commander La Forge. There were a lot of tasks left undone at McKinley, and the engineering section was seriously understaffed. And thus, Chen found herself on her hands and knees in the gap between Decks 5 and 6, tricorder at the ready, confirming the ship's internal sensor system was working properly by scanning each of the sensor array clusters, set at ten-meter intervals in the walls off the passageways, one by one. "I'll just bet Dina is behind this," she spoke aloud again as she confirmed yet another of the devices to be functioning perfectly.

After verifying the next eight sensor clusters were sensing accurately, and muttering curses against Elfiki, Worf, the staff of McKinley Station, and the late Admiral Jefferies, she finally received an anomalous reading from her tricorder. "Uh-oh," she said, and tapped her combadge. "Chen to engineering."

"La Forge here. What is it, Trys?"

"Sir, I think I just found a bad unit. Section 06-43-F-Eta," she read off the nearest crossbeam.

"Okay, sit tight there," La Forge said, and cut the connection.

Chen sat on her haunches and felt her muscles tighten for several minutes, until finally, a hatch opened around a bend somewhere ahead of her. Seconds later, Commander La Forge appeared, crawling her way with an equipment case strapped over his shoulder.

"All right . . . let's have a look." La Forge took the tricorder from Chen and quickly reviewed the diagnostic of the suspect unit. "Oh, yeah, this one is shot," he said, and then cracked open his case, taking out a small handheld tool. "Good job, Trys," he said with an easy smile.

"And I only had to check five thousand other good ones to find it," Chen said, making sure she blunted the comment with a smile of her own.

La Forge gave her a sympathetic look as he worked the cluster assembly loose from its socket. "I know, it's a dull, monotonous, tiring job. But it's better that we find these now, rather than discovering in the middle of a crisis that we have gaps in the grid. And I really do appreciate your pitching in," he added with a grin.

The commander's positive mood was contagious, and despite the pain in her knees and shoulders, Chen's smile became a bit more genuine. "Thanks," she said. "You're in a pretty chipper mood, considering it's your butt on the line if all this work doesn't get done."

La Forge glanced up from his work, with an odd look in his mechanical eyes. For a second, Chen thought he would snap at her to never mind about where his butt was or might end up. Instead, what he said was, "I had a really good leave. I went home, spent time with my sister and her daughter, and . . . worked my way through some things that I've been letting eat at me for a while. So . . . yeah, I've got my life, I have people who love me, and a career that I love. I'm a lot better off than a lot of people are right now."

Chen nodded somberly. "Like Taurik."

La Forge raised his head again. "Yeah . . . Why Taurik, specifically?" he asked, concern for his assistant plain on his face.

"No reason," Chen said. "It's just . . . well, you know, he was on board the whole time we were at McKinley, supervising the repairs."

"Yeah. I couldn't have taken my leave if he hadn't volunteered."

"Volunteered?" Chen's jaw dropped. That meant he had never had any intention of going back home following the attacks, which meant . . . "Son of a *targ*!"

"What?" La Forge asked, looking ready to back away from her.

"He was pulling our legs! A joke—some kind of payback for all those pranks."

"Taurik, joking?" La Forge asked, and as soon as

he did, Chen realized how unlikely that really was. "Joking about what?"

"He said he had a wife and daughter who were killed in ShiKahr."

Geordi La Forge's face fell. "He did." The way he was looking at her made Chen feel a half meter tall. "What makes you think he would lie about something like that?"

"Well . . . he didn't go back to Vulcan for the big mass memorial they had there." Chen had no idea what such a service for mourners who refused to mourn would be like, but the news reports had said close to fifty million had gathered in the shadow of Mount Seleya, so there must have been something to it.

La Forge shook his head as he scanned the replacement sensor unit with his tricorder. "What he told me was, it was more logical to allow those of us whose families survived to spend our limited time with the living, rather than for him to deny someone else that chance so he could honor those who would be dead for eternity."

Chen frowned as she tried to reconcile all of this in her mind. "I don't think I'll ever understand Vulcans," she said.

La Forge gave her a shrug as he closed up his case and started back the way he had come. "Well, why should you be different from any of them?" he asked, before disappearing back around a corner of the tube.

6

———

Picard leaned forward in his seat, gripping both armrests as he watched the invading ship turn and prepare to jump to warp. "Fire phasers!" he ordered.

Energy beams bolted out from the *Enterprise*'s ventral emitters, one hurtling across the other vessel's bow, and the other striking its warp coil. Their shields took most of the blow, but not enough; flashes of light and energy showing through the warp plasma vents indicated a cascading series of overloads, temporarily crippling the smaller craft's warp drive.

"They're hailing us now," Choudhury reported from her station.

"Yes, *now* they want to negotiate," Picard muttered bitterly under his breath. He stood from his seat and said, "On-screen."

The image of the Ferengi ship was replaced by that of its young commander, a boy barely past the Age of Attainment. *"My Federation friends, please,"* he said, holding out both hands, wrists together, in the customary sign of submission. *"I fear there has been a terrible misunderstanding."*

"Indeed there has," Picard said. "Apparently, Dai-Mon, you are under the impression that there's some profit to be made in desecrating the wreckage of Starfleet vessels and facilities within Federation space."

The Ferengi put on a wounded expression. *"Captain! I'm saddened that this negative perception of Ferengi still persists among you hew-mons to this day! I am an honest businessman, hoping to provide my services and help the people of the Federation in this, their time of need."*

If the DaiMon was trying to pacify the captain with his sympathetic tone, he was having the exact opposite effect. "We tracked you here from the former site of Starbase Leonov," he said as he stepped closer to the viewer, his voice rising. "And our sensors are reading significant amounts of Federation-manufactured duranium and tritanium alloys in your cargo holds!"

"Which I will offer back to the Federation—for a very reasonable reclamation fee—so it can be reused in your rebuilding efforts." The Ferengi smiled, as if this were the most generous offer ever imagined—which, to him, it may have been. *"So, you see, we are both on the same side—"*

"And who asked you to collect this material from our battle sites?" Picard demanded, making no effort to rein in his outrage.

"Nobody asked me," the DaiMon said, with evident pride in his initiative. *"But, as the Ninth Rule says, opportunity plus instinct equals profit."*

"Yes, well, in this instance, your math is off," Picard informed him. "You will drop your shields and release your cargo to us. And then you will leave Federation space."

The Ferengi's snaggletoothed jaw dropped. *"What? Captain, that's outrageous! You can't simply—"*

But Picard had turned his back on the protesting alien. "Lieutenant," he said to his tactical officer as he moved back to his seat, "arm quantum torpedoes."

Choudhury was caught off-guard by that order, and it took her a moment, even after Picard signaled her with a wink, to respond, "Quantum torpedoes. Aye, sir." Picard turned back to the screen just in time to see the properly intimidated DaiMon reach forward to his control globe. The transmission ended then, and on-screen, Picard and the bridge crew watched as the Ferengi ship's cargo doors slid open.

"Their shields are down," Worf reported, reading from his chairside display. "Have all the surrendered material beamed into Cargo Bay Four," he ordered the officer at ops, then said to Picard, "Well played, sir."

Picard answered with a dismissive snort. "Any schoolyard bully can issue threats," he said, even though he had no regrets about using such blunt tactics against the scavenger, who was now moving off at impulse, its holds empty.

"Still," Worf said in a low grumble, "we have at least now accomplished something."

Picard raised an eyebrow at Worf's sarcastic response. The *Enterprise*'s mission was officially termed a rescue and recovery patrol, though the job they were actually charged with, as the president had phrased it, was "roving troubleshooter." The captain had been given a significant degree of latitude and autonomy to respond to whatever crises he discovered, in whatever way he, in his best judgment, saw fit.

Initially, Picard had thought it an unqualified vote of confidence from his superiors, one that would allow him to help in ways he couldn't if given a single specific assignment, such as ferrying emergency supplies to Vulcan or Qo'noS. In reality, though, being roving troubleshooters meant they were traveling rather aimlessly, like Don Quixote wandering a landscape mostly devoid of windmills. They had encountered two small evacuation ship convoys, though neither had been in need of any assistance. And the "accomplishment" of tracking and recovering a few tons of debris paled when one considered how much more of what had been lost at Starbase Leonov could never be recovered.

There was, however, one remarkable incident during their recent travels. "Computer," Picard said, "replay visual log of our fly-by of the Axanar system yesterday, twenty-two forty-two hours, full magnification."

On the main viewer, the stars jumped, and a blue-white globe filled the bottom-right quadrant of the screen. As the planet slowly grew larger, a strange speck of light appeared above one of the small islands in the world's primary ocean. The light expanded, and then divided, until it became visible as separate distinct streaks, now clearly identifiable as torpedo trails. They flew upward through the highest reaches of Axanar's atmosphere, and then the torpedoes detonated, one after another.

"A twenty-one-gun salute," Picard said, as the sequence of brilliant starbursts continued. He turned back to Worf, but addressed the entire bridge. "What we are doing is of value . . . if to no one else, then to these people, and others like them. The entire Federation has suffered a traumatic blow, and they need reassurance that they are now safe. We are that assurance. We are that security. It is the heart of our pledge as Starfleet officers: to serve and to protect the people of the Federation. It is a responsibility that we should take pride in performing."

Picard looked again to Worf. "Understood, sir," the first officer said, matching the captain's tone and also looking about the bridge and making sure the rest of the crew received the captain's message. Picard could tell that his Klingon heart was not in it. Silently he sighed, grateful at least that Worf's ambassadorial experience enabled him to hide his feelings from the rest of the crew.

The captain took his seat again. "Helm, resume on heading—"

"Sir?"

Picard and Worf both turned as Lieutenant Choudhury stepped down from her tactical station, padd in hand, moving between them. "Excuse me, Captain, but I'd like to recommend a variation to our current patrol route."

"Oh?" Picard said.

Choudhury nodded and offered him the padd. "There were four Andorian cargo vessels that were part of the evacuation of Andor, though in the chaos of the last hours before the Borg attack, they never formally received clearance to break orbit, and so, they were officially assumed destroyed. But, we have evidence they may in fact have left before the Borg arrived: radio communication between an unidentified Andorian ship and Ivor Prime, right after the news broke about the end of the war."

"And their most likely return route would be right along here," Picard said, tracing a finger across the padd's display of an empty region of Sector 003. "Have we picked up a distress call from this region?"

"No, sir. But neither have they returned to the Andorian system, and they certainly should have by now," Choudhury said, fixing him with a direct look that spoke of her professional conviction.

Picard considered the padd, and Choudhury, thoughtfully. In the prelude to the Azure Nebula invasion, Choudhury was able to make the leaps of logic that allowed her to accurately predict Korvat had been in imminent danger of attack.

He then stepped up directly behind the flight controller's forward station. "Ensign Faur, lay in a new course, bearing 0-6-7 mark 3-4-4, and engage at warp five. Initiate and continue long-range sensor scans for anything that could possibly be a ship in distress." Picard turned back and gave Choudhury a broad smile. "Excellent work, Lieutenant."

"Only if we're able to find and save anyone," Choudhury demurred. "Even then, most of the credit has to go to Ensign Rosado."

Picard turned to the bridge library station, where the older human woman stood. "She's the one who's been able to pull together all the Andorians' fragmented data—what wasn't lost once Andor itself was attacked," Choudhury continued, "and then sync it with communication logs, Starfleet logs, and civilian space traffic movement, triangulating all that across the subspace comm relay grid."

Picard was duly impressed. Rosado had been head librarian at the University of Bologna on Earth for close to fifty years before resigning, and had then decided to start her second career in Starfleet. Clearly, her experience in information sciences was proving an asset in her new career. "Well done, Ensign," the captain told her.

"Is there a reason this search protocol was limited to Andorian vessels and records?" Worf asked.

"Just to limit the volume of raw data while we were testing the program," Rosado explained as she moved back to the operations console. "And since Andor is the closest affected system . . ."

"Then this protocol could be used to likewise track unaccounted-for ships from any system?" Worf asked. Picard noticed a look passing between his first officer and Choudhury, and noted that the Denevan woman looked away, an uncharacteristically haunted expression on her face.

"Yes, sir," Rosado answered. "Although Andor suffered . . . relatively limited damage." From her hesitation and expression, it pained Rosado to describe the annihilation of at least five major population centers and the deaths of close to one hundred million as "limited damage." "For those worlds that suffered more complete destruction—" Rosado's eyes, along with, it seemed, the entire bridge's, flicked to Choudhury. "—the available data may not be sufficient for the computers to extrapolate from."

"I see," Picard said softly. "Still, if there's even the slimmest chance of finding and rescuing any lost evacuees . . ." Picard handed the padd back to Choudhury. "I'd like you to share this search protocol with your counterparts on all vessels currently assigned to patrol and rescue-and-recovery duties."

The tactical officer nodded. "Aye, sir."

"And," Picard continued, stopping her as she started to turn back to her station, "we should endeavor to refine the protocol to enable us to search for information from any and all impacted worlds."

"Yes, sir," Choudhury answered, and again, for just a fleeting moment, he thought he saw that strange, haunted look pass behind her dark eyes.

Then she dropped her gaze to her panel, rapidly keying in instructions, and Picard dismissed it. He turned back to the forward viewscreen, watching the stars warp by. Somewhere, up ahead, were people in trouble, in need of help.

Picard allowed himself a small, private smile. *And the* Enterprise *is on its way.*

At the end of her shift, Trys Chen climbed out of a hole in the wall. She spent several minutes in the middle of the corridor, twisting this way and that, ignoring the odd looks she got from the shift-change foot traffic passing by. Then she made her way back to her quarters, stripped off her dusty, grease-stained uniform, and took a long sonic shower. It had been a long day of mind-numbing repetitiveness, allowing her normally overactive mind to wander aimlessly in places she thought better not to explore. *What do I care about Taurik or how he mourns his dead family?* she asked herself as she finished her shower, pulled a thin wrap around herself, and walked across her living quarters to the replicator to order herself a beer.

As she savored the first cold sip and let herself relax even further, she noticed that her computer station was signaling a saved message. She slipped into her desk chair and keyed the playback function, but the only message was that there had been an attempt to contact her by someone at the Raal Provincial Hospital on Vulcan. Trys stopped with the glass halfway to her lips as she stared at the screen. Why would anyone on Vulcan—in a Vulcan hospital in a backwater province—be calling her? The only possible person she could think of would be—

Well, no, that couldn't be possible . . .

Except, who else . . . ?

No.

The beer mug sweated in her hand as she stared at the screen, frozen. Trys was rarely indecisive, and she didn't like the way it felt to be so now. So, she hit the tab that initiated a return signal, and she watched as the screen cycled through a number of frames, from the Starfleet delta, to the UFP seal, then the stylized IDIC representing the Vulcan government, and then the unfamiliar emblem of a Vulcan medical facility.

Finally, that static image was replaced by the face of a Vulcan man. He wore a large surgical healing patch that covered his right eye socket and wrapped around to his ear. An ugly black-green blotch on the top of his stubble-covered head suggested his hair had recently caught fire and burned to the scalp. He looked out from the screen with his one good eye and said, *"T'Ryssa Chen?"*

"Yes?" she said, wishing to the gods of at least a hundred cultures that she'd ignored that damned message.

The man lifted his left hand, fingers splayed in a V, and told her what she already knew: *"Live long and prosper, T'Ryssa. I am Sylix."*

Trys felt an entire lifetime of emotion roiling in the pit of her stomach. "Yeah, and?"

"You know who I am?"

"Sure. You're the guy who went all *Pon farr* on my mom twenty-seven years ago, and then ran away to let her raise the result all by herself."

The man on the screen hesitated before dipping his chin and saying, *"That is . . . sufficiently accurate."*

Trys felt ready to burst out of her skin. For years, she'd wondered what she'd say to this man if she ever saw him again. Now here he was, and the only sound coming out of her mouth was a slow, hoarse breathing.

"T'Ryssa, I—"

"I prefer Trys," she said curtly.

"Trys—"

"Actually, from you, I think I prefer 'Lieutenant Chen,' instead."

No doubt pained by his spawn's undisciplined show of indecision, Sylix took a breath and said, *"I contacted you, Lieutenant Chen, because I have* been unable to find the current whereabouts of your mother, Antigone."

"Probably because she doesn't want you to find her." *Too bad I wasn't as successful at avoiding you.*

"I had hoped you would help me in this regard."

"Really. Why?"

"Because I'm a civilian, Starfleet Command would not—"

"No, not 'Why would you ask for my help?'—although that is a damned good question. I meant, why would you want to find Antigone?"

Sylix hesitated almost imperceptibly. *"I simply wish to ascertain whether she survived the recent hostilities."*

"Yeah, bullshit," Trys snapped. Her mother's current assignment, the *U.S.S. Wounded Knee,* came through the war without ever seeing action, but she wasn't about to volunteer that information to the son of a bitch. "Did you try to contact her after the *Odyssey* went boom? Did you try to find her any time during the entire Dominion War? No, this is about *you.* You had a near-death experience when the Borg hit Vulcan, and by some miracle, you lived. You managed to get rescued, fixed up, and flown to a hospital on the other side of the planet, where you got a lot of time to just lie there and think about how close you came to being just more sand piled on the Forge." Sylix said nothing as he listened, but the small twitches of his injury-weakened facial muscles told her she had his number to the last decimal place. "Now you've got this big second chance, so now you want to reach out to all those you've hurt and make amends for all your wrongs."

The Vulcan stared stock-still at her for a moment. Then, he lifted his one exposed eyebrow and said, *"You are very human, aren't you?"*

"Damn straight, Skippy."

"I should think that you would want to help me, given—"

"Given what? That you're my daddy?" Trys erupted. "What's that, an appeal to *emotion*? You want to make up for being a lousy person all your life, fine; but don't you dare ask me for my help!"

And with that, Trys cut the connection, hard enough to cut her knuckles. Cursing as she put her fingers to her mouth, she went to the 'fresher to run cold water over her hand. Once the flow of green blood had stopped, she dried her hand with a towel and walked back out into the cabin. *Goddamned Vulcans,* she thought as she took a long swig of beer to wash the taste of copper from her mouth.

Beverly Crusher had been to Pacifica several times in the past, on both official Starfleet business and for her own personal pleasure. But on all those occasions, she had only ever seen the surface of this pelagic world. This was her first time visiting hi'Leyi'a, Pacifica's underwater capital city, and it was with a sense of awe that she stood in the center of hi'Leyi'a's main plaza, on the ocean floor, staring up at a kilometer of seawater above her.

"This is fantastic!" Miranda Kadohata said, her breath having been, figuratively speaking, taken away. Their beam-down coordinates had placed them in a small air pocket, with invisible force fields holding in enough gaseous oxygen for the visiting air breathers to continue doing so comfortably. Both Kadohata and Crusher gaped at the alien cityscape that surrounded them. Multi-hued, coral-like spires rose upward, illuminated by bioluminescent seaweeds clinging like kudzu to every surface. Spiraling shells and fractal-patterned sponge-like structures decorated every surface, and the tiny, gemlike sand grains that made up the flooring of the open courtyard reflected and intensified the limited ambient light of the depths.

Paul Dillingham grinned amiably at the two women. "Well, I feel a lot better about gawking at all this like a hick tourist, seeing you veteran Starfleeters acting just the same way." A school of what looked like small Earth jellyfish swam by, flashing like oversized blue-green fireflies. And of course, hundreds of Selkies, Pacifica's water-breathing humanoid natives, swam to and fro, carrying out the business of their daily lives.

"Well, this is what we live for, you know," Kadohata said. "Strange new worlds and all that."

"Pacifica is hardly a new world," Dillingham

countered, but before he could get any further in what was sure to be a pedantic monologue on Pacifican history, the sound of the energy field changed pitch, and the field rippled behind him. For a split second, Crusher envisioned the invisible barrier popping like the bubble it was, and the three of them being crushed by hundreds of atmospheres of seawater.

It held steady, however, even as a mottled green humanoid limb, ending in a web-fingered hand, passed through the energy membrane, followed in short order by the rest of the body of a male Selkie.

A *naked* male body, Crusher couldn't help but notice. While the Selkies who lived on the surface and interacted regularly with other, more modest species normally wore some sort of attire in deference to their guests, for those living underwater clothing was a hindrance.

Once inside the bubble, the Selkie drew a deep breath—*a younger, amphibious Selkie, then,* Crusher realized—and said, "Welcome to hi'Leyi'a. I'm Uthdel Evelth, Secretary Bemidji's personal assistant. Would you come this way, please?" As Evelth gestured toward the nearest of the structures surrounding the plaza, the energy-enclosed dome morphed, expanding toward their destination and, as they drew closer, retracting behind them.

Off to the side of a wide, elaborately decorated portal, through which several fully aquatic Selkies entered and exited, there was a smaller set of doors, adorned only with a sign warning of the nonaquatic environment beyond. The air bubble pressed over this opening, and the doors opened for them with a soft hiss. Crusher, Kadohata, and Dillingham entered a corridor that, in marked contrast to the exterior, was constructed of the same plain, unadorned polymetal that typified practically every Federation facility across the quadrant.

The corridor led to an equally plain conference room, split in half by a transparent plate. The other half of the room was flooded, floor to ceiling, with clear Pacifican seawater, putting Crusher in mind of visiting an old-style aquarium. On the other side of the transparency was Pacifica's Secretary of Interplanetary Affairs, Osseo Bemidji, a venerable old member of the planet's ruling party, with sagging facial features and random spots of white all over his fully exposed body. "Finally!" he said as he stood and leaned across the table on his side of the room. Whether it was intentional or not, the water and the transparency both acted to magnify Bemidji's large, all-black eyes to intimidating proportions. Crusher suddenly got the feeling that it was she and her colleagues who were in fact in the proverbial fishbowl. "We need to get all these so-called refugees off the surface!"

The Federation team was momentarily stunned. "Mister Secretary, excuse me," Crusher eventually said, "but we're only here to assess the refugee situation here, not to remove them."

Dillingham then piped in, "Which, under Article 51 of the Articles of the Federation, cannot be done without proper cause, nor without due process for those persons who—"

"Do not quote the Articles at me!" Bemidji cut him off, waving his finned arms in a wide arc. "Pacifica has been a proud and stalwart member of the Federation for generations. But the Articles are not a suicide pact. Pacifica is facing a dire threat from this sudden, massive influx of off-world air-breathers!"

"What kind of dire threat?" Kadohata asked.

Jets of small bubbles streamed from the secretary's gill crests—the equivalent of an air-breather's sigh. "I know you are probably not aware of this, but the beginning of the Selkies' life cycle is not lived in the oceans, but on the surface—"

"In an amphibious stage," Crusher interrupted, "which lasts through childhood and the child-bearing and -raising years, approximately the first thirty-five years of life, on average."

Bemidji scowled at her, then nodded. "And it is our young, our future generations, these refugees are putting at risk."

"How is that, Mister Secretary?" Dillingham asked.

"Our children have very exacting environmental needs," he explained, making what looked like a determined effort to maintain his patience. "For centuries, we've welcomed off-worlders who wanted to visit our smaller islands and build there—their lack of natural shelter, exposed shorelines, and sandy ground make them all but worthless to us. But the refugees have already overwhelmed those existing resorts, and they're demanding to be placed inland on the larger landmasses, where they will be a disruption to our young and jeopardize the region's ecological stability."

"Mister Secretary," Crusher started, hesitated, and then said, "while I respect your concerns, these people you want us to remove from your planet have suffered a far greater disruption to their lives than your young are likely to."

"Yes, well, that's a fine thing for you to judge, Commander Crusher, but these are our children you're so cavalierly dismissing!"

Beverly's right hand unconsciously went to her stomach in a protective gesture. "First off, Mister Secretary, I would prefer to be addressed as Doctor, given that I am a physician. And as a doctor, and a Starfleet officer, I would never dismiss or intentionally endanger any life. That said, I know as well as you do, sir, that your young people do frequent off-worlders' resorts."

Bemidji stiffened visibly at that. "And they have no qualms about interacting with air-breathers, either," Kadohata interjected, in a way that suggested, to Beverly at least, that the second officer was speaking from direct knowledge. Kadohata caught her stare from the corner of her eye, turned, and gave her a look that said, *What? You know I had a life before meeting my husband.*

Meanwhile, after several seconds spent seething over the humans' insinuations regarding his fellow Selkies, Bemidji said, "There is a difference between mature adults choosing, of their own free will, to travel to other parts of their own planet and initiate contact with visitors, and being compelled to allow outsiders to invade the sanctuaries of our newborns, as is happening on iy'Dewra'ni."

Crusher recognized iy'Dewra'ni as the name of one of Pacifica's largest landmasses, and the site of the primary resettlement area that Barash had concerns about. "Mister Secretary, I'm certain that, despite all the challenges, we will be able to find a solution that will address both the needs of your citizens and those of the refugees."

"Yes, well, there had better be. Because when it comes to protecting our own, we will do so, Federation or no Federation." And with that, Bemidji turned, put his arms out to his sides, and with one mighty stroke swam up to the ceiling and through a door Beverly had not noticed until now.

"Cheery fellow," Kadohata noted after the secretary had exited and the portal had closed behind him.

"Just how endangered do you think their nurseries really are, Doctor?" Dillingham asked.

"I couldn't even hazard a guess without taking a firsthand look," she told him. "But I find it hard to believe that, even with the limited land area on this planet, the situation can be as dire as he suggests."

"Well, it's not just about available land; it's about civic organization," Kadohata said. "Cestus

III was able to take in all the refugees from the Cardassian DMZ back when, because Governor Bacco and her cabinet were dedicated to making it work." Crusher caught the pride in Kadohata's words as she spoke about her fellow countrywoman, who was now president of the Federation. "Here, though . . . being a water breather, Bemidji is pretty far removed from what's happening on the surface. Can we really take what he says at face value?"

"I should hope a government official at his level would make sure of his facts before risking a rift with the Federation," Dillingham said.

"Sure," Kadohata allowed, "but he wouldn't be the first politician to try to put up an assertive front while talking out his . . . blowhole."

Dillingham shook his head. "Selkies don't have blowholes."

"Whatever orifice he's talking out," Crusher interjected, "it hardly matters. We came to get our own firsthand look at the refugee encampment. So let's see it. Crusher to *Genesee*," she said, hitting her combadge. "Three to beam up."

7

The *Enterprise* discovered all four of the Andorian transports within two light-years of the path where Rosado and Choudhury's model predicted they would be found.

Unfortunately, they did not find the ships intact.

"The *Shratha's Pride Three* was the first of the four ships to be destroyed," La Forge briefed the assembled senior officers, "when it suffered a warp core breach at zero-three thirty-two hours three days ago." He gestured to the screen at the far end of the conference room table, where a computer-created animation showed, in slow motion, the first of the Andorian-designed transports violently break apart. "The exact cause has not yet been determined, but right now, it looks like structural fatigue."

"How old was the ship?" asked Lieutenant Elfiki.

"Well, the *Atlirith*-class transports were in general production from the late twenty-three tens to the mid fifties," La Forge answered. "The physical analysis we did of the remains indicates all four ships were on the older end of that scale, and hadn't been significantly refurbished in at least twenty years." The chief engineer turned back to the screen, and as the animation continued he explained, "The resonance wave from that event was enough to send a disharmonic vibration through surrounding subspace, knocking the *Pride Two*'s dilithium chamber out of alignment." Onscreen, the second of four ships exploded.

"Aren't there supposed to be safeguards against that kind of thing?" asked Ensign Rosado, shocked and angered by the scenario the chief engineer had just described.

"Supposed to, yes," La Forge said with a sigh. "The Shratha Transportation Company, from what I've gathered, had a long history of cutting corners and fudging their way through standard safety inspections. But, when the call went out for all available ships to assist in the evacuation of Andor . . ."

"It probably didn't make much difference," said Doctor Tropp, sitting in on the briefing in Doctor Crusher's absence. "They were risking their lives either by boarding the ship or staying behind."

La Forge nodded. "The debris and subspace shockwaves from the first two explosions breached the other two ships' shields, tearing multiple hull breaches in both *One* and *Four*. It was all over in under ten seconds," he concluded as the last ships disappeared and the screen went blank.

A silence fell over the conference room. This was far from the end result anyone had hoped for. What had seemed an opportunity to find some small victory in all the destruction the Borg had wrought had only served to cast a darker shadow over the crew.

After a moment, Picard said, "Well, at the very least, the families will not have to live with the uncertainty of not knowing what's happened to their loved ones." It was small consolation, but it would have to do. "Geordi, does your investigation require that we remain here for very much longer?"

La Forge shook his head. "No, sir, I think we've gathered all the evidence we can."

"Very well, then. Lieutenant Choudhury," he said, turning to the security chief, who had sat strangely silent throughout the briefing, "have you identified any other potential emergencies we should investigate?"

"No, sir."

The bluntness of that seemingly defeatist answer brought the room to dead silence again. This one seemed to stretch out for far longer, until Elfiki spoke up. "We are still running more data. It does take time, with the volume we're dealing with, but . . ." She looked to the captain with a cautious and uncertain smile. "We should, hopefully, have more soon."

"Thank you, Lieutenant," Picard said, genuinely

grateful to be able to end on a more upbeat note. "We shall resume our patrol course and, needless to say, continue to keep on the lookout for those in need of help. Dismissed." As everyone rose from their chairs, he added, "Lieutenant Choudhury, a moment, please?"

Obediently, she lowered herself back into her chair. Worf also stopped, turning to direct a look of concern toward first the lieutenant and then the captain. Picard waved his first officer off. He knew these two had formed a seemingly unlikely friendship early on, and he suspected that there was more than just professional camaraderie behind Worf's decision to accompany Choudhury to Deneva during his leave. But Worf made no protest, and followed the rest of the staff out.

Once the room was empty, Picard stood up from his seat at the head of the conference table and moved to the one directly to Choudhury's left. "Lieutenant," he asked gently, "are you all right?"

"I'm fine, sir," she said, all too automatically, as she snapped upright in her seat.

Picard fixed her with a piercing yet kindly look. "We were all disappointed by the way this recovery ended. But we mustn't let this setback demoralize us. After losing so much, we can hardly allow ourselves to give up hope as well."

"Of course not, sir," she quickly agreed. "You're absolutely right, and I should have been more mindful of how I was presenting myself before the rest of the senior staff. It won't happen again."

Picard said nothing as he considered the woman beside him. In the relatively short time she had been aboard the *Enterprise,* the captain viewed Jasminder Choudhury as a steady, reassuring presence at the heart of the crew. Even at the height of the recent invasion, when the captain himself felt about to fall apart, Jasminder had remained as calm and centered as the Buddha himself. And at a glance, she still appeared just as poised and calm as ever. But, just as she had during the ceremony in the shuttlebay, she refused to make direct eye contact with him. "Lieutenant . . ." he started, then stopped. "Jasminder."

She briefly turned her head, and in her eyes Picard saw all the pain she'd been trying to keep hidden. "All of us, the entire crew, share in your loss," he told her, lightly touching his fingertips to her forearm. "What you are going through . . ."

"Sir, please," Choudhury interrupted, her eyes shut and her lips pressed to a thin, tight line. Suddenly, her serene exterior was revealed as a very carefully maintained façade masking a rampant storm of feelings. "I appreciate the sentiment, but I'm fine." She opened her eyes then, and offered him a tiny sliver of a smile.

It was actually a very good show of reassurance, and might well have worked under different circumstances. But the events of the past several weeks were still fresh in his mind, as were the pains he had taken to deny the feelings of depthless despair and hopelessness that had nearly overwhelmed him not long ago. "What you have suffered—the loss of your entire world—is unfathomable to most of us," he began sympathetically.

" 'Whatever is subject to origination is all subject to cessation,' " Choudhury intoned in response. "That's one of the most basic truths of this existence: all is impermanent."

Picard hesitated, unsure how to reply to that. He recognized the quote from the *Tipitaka*, as well as the truth behind this piece of Buddhist teaching. But it struck him as being a disturbingly dark sentiment, particularly in the current context.

Choudhury must have sensed his confusion, because she added, "Grief is also impermanent. I wouldn't expect you to understand, sir, but . . . my spiritual beliefs have sustained me throughout my life, through all the changes I've experienced. It's not always easy," she admitted, allowing the captain another fleeting glimpse of her deeper being, "but I am coping, sir."

Picard considered Choudhury a moment longer, wondering just how skeptical he should be about that claim. He had never been a religious man, and while he knew something of Choudhury's beliefs and their historical roots, he couldn't claim to genuinely understand them. He did, however, understand the importance of faith—it was a lesson that had been driven home for him in that desperate last hour of the Borg assault, by holding on to hope when reason told him all was hopeless.

Finally, he gave her a nod, and said, "If there's anything . . ."

"Thank you, Captain," she said quickly, "but there really isn't."

And he knew there wasn't. "Very well, Lieutenant," he said, his voice thick with regret. "Dismissed."

Jasminder Choudhury stepped out of the lounge, onto the bridge, and turned to the turbolift doors after a silent exchange with her relief, Ensign Abby Balidemaj. The ensign indicated that she would be fine manning the tactical station for a while longer, and Choudhury smiled back at her gratefully, since she was in no state to be on the bridge at that moment.

It was ridiculous, she knew, and wholly unprofessional. But the discovery of those Andorian ships, and then watching a depiction of their destruction in cold clinical detail, had triggered a renewed wave of grief, which seemed to rise up from the small hard knot in her stomach, push the air from her lungs, and wrap its sharp claws around her heart. She folded her arms across her midsection and paced the small space inside the car, unable to keep her body still. She wished she didn't have to mislead Captain Picard. She was trying to the best of her ability to cope with the death of her family. But to say she was, indeed, managing to do so . . .

She put a hand over her mouth to stifle a sob and willed the turbolift to move faster. When it finally came to a halt, she held back a moment, making sure no one was in the corridor, before darting out and quickly slipping into her quarters. Choudhury ordered the lights up only a fraction of full illumination, just enough to make her way through the living area to the small corner she had set aside for meditation.

She lowered herself onto the large cushion on the floor, folded her legs into the lotus position, and closed her eyes. Jasminder left the incense sitting on the small table underneath her mandala unlit; lately, the normally pleasant scent of smoldering wood only triggered memories of Deneva's scorched surface. She willed her mind to go blank, drawing a slow, cleansing breath in through her nostrils, following the air as it flowed into her lungs and then back out through her mouth.

Her mind refused to cooperate, though. Rather than emptying in the dimness and near silence, it pulled up old images from her memory: Her father and her, planting the oak sapling in front of their new house. Grandma Basma leading her into her mother's bedroom to meet her baby sister, Divya, for the first time. The whole family in the stands at the Junior Parrises Squares finals, on their feet cheering her after she had scored the winning point. Laughing and clapping as Divya and Guarav danced at their wedding. All juxtaposed with the deathscape where she and Worf had walked just days earlier.

All is impermanent. The words mocked her now. All of it was gone now. These people and places existed now only in her mind and memory. And her mind stubbornly refused to put them aside.

She felt tears leaking through her closed eyelids and angrily swiped them away. Choudhury was no stranger to death. She'd lost her best friend from the Academy their first year out, during a pointless shooting match near the Cardassian border. She had risen to security chief aboard the *Timur* only after Lieutenant Ang was killed at the First Battle of Chin'toka. And following that, she had been responsible for more deaths than she cared to think about. She'd mourned them all, friend and foe alike, but she had always been able to move past mourning with the help of her faith, and reclaim her tranquility and balance.

But these weren't Starfleet officers, she chided herself, *or Jem'Hadar soldiers bred to disdain the divine life force within them. This was your* family. *These were the people who begged you not to leave Deneva, who tried to convince you that you didn't need to join Starfleet to fulfill your calling as a protector. And now, those people and that home you swore to help protect . . .*

Choudhury sat there for nearly fifteen minutes, mourning her family and her world, and all that she had held dear for so much of her life. Until finally, she had no more tears to shed, and she got up and went to the 'fresher to splash a little cold water on her face. She patted her face dry with a towel and studied her reflection in the mirror, checking for redness and puffiness around her eyes. Convinced that she could at least project the image of a protector, she shoved her feelings down, put her shoulders back, and headed for the bridge.

Over the course of her career, Meron Byxthar had visited dozens of refugee and displaced persons settlements. She'd been to the near-permanent Bajoran settlements in the Valo system, and traveled with a nomadic clan of Xindi Arboreals across five star systems over the course of two years. She'd visited the Thallonian camps on Nelkar, the Skrreean communes on Draylon II, and even a small Kreel asylum on Archanis IV, prior to its discovery and dismantlement by the Klingon Defense Force.

Given all this, she should have been prepared for what greeted her when the transporter rematerialized her on the perimeter of the iy'Dewra'ni refugee camp, and much of it was indeed familiar. Byxthar found herself, along with the rest of the team, before a small prefab structure that was serving as the infirmary and administrative office, just inside the camp entrance. Looking out across a broad, rolling pasture, she saw row upon row of cloth tents stretched out for hundreds of meters.

Filling the makeshift streets of trampled grass that ran through this instant city were hundreds upon hundreds of humanoids. They seemed to move in slow motion, and without any apparent destination. Some were engaged in conversation with one another. Others were engaged in conversation with themselves, or perhaps the gods that had apparently abandoned them. And others simply sat silent, staring vacantly into space. Byxthar opened her telepathic senses to the faceless mass and felt their grief, helplessness, hopelessness. All extremely common in her experience, except for the fact that all these people were citizens of the United Federation of Planets.

"Oh, my . . ." said Kadohata, giving voice to the horror and shock Byxthar had also sensed from her colleagues. "This looks like something out of the Dark Ages." Byxthar didn't know much Earth history, but guessed, from the evidence before her, that "the Dark Ages" referred to the late twentieth and early twenty-first centuries, a period of near-continuous small and large wars just prior to first contact by the Vulcans.

And these are the lucky ones, Byxthar heard Doctor-Commander Crusher note to herself as she shook her head in mute disbelief.

"What is with these cloth tents?" Dillingham demanded of no one in particular.

"The cellulose fiber fabric would be far more efficient to replicate than hundreds of plastiform panels for standard prefab shelters," Gliv said, brushing a tuft of windblown fur away from his eyes.

"Those can't be sturdy enough to qualify as

adequate shelter," Dillingham said, shaking his head. "They're bound to be blown away during the next significant storm."

There's not a cloud in the sky, and they're worried about storms—like we need to start inventing things to worry about. That last comment was unspoken by someone approaching them from behind. The Betazoid turned and saw a bulky Grazerite man in a filthy Starfleet sciences-blue shirt rounding the corner of the building. "At last, you're here," he said as he belatedly became aware he'd been noticed. "Please tell me you're ready to start beaming these people up right now," he said, even as he took mental note of the civilian garb Byxthar and Dillingham wore.

Doctor-Commander Crusher fixed the Grazerite with a look that mirrored her troubled thoughts. "And you are . . . ?"

"Lieutenant Commander Amsta-Iber, chief meteorologist, Aronnax Station."

"Aronnax Station?" Crusher asked. "What are you doing here?" Aronnax Station was a Federation scientific facility, dedicated to exploring the remote regions of Pacifica's global ocean, located on a small island nearly halfway around the planet from their current position.

"I'm here because the Selkies wanted a Starfleet officer here, overseeing this . . . this." He tossed a hand up in the air as he silently dismissed a number of colorful ways to describe the scene laid out before them. "The Starfleet presence at the Federation embassy was reassigned after Barolia and Acamar, and so were the guards and other support personnel at Aronnax. It was me or the ichthyologist."

"So you've been running this all on your own?" Crusher asked.

"Trying to," Amsta-Iber said wearily. "The locals have been a help, but they're not happy about it. Apparently we're in close proximity here to one of their major spawning areas, and they don't want these people lingering. So, the sooner you can start relocating them, the better."

"We're not here to relocate these people," Crusher told him. "And even if we were, there's little we could do with just one runabout."

"One runabout? That's all they sent to sort this mess out?" he cried, as a number of colorful phrases flashed through his mind.

"Never underestimate what a determined group can accomplish," Crusher told him with a small half-grin. "What's the medical situation, Commander? Is there a doctor on site?"

"We have an EMH set up and running," he answered.

Crusher sighed, and Byxthar heard the string of unflattering comments she left unspoken. "Fine," she said. "Do you have an up-to-date map of the camp layout? How about a census? Do we have an accurate accounting of the people we have here?"

Amsta-Iber blinked, caught off guard by the sudden barrage of questions by a superior officer.

"Um, yes, sir. I have the map in the office, and the census is being taken at Eden Beach as the refugees are beaming down."

"How many are there?" Kadohata asked.

The Grazerite drew a long, noisy breath through his nostrils. "We're at over seventy thousand by now."

My God, Crusher thought to herself, but didn't let that reaction show as she turned to the entire team. "Okay, we need to survey this entire camp, and make sure everything is up to standards—food, water, shelter, clothing, waste disposal, hygiene, medical care. Miranda, I want you—"

A high-pitched unintelligible cry interrupted the doctor-commander's instructions. Looking out toward the tent city from where the scream had come, Byxthar saw a young human woman in a filthy dress running in their direction, a bundle of some sort in her arms. The Betazoid was able to sense what it was the woman was carrying, and why she was crying. *It's her baby; he won't wake up,* she thought as she started to turn to tell Crusher.

Whether the physician had heard her telepathically or was acting on her own instincts, Crusher rushed forward to intercept the crying mother, moving at a slightly irregular gait due to the child she herself was carrying. Kadohata followed, and then so did Byxthar and the others, including Amsta-Iber.

Crusher caught and stopped the woman, got her

to sit down on the ground, and had her tricorder out to examine the child by the time the rest came up behind her. The mother, between sobs and gasps for air, was saying, "Matthew, oh Matthew," over and over. Byxthar saw the baby, a boy not even a year old, lying limp in his mother's arms. She sensed that the little one was in excruciating pain, but was too weak to do more than softly whimper as he struggled to breathe.

Crusher finished her scan, interpreted the tricorder readings, and almost without a pause for thought slapped at the combadge on her chest. "Crusher to *Genesee*," she called, and the small ship's computer beeped an acknowledging tone. "Medical emergency. Three to beam out, these coordinates." She then looked up at the rest of the mission team from her crouched position. "Miranda, you're in command. Get the survey under way," she told Kadohata, and then lifted her eyes skyward. "Energize!"

Once the doctor and her patients were transported away, Byxthar shifted her attention to the growing crowd of curious refugees drawn by the commotion. "Hey, what about the rest of us?" a Solari man demanded after the three had gone. "When do *we* get off this rock?"

That question was echoed and repeated by more of the frustrated refugees gathering around him. None of the team members had an answer, and could only stare back as the crowd grew in both number and in volume.

• • •

Doctor Crusher left the wailing woman sitting on the transporter pad as she stepped off and reached for a small hatch an arm's length away. She grabbed the emergency medical kit there and went back down on her knees as she threw the lid open and snatched a hypospray. She took special care to check and recheck the instrument's settings—not only the dosage, but the force of the injecting spray, both of which she adjusted down for her small patient. She put her hands out to take the baby—

"NOOO!" the mother screamed, clutching the child tight to her chest. "What are you going to do with him? You can't take him away from me!"

"I'm not going to take him away," Crusher said, in her most soothing tone. "My name is Beverly. What's yours?"

The girl took a moment to recollect herself before answering, "Peggy. And this is Matthew."

"I'm not going to do anything to hurt Matthew," Crusher assured her. "I'm just going to give him some medicine," she said, holding up the hypo so she could plainly see. "It will make him better." Crusher spoke simply but authoritatively. Peggy didn't need to know Matthew had picked up a foreign microbe—undoubtedly one she had picked up first herself and passed on through her milk—resulting in a severe case of gastroenteritis and dehydration. What she needed to know—and believe—was that the doctor was going to help her baby.

The woman—really no more than a girl, maybe nineteen at the oldest—considered the doctor's words uncertainly for several long moments. Her eyes then went down to the pronounced bulge of Crusher's midsection and lingered there a moment before she finally loosened her hold on the child.

Crusher slowly reached forward, putting a hand on little Matthew's back, and pulled down his pants and his diaper. A nearly overpowering stench filled the cabin as the diaper's contents were exposed to the open air. *I'd almost forgotten this part,* Crusher thought to herself, quickly reining in her gag reflex before putting the hypospray nozzle to the baby's bottom. With gentle pressure, Crusher intravenously pumped a mild antibiotic solution into his system, along with several milliliters of saline solution.

Crusher threw the medkit strap over her shoulder, then lifted the baby out of his mother's arms, eliciting only a mild squeak of protest. She stopped in the 'fresher, where she stripped Matthew's diaper completely off, dropped it into the waste extractor, and dematerialized it. At the same time she grabbed a towel, went back to the main cabin, swept the game tiles off to one side of the table, spread the towel, and lay the baby down.

He was still unresponsive, but his breathing was a bit more regular now. As Crusher ran her tricorder over him again, she saw that Matthew was responding to the treatment, if a bit slowly. The doctor gave him another few cc's to combat his dehydration; beyond that, she just had to wait and hope little Matthew could rally by himself.

"Is he going to be okay?" Peggy stood on the threshold of the living area, leaning her full weight onto the doorframe, the picture of exhaustion. She showed physical signs of dehydration, too; Crusher would have to check the refugees' water source for infestation, and probably half the refugees as well.

Crusher avoided her eyes, looking instead into the medkit. "How long has he been ill?" she asked as she pulled out a silvery package, which she tore open, and extracted a sterile cleansing cloth. She quickly but thoroughly cleaned the baby's bottom, all the while watching for the slightest sign that he was coming around.

The girl seemed confused by the question. "Well, he was being cranky on the transport, but everyone was." A new, haunted expression crossed the girl's face.

"What about the diarrhea?" Crusher asked. "When did that start?"

"Did they really destroy everything?"

Crusher felt her stomach clench. She hesitated, debating how to answer that non sequitur, until Peggy clarified, "The Borg, I mean. They said they were coming to Danula II. They made me leave, me and Matthew. They said I had to make sure he was safe. They said I had to leave them all."

"And you are safe now," Crusher told her in her

most reassuring tone, sidestepping the question altogether. Crusher hadn't heard any reports specifically mentioning Danula II, a small Federation colony that was home to one of Starfleet Academy's physical training and athletics facilities. But she knew it was located about fifty or so light-years from the Azure Nebula, right in the "dead zone" created by the Borg invasion; there was little doubt as to the fate of Peggy and Matthew's homeworld.

The doctor told Peggy none of this, though. Instead, she pressed the young mother again: "I need you to tell me how long Matthew has been sick like this."

"Uumm . . . a couple days?" Peggy was looking everywhere but in Crusher's eyes. "I think . . . after the fourth day after we got here?"

"Did you drink any water from the lakes or streams down there? Without sterilizing it first?"

"It looked clean," Peggy answered, as tears of realization and guilt started to well in her eyes. "And the lines for the replicators were so long . . ."

Suddenly, the doctor's tricorder began to emit a number of shrill warning tones. Crusher spun back toward her tiny patient and picked up the scanning device again. "Damnit," she whispered, as she watched the child's vital signs dropping. "No, no, no . . ."

"What?" Peggy cried, rushing around to the other side of the table, knocking most of Byxthar's ceramic game tiles to the deck, with a sound like a building collapse. "What's wrong?"

Crusher kept her eyes fixed on the tricorder, avoiding the young mother's eyes. The contagion was playing havoc with young Matthew's autoimmune system, and resisting the antibiotic treatment. Crusher cursed silently to herself as she looked vainly at the medkit lying open beside her. If she could isolate the specific microbe the boy had picked up, she could synthesize a targeted treatment, but not before the boy's already strained internal organs would start to shut down.

Matthew was dying, and Crusher was running out of options.

Literally tossing the tricorder aside, Crusher scooped up the baby in her arms and ran out of the runabout living area. In the short, narrow passageway that led to the cockpit, she used her elbow to knock another door control panel, and stepped into the small science lab that was part of the runabout's replaceable standard mission module. Though rudimentary and somewhat poorly equipped compared to a starship laboratory, the standard module lab did include a small stasis chamber, normally used for small biological specimens gathered during science survey missions. Crusher hit the button to open the roll-out drawer and lay the baby in the specimen tray. Even though the chamber was far too small for an adult human patient, it was large enough to make the baby look even tinier. It was with no small degree of regret that Crusher hit the button again, and watched the little boy be swallowed up into the bulkhead.

"What are you doing? What are you doing?!" Peggy screamed as Crusher spun and caught her by the wrists, warding off her furious balled-up fists. The fight left the young girl quickly, though, and then Crusher was supporting her sagging, dejected weight. "I was supposed to keep him safe," she half-whispered, half-sobbed.

"He is safe," Crusher told her. "He will be, I promise."

"We were the only ones they put on the ship," Peggy continued as if she hadn't heard the doctor at all. "Just us. They stayed—his father, my mother and father. They said it was more important that the baby and I were safe." Tears started to course down her face. "And now, we're the only ones left." She didn't ask this time about Danula, or her loved ones who stayed behind there; Crusher was rather sure she already knew, and was repressing much of what had happened in the last several days.

The doctor guided her by the elbow back to the living area, and sat her down at the table. She then went to the replicator, and while waiting for the two cups of tea she had requested to materialize, she struck her combadge. "Crusher to Kadohata."

"Yes, Doctor," came the response. *"Is the little boy all right?"*

"I had to put him in stasis," Crusher told her in lieu of an actual answer. "Miranda, there's a contaminated water source down there, and odds are, these two aren't the only ones to get sick from it. I need you to find it so I can track down whatever it is that made him sick."

"I'm on it, Bev."

Crusher thanked her and cut the connection, then brought the two steaming mugs back to the table. She placed one in front of the puffy-eyed Peggy, and took her own seat opposite. "I should have been a better mother," the girl muttered. "I should have known . . . I should have realized . . ."

Crusher reached across the table and laid a hand on the young woman's forearm. "Don't punish yourself like this, Peggy."

"He's all that I have!" Peggy burst into tears again. "He's all I have left!" Crusher moved around the table to her side, letting Peggy throw her arms around her. "Everything is gone . . . Doctor, if I lose him, too . . ." she sobbed into the doctor's shoulder.

"Don't think that way," Crusher told her. "You're not going to lose him. And you're going to be strong for him. You have untapped strength inside you that will get you and him both through this."

Peggy's sobs stopped briefly for a deep, sniffling breath. "How do you know that?" she asked.

Crusher, her own face buried in Peggy's hair, simply answered, "I know . . ."

Starbase 32 sat on the edge of Federation space, where it served as a jumping-off point for Starfleet's exploration of the unknown region beyond. In addition to being the home port to a dozen star-ships whose mission it was to seek out new life and civilizations in this part of the galaxy, it was also home to many of the families who crewed those ships. Beverly Crusher had requested a posting at Starbase 32 following the end of her internship on Delos IV, so that she and Wesley could be that much closer to Jack, out there aboard the *Stargazer*. His ship's mission was an open-ended one, so there was no way of knowing when he might come back, but as far as Beverly was concerned, that was beside the point; his family would be there waiting for him when he did.

She had just come off shift at the base infirmary and had gone to Christof Schuster's quarters to pick up Wesley. Schuster was a sciences-division lieu-tenant who, like Beverly, had a spouse serving on a deep-space explorer, and a young child—a seven-year-old daughter named Elle—whom he was rais-ing by himself. He was an ever cheerful man who had happily volunteered to let Wesley sleep over when Beverly had to respond to a late-night medi-cal emergency during her third week as assistant CMO. The two had formed a close friendship and mutual support network after that, and their chil-dren, who shared a number of classes at the base school despite their age difference, became all but inseparable.

Christof invited Beverly to sit down and have a cup of coffee, which she gratefully accepted. A shipment of spoiled Owon eggs had come to the station earlier in the week, and the infirmary had been run ragged with a steady stream of food poisoning cases since. While Wesley and Elle played Parcheesi in the living area, the grown-ups sat and relaxed and chatted about nothing in particular—their jobs, current events, recent news from their respective spouses.

The peace of the moment was then broken by the chiming of the cabin door. Elle jumped up to answer, and everyone was surprised when the base commander, Admiral Naomi Jerusalmi, appeared in the open doorway.

Both officers leapt to their feet as Schuster invited her in. "Lieutenants," she said, giving them a smile that somehow looked out of place on her soft, round face. Alarms started going off in Beverly's mind. Though the admiral was a perfectly nice and personable woman, she was not in the habit of casually dropping by to visit junior officers. Her visit to Schuster's home, Beverly thought, could not bode well.

The admiral gave a wary look at the children, both mirroring their parents by standing at full attention, then looked back to the adults. Schuster caught the hint, and said, "Elle, why don't you and Wes go play in your room for a few minutes." Beverly studied the admiral's face as the kids made their exit, and then gave Christof a quick look of sympathy out of the corner of her eye.

The admiral took a breath as she stepped further

into the room, closing the gap with her officers. "I'm sorry to do this this way," she said, looking back and forth between the two, "but you weren't in your quarters, and this isn't something a commanding officer should put off."

Beverly was momentarily confused. Why would Jerusalmi have gone to her quarters? And why was she not looking at Christof . . . ?

"Doctor Crusher, I regret to inform you that your husband, Lieutenant Commander Jack Crusher, has been killed in the line of duty."

Time stopped. Her mind felt as if someone had opened an airlock door and blew every thought in her head out into the vacuum. At some point, she remembered she needed to breathe, and she spoke the only word she could find. "No."

Beverly felt Christof's hands around her shoulders, and then she felt a chair underneath her. It took a few more seconds to realize that her legs had given out on her.

"I'm sorry," the admiral said, empathy in her gray eyes. "It was an accident of some kind, during an EVA repair mission. Captain Picard didn't provide many details, but the *Stargazer* is on its way back . . ."

And Beverly felt a jolt of elation shoot through her when she heard that. *He's coming home!* That brief spark of joy was quickly snuffed out, though, as she realized that in the truest sense, he would never come back to her again.

The next few days went by in a haze. Doctor

Meather, the base CMO, had relieved her of her duties in the infirmary, leaving Beverly with nothing to do but sit and stare at the bulkheads. Wesley became strangely withdrawn; to him, "Daddy" was a vaguely remembered visitor from long ago, yet he knew from seeing Elle and her father together that he had been denied something far greater.

Still, a part of Beverly's mind clung to denial. She and Jack had been apart for so much of their marriage, so really, nothing had changed, had it? She hadn't heard from him for almost two weeks, but he was always terrible about letter writing, claiming the few times he did respond to Beverly's letters to be too busy to do so more often. (Even after making a big deal about that one holorecording he made for Wesley before heading back to the *Stargazer* five years ago, he'd never found the time to make more.) So, as long as the *Stargazer* was still out there, nothing was really wrong.

That delusion was challenged by Jean-Luc Picard's appearance at her door four days later. His light brown hair had receded even further since the last time Beverly had seen him, and he wore a dermal regenerative patch on his right temple. And in his eyes, Beverly could see how deeply he too was mourning for Jack. The two had been friends longer than Beverly had known either, and Picard had worked with him on a daily basis for years. Seeing his pain, she wanted to wrap her arms around him so they could both cry over their loss.

Of course, they both maintained perfect Starfleet

decorum, even though she was in civilian dress. Picard stood there for a moment looking uncomfortably first at her, then at her son. Wesley held himself like a tiny cadet during inspection, as Picard knelt down to speak directly to him. "Wesley . . . Wes . . . you're called Wes, right?"

The boy nodded, trying desperately to keep his brave, grown-up face from slipping.

"I am very sorry about your father, Wes. I . . . erm . . ." Jean-Luc clearly had no idea how to talk to children, much less on such a topic, and after stammering a bit, he simply gave Wesley a pat on the shoulder, and stood again. "Beverly, I cannot begin to tell you . . ." he started to say to her, but he was still discomfited by the small boy there, staring up at him with a mix of pain, awe, and hate.

Beverly cut Jean-Luc off by looking to Wesley and saying, "Honey, Captain Picard and I have to go do something. Why don't you read your book for a little bit, and we'll be right back."

"Okay," Wesley said in a whisper, and after giving Picard a last sullen look, turned back into the cabin. Jean-Luc followed Beverly out, and fell in step beside her as she moved away from her door.

"I am so sorry for your loss," he said as they walked down the empty, strangely peaceful corridors of the station's residential section. "But you should know Jack gave his life to save his ship and the rest of the crew." Beverly only barely listened as Jean-Luc went on, explaining how one of the *Stargazer*'s warp nacelles was overloading and threatening to explode. Jack and the other member of the EVA team, Lieutenant Joseph, blacked out from radiation, and Jean-Luc had gone out after them himself. But he could only reach one of them in time . . .

Picard only stopped when he saw that Beverly had guided him down a dead-end corridor to a turbolift and had pressed the call button. "Where are we going?" he asked.

"The morgue," Beverly said in an even tone. "I need to see . . ."

Picard's face fell. "Beverly . . . there's really no need. Jack . . ."

"I have to see him."

"Beverly, he was injured rather severely. I don't think . . ."

The turbolift car arrived, and Beverly stepped on without seeing or caring if the captain would join her. "Morgue," she ordered the computer, and only when the doors had slid shut again did she notice she was not alone.

As the car started to rise toward the station's upper levels and the main medical facilities, Jean-Luc again told her, "You don't have to do this."

Beverly shook her head and refused to look at him. "Yes, I do. It's important to me. I have to face the fact that he's gone."

The captain thankfully dropped his protests, understanding this was one area in which he could not pull rank. They rode in silence the rest of the way, and then continued wordlessly through the white, sterile corridors that led through the lower level of the medical section. "It's good of you to come with me," she said, breaking the uneasy silence that had fallen between them.

"It's the least I could do."

They continued in silence until they reached the morgue and entered the autopsy room, a two-level room with a bioanalysis station, a dedicated LCARS access station, and on the lower level, a two-meter-long table, a white sheet draped over it, covering the unmistakable shape of a humanoid body. Beverly forced herself to keep walking, to move down the steps, to approach the table . . .

And she froze. This was it. When she lifted the sheet and finally saw the face of the person underneath, there would be no more denial. Jack's death would be part of her reality. She stood there and stared at the shrouded figure for what felt like an eternity.

And then Jean-Luc was at her side, studying her, reading her face. And as he continued to watch her, ready to react to any change in her demeanor, he reached across, took hold of the sheet, and lifted it.

It was Jack. The right side of his face was marred by a grotesque network of lacerations running from his throat up around his jaw and up over his brow. The skin and muscle had been crudely rejoined and the blood cleaned away, but the doctor could see how horrible the injuries from the explosive concussion had been—bone shattered, flesh torn away and hanging loose, blood and viscera floating free in zero g, splattering the inside of his helmet . . .

Jean-Luc lowered the sheet again. "You shouldn't remember him like this," he said, his voice surprisingly gentle and compassionate. Beverly nodded, and thanked him for helping her through this moment.

But her last memory of Jack would now be forever burned in her mind.

Jack's final request was that his ashes be scattered over the Hermosa coral reef, just south of San Francisco. Beverly didn't know why that place was so special to him, and she couldn't ask him anymore. But she and Wesley dutifully made the trip back to Earth and solemnly carried out this final request. It actually turned out to be therapeutic, letting mother and son get away and spend time alone together, and the Hermosa Reef—a thing of incredible beauty created as the result of a terrible disaster centuries earlier—was indeed a most tranquil spot, ideal for creating the closure that both of them needed.

When they returned to Starbase 32 nine days later, they discovered the Schusters were gone. Elle had been sent to live with cousins in Salzburg while Christof grabbed at a sudden career opportunity: a posting as the new senior science officer aboard the *U.S.S. Stargazer*. Beverly was stunned by this betrayal. That's what it felt like: a betrayal of their friendship, of his daughter and her friendship with Wesley, and even of Jack, whom Schuster had never even met.

The following day, Jerusalmi stopped by the infirmary and asked to speak with Beverly privately in Meather's office. The admiral welcomed her back, and reiterated the same standard sympathies she'd offered two weeks earlier, so long ago. Then, apropos of nothing, she mentioned that the position of chief medical officer aboard the *U.S.S. Hammarskjöld* had recently opened. Beverly was still waiting to find out why the admiral had wanted to talk to her when, to her surprise, Jerusalmi offered to recommend her for the position.

Beverly was dumbstruck. The admiral said something more about understanding this was a difficult decision, and acknowledging that it was "poor timing." She also stressed that it was a great opportunity that Beverly had more than earned, and that she should give it serious thought.

Beverly did think about it as she continued her uneventful shift. Chief medical officer on an *Ambassador*-class ship—all else aside, it would indeed be an incredible opportunity, the kind she had dreamt of at the Academy. Back then, everything was about building her career and climbing the ranks. Instead of a ring, Jack had given her a book, *How to Advance Your Career Through Marriage,* as his way of proposing.

But now, of course, she couldn't accept. The idea that she could leave Wes now of all times, just ship him off to his great-grandmother, was unthinkable. Not that she expected Starfleet to concern itself with such things; they just moved their people about wherever they needed to put them, treating them like generic, easily replaceable cogs, never mind the effect on spouses, children, friends . . .

She returned to her quarters after the end of her shift, and the moment she walked in the door, she was welcomed with a full-speed tackle that nearly knocked her to the deck. Looking down, she found her five-year-old with his arms wrapped fiercely around her waist, his face buried in her side.

"Wes?" She gently pried him away, and squatted down to look into his red-rimmed eyes. "Wes, what is it, honey? What's wrong?"

He took a couple hitching breaths before he was able to say, "I . . . I was 'fraid I was . . . was left alone."

Beverly's breath caught and her heart tightened. Her schedule for this week matched with the school's; Wes couldn't have been home more than ten minutes ahead of her. Looking over his shoulder, though, Beverly saw the chest of Jack's personal effects, which had been offloaded from the *Stargazer* during their trip to Earth, sitting open at the far end of the room. One of the old-style maroon uniform tunics had been pulled halfway out; that surely would have been enough to trigger a young child's feelings of loss and insecurity—it certainly triggered a reaction in his mother.

"No, Wes," she said softly, looking him straight in his huge hazel eyes. "You're not alone. You have me. You will *always* have me, sweetheart. All right?"

Wes looked back at his mother, wanting to believe her, but . . . "But, Elle . . . her dad . . ."

"I will never do anything like that to you, Wesley," Beverly told him with all the conviction she had in her soul.

"Promise?"

Beverly glanced again at Jack's uniform, and down at the modern blue one she wore. And then she looked to her son again. "I promise you, Wes."

The following morning, Beverly Crusher went to Admiral Jerusalmi's office to turn over her combadge and rank pips. Then she and Wesley left Starbase 32, and Starfleet, intending never to return.

8

———————

Worf walked into the engineering section and found it very much as it always was: abuzz with activity. Personnel were moving about with purpose and confidence, ensuring that the heart of the mighty starship, the warp core, and all its peripheral systems continued to operate consistently at peak efficiency. Worf was impressed and pleased. If not for the mix of red and blue uniforms in with the normal gold, one would never know this department was without so many of its regular crew.

"Can I help you, sir?"

Worf turned to face Lieutenant Taurik, who was working on the central systems console. "Yes, Lieutenant. Can you tell me where Commander La Forge is?"

The other man looked confused for a moment. Vulcan stamina being what it was, Worf couldn't help but note how very fatigued the assistant chief engineer looked. "He had gone to check on the main computer core," Taurik answered after only an extra second's thought. "However," he continued, "I believe I hear him approaching at this moment."

Worf followed his eyes as Taurik turned in the direction of the wall-sized main systems display. A moment later, he also heard La Forge's voice moving closer, just before he rounded a corner and entered main engineering. ". . . is not good enough, Sonol," he was telling the Payav ensign walking with him. "Gather up ten of the temps, and have them double-check the trigger responses on the emergency force-field emitters on decks two through six."

Sonol acknowledged his orders and moved off in another direction, calling for volunteers. La Forge, spotting Worf, continued walking in his direction, but once he reached him, turned to his assistant instead. "Taurik, I told you when I left I didn't want to see you here when I got back. Go to your quarters and get some rest."

"That is not necessary, sir," the junior officer said, trying—and failing—to shrug off his exhaustion.

Worf turned and glowered at him. "Are you refusing to obey an order from a superior officer, Lieutenant?"

Taurik looked up at Worf. "No, sir," he said in a plain, neutral tone. "If you'll excuse me, sirs," he added before turning and leaving engineering.

La Forge shook his head as he watched the young man go, then turned his attention to Worf. "So . . . what brings you down here?" he asked as he started walking again, making a circuit of all the section's monitoring stations.

Worf paced along beside him. "How are your repairs proceeding?"

Geordi sighed. "As well as can be expected, I suppose. We've got the internal sensor network finished, and with that, we've discovered a whole slew of other things that need attention. But we're making good progress, all things considered."

"Good," Worf said, giving La Forge a grin. "You should take great pride in how well your department has continued to perform in the face of many formidable challenges."

"Thanks," La Forge replied, somewhat surprised. "High praise, especially coming from you."

"It is deserved—and long overdue, my friend," the first officer answered. He had been looking at his long-time colleague in a very different light since the recent incident when La Forge had stood up to the captain and refused to follow his illegal and dishonorable order to build a thalaron weapon. In the years since the two of them had both joined the old *Enterprise*'s crew as junior grade lieutenants, Worf had held more than half a dozen different positions, while Geordi had remained in one place, seemingly stuck there like a *gobfly* caught in tree sap. Yet, he had shown great strength of self and spirit at a time when it had seemed the entire galaxy was on the brink of destruction. Worf regretted underestimating him for so long, and resolved to reinforce and build upon the bonds between them.

"Thanks, Worf," La Forge said, and gave the Klingon one of his wide, easy smiles. "Now's when you hit me up for a favor, right?"

Worf stopped in place. "I am the first officer," he said forcefully, making La Forge spin back just as he was about to enter his office. "If I have a task for you to complete, I will not resort to spewing false compliments to compel you to do it."

La Forge reeled back. "Hey, I was just teasing. I didn't mean to suggest . . ." he said in a rush.

But he trailed off when he saw the unexpected expression on Worf's face. "Yes, I am familiar with the concept of 'teasing,'" he said with a smirk.

La Forge stared a moment more, then laughed. "Okay, yeah, you got me good, there," he conceded. "So . . . was there something else you wanted?"

"There is something I'd like for you to take a look at," Worf said, nodding. La Forge gestured for Worf to follow him into his office, and both sat. "We've run and completed the records search protocol for any unaccounted-for evacuation ships out of Deneva. In the course of reviewing the data, a curious item was discovered. Shortly after the global evacuation order was issued, the Denevan president invoked something called Plan 2757. This is the only time it is mentioned; there is no indication of whether this plan was carried out, or what it in fact entailed."

"That is curious," Geordi agreed, leaning back in his chair. "And you have no idea what 2-7-5-7 is supposed to stand for? A code of some kind, maybe?"

"I have a theory," Worf said. "I suspect it is a reference to the events on and around stardate 2757, when Deneva was invaded by a swarm of extraplanetary neuroparasitic life-forms. The entire planet's population was all but incapacitated by these alien creatures."

"Right, I remember," Geordi said, nodding. "It was Kirk's *Enterprise* that discovered what happened, and was able to exterminate the infestation."

Worf nodded. "Yes, though not until eight months after the initial infestation." That had been a most serendipitous event for the Denevans; had the *Enterprise* not already been en route, the entire colony surely would have perished. "Given this, and the timing of the president's order, it would seem that Plan 2757 was to be put into motion in the event of another global emergency."

"And you don't think it was part of the overall evacuation?" La Forge asked.

Worf shook his head. "We've been in contact with several other Denevan evacuation ships; none of them were aware of any such plan. I believe it was in addition to the official evacuation plans, kept secret in case the next threat was from sentient invaders."

La Forge nodded thoughtfully. "Okay. Well,

if no one was talking about this plan after the president authorized it, let's see what they were talking about." He activated his desktop computer interface, called up the results of the Elfiki-Rosado search protocol for Deneva, and keyed in his own set of search instructions. He hit a final control, and the word WORKING appeared on the screen. The two watched in silence for a moment, then La Forge asked, "So . . . with the Deneva search done, did we find anything about Jasminder's family?"

Worf scowled and shook his head. "No, there is still no information either confirming or disproving that any members of the lieutenant's family were evacuated." It was a terrible thing, to be left without knowing if a loved one had met their end, or how. Geordi's expression mirrored his own, and Worf recalled that he still, to this day, did not know the true fate of his mother.

"She was in pretty rough shape after we found the Shrathra ships," La Forge noted. "Has she been doing any better at all?"

Worf felt the muscles of his neck and jaw tighten. "Why would you ask me?"

La Forge started to grin, but then let it fall as he got a good look at the very Klingon expression on Worf's face. "You're not teasing this time."

Worf looked away from the engineer, and cursed himself for his overreaction. "Hey, Worf?" said La Forge. "Hey . . . are *you* doing all right?"

Worf looked up, and put on his best stone-faced expression. "I am fine."

La Forge narrowed his mechanical eyes at him skeptically. "Come on, Worf, 'my friend' . . ."

Hearing his own words thrown back at him in a derisive tone shamed the Klingon. And he had no one else to discuss his situation with—not Jasminder, of course, and he did not feel comfortable talking with Hegol, given their earlier conversation. Worf took a deep breath and said, "Jasminder and I have been physically intimate."

La Forge stared back wordlessly for a moment. "Okay, I wasn't expecting that," he finally responded.

"The first time was while we were preparing to face the Borg in the Azure Nebula, and it was not planned. Then, after our visit to her family's land on Deneva, she said she felt it had been a mistake."

La Forge absorbed that information. "Well, she's been through a lot, Worf. She's in mourning, and that can confuse a person as to what they really want."

"Yes, I understand that," Worf said. "However . . . I am no longer certain . . . Klingons traditionally frown upon casual sexuality without a more permanent bond." Worf didn't mention that this tradition was considered archaic by most of contemporary Klingon society. Nor did he mention how he'd largely disregarded those strictures during his courtship of the decidedly untraditional Jadzia Dax. What he did say was, "Our initial intimate liaison was not long after Captain Dax's visit to the ship."

"Ohhh," Geordi said in understanding, though Worf knew he really could not understand, not completely.

It had taken until now for Worf himself to understand. "I have never truly let myself believe Jadzia had reached Sto-Vo-Kor," Worf said, "because a part of her existed here still, in Dax." It had been over five years since he and Ezri Dax had parted ways at the end of the Dominion War. At the time, she was only just beginning to come to terms with being a joined Trill, a counselor who didn't even know her own mind, still uncertain of how to assert her own identity over the chorus of all the Dax symbiont's past lives—including the life that Jadzia Dax had pledged to share with him.

Ezri had changed dramatically in the time since then. Now she was a starship captain, commanding one of the most advanced ships in the fleet, unafraid to go toe-to-toe with a legendary captain like Picard. "Seeing Ezri now . . . seeing the person she has become, and how different that person is from Jadzia . . ." He paused and said, "I have no more doubts. I understand now that Dax is no more who Jadzia was than . . ."

"B-4 is who Data was."

Worf noted the very matter-of-fact way Geordi said that. The human had been deeply affected by his closest friend's death for a long time, and it was good to see signs that Geordi, like Worf, seemed ready to move on. "Exactly," Worf said.

La Forge nodded, then after considering the matter a moment longer, gave his head a shake. "Okay, well, wait, I'm still confused. It sounds to me like you had a positive psychological breakthrough. So, why now is your . . . relationship with Jasminder a mistake?"

"Because she is a human. She is a very tranquil, peaceable, nurturing human woman. Klingons are rarely any of these things—particularly not in our most primal behaviors."

"Ohhh," La Forge again said, this time in a tone that indicated that he didn't want to understand any more than he already did.

"She is a fascinating woman," he said, more to himself than to Geordi. "Brilliant, insightful, selfless. I do not believe I have ever enjoyed the simple companionship of another person so much." He paused and sighed. "It's best that we keep this relationship simple."

Geordi gave him a sideways look. "Yeah. Good luck with that . . ."

Picard sat at his ready room desk, scanning the reports coming in from all over the Federation, and tried to keep his mood from plunging any further than it had since leaving Earth.

It wasn't easy, though. Chancellor Martok had ordered the evacuation of Qo'noS, and the temporary relocation of the seat of the Klingon government to Ty'Gokor. An attempt had been made on the Cardassian castellan's life by a would-be assassin upset by the loss of their fleet at the Azure Nebula. Romulan Empire warbirds had destroyed at least three ships full of refugees from the breakaway Imperial Romulan State—reportedly by using the *Enterprise*'s search protocol, which Starfleet had shared with all the local powers.

And that protocol, though wildly successful in locating and saving over three hundred evacuation ships and thousands of lives across the Federation, had apparently reached the limit of its effectiveness. The greater problem now was what to do with all those ships and their passengers, and more and more worlds were expressing urgent concerns about all the refugees they were being asked to take in. Again, Picard's thoughts went to Beverly, and he hoped she was making better headway addressing the problems on Pacifica than he was out here.

The chime to his ready room door sounded, and he welcomed the excuse to put his padd aside. "Come," he said, admitting Lieutenant Choudhury.

"I'm not disturbing you, am I, sir?" she asked, pausing just inside the threshold.

"No, please," he said, gesturing for her to enter and take a seat as he stood up to refresh his empty teacup. "Can I get you anything?"

"No, thank you, sir."

Picard recycled his used cup and ordered another Earl Grey, surreptitiously studying the security chief as he waited for the materialization sequence to complete. She was tense and serious, but did seem a bit more poised than she had been of late. "So, what can I do for you, Lieutenant?" as he moved to the couch and sat facing her.

"Sir . . . Rosado, Elfiki, and I were trying to expand the scope of our search protocol. Until now, the parameters were set to gather data in a time period starting with the Azure Nebula invasion. We've adjusted that back, to cull information starting with the attacks on Barolia and Acamar."

Picard nodded his approval. Those were the first two worlds the Borg attacked, beginning five weeks of scattered surprise attacks leading up to the start of the Borg's final offensive, and there were a number of smaller-scale evacuations during that period. Although they faced much longer odds of rescuing any ships that had been missing that long, they owed it to those citizens to make every effort.

"In the course of putting together a sequence of events," Choudhury continued, "we found the first really big Borg panic occurred on Cestus III, starting in the city of Lakeside." She paused, giving Picard a significant look. "We also determined from comm traffic records that, less than thirty minutes before the panic started, there was a personal subspace communication on a Starfleet channel, from Commander Kadohata to Cestus III. The connection is only circumstantial, sir," Choudhury hastened to add, as Picard dropped his head and pressed his hand over his eyes. "But, I felt you had to be told, sir, particularly given the . . . 'incident' last year."

Picard sighed. "The incident," as he well knew, was the short-lived mutiny Kadohata had taken part in after Picard had refused a direct order from Admiral Nechayev during last year's Borg episode (it seemed an exaggeration now to call any of the Borg encounters previous to the just-ended war crises). Given the circumstances, along with Kadohata's service record and her desire to rebuild his trust, Picard had opted to officially forget her role in the "incident." So willing was he to put it behind them that, when her name came up on the promotions list four months ago, he ignored the residual misgivings he'd had and advanced her from lieutenant commander to full commander. *Good heavens, I even entrusted her with the safety of my wife and unborn son,* he thought to himself, *and now this betrayal.*

It occurred to him then how insane that attitude really was. What she had done—if she had in fact done it—was with the purpose of ensuring her family's safety. Wouldn't that be reason to trust her more?

"It's probably just a coincidence," Picard finally told Choudhury.

Choudhury nodded. "Yes, sir. As security officer, I felt I had to bring it to your attention—"

"As you should have, yes. Now . . . have these new parameters yielded any promising leads?"

Choudhury made a noncommittal face, and was about to expand on that response verbally when the door chimed again. Picard gestured for her to hold her thought, and said, "Come," admitting Commanders Worf and La Forge. The latter wore an optimistic smile on his face, and the former, while far less obvious, also had a glint of excitement in his eyes. "Gentlemen, do I take it you've come with some encouraging news?"

"We think so, sir," La Forge answered. "Jasminder, you'll want to hear this, too," he added to Choudhury, who had stood as they entered, and looked ready to be dismissed. Instead, she moved behind La Forge and looked over his shoulder as he crossed to the captain's desk and activated his computer monitor. The captain stepped forward, between Worf and La Forge, to see what had gotten his officers so excited.

On the screen appeared an image from what looked like a sort of advertising brochure: a picture of an old twenty-second-century cargo hauler, in dock, surrounded by the legend THE DENEVAN COLONIAL MUSEUM—SEE DENEVA'S HISTORY FIRSTHAND! "This is the S.S. Libra," La Forge explained, as Picard's face twisted in incomprehension. "It was one of the longest-serving ships in the Resources Corporation of Deneva's cargo fleet, and after she was finally retired in the early part of the twenty-third century, she was placed in permanent drydock and made into a museum ship. It's been in synchronous orbit for over a hundred years."

La Forge hit a key on the base of Picard's computer, and the image switched from the still illustration to a moving image of a star field, with a blue-and-white planet quickly filling the lower left-hand corner of the screen. An ID code and time stamp identified it as having been recorded by the *U.S.S. Musashi*. Picard readily recognized this as Alex Terapane's command, one of the six ships destroyed while defending Deneva. "Now here," La Forge said, tapping another sequence of keys, "is the museum spacedock." A yellow square appeared just above the curve of the planet, and then the image zoomed until the area within that square filled the display screen. Picard could then clearly make out the spacedock; however . . .

"The *Libra* is gone," Choudhury said softly. There was no debris around the docking facility, nor any noticeable sign of damage. "It was gone before the Borg. . . . But that ship's been a museum piece for centuries!"

La Forge's smile grew wider. "Exactly. A museum display visited by thousands of people a year, so they can walk through and see the entire ship, including its huge cargo areas, with their full life support!" Picard's breath caught as he realized what La Forge was driving at: the ship could potentially hold thousands of escapees.

"*This* was Plan 2757," Worf told Picard and Choudhury.

"Plan 2757?" Picard asked.

"An ambiguous nonrecurring reference we discovered in the Denevan government's comm records," Worf told him. "It seems to have referred to stardate 2757 . . ."

". . . but stardates aren't used by planet-based organizations," Choudhury said, obviously repeating a point she had already tried to impress upon her listeners. Picard nodded at her objection; the stardating system was developed to account for relativistic effects and other time-space shifts encountered by warp vessels. While it wasn't impossible that "2757" was a reference to a stardate, it didn't seem likely.

"Yes and no," La Forge said. "The number has a dual meaning. Stardate 2757 is approximately when Deneva's parasite crisis first struck—'approximately' because, like you said, Jasminder, a planet isn't a spaceship, and the old conversion formulas didn't quite apply. But, if 2-7-5-7 is an Earth calendar date . . ."

La Forge reached for the desktop monitor again and brought up another page from the Denevan Colonial Museum brochure, this one an illustrated timeline of Denevan history. Picard spotted the relevant twenty-second-century event immediately: *2/7/57: The R.C.D. cuts ties with Earth Cargo Service, establishing Deneva's economic independence. E.C.S. Libra renamed S.S. Libra.*

"They expected Starfleet to see a stardate," Worf said, sounding vindicated, "and used it to direct them to this information, alerting us to the secret launch of this escape vessel."

"That's a bit of a leap, isn't it?" Choudhury asked the first officer. It was a legitimate comment, and Jasminder voiced it in a respectful and tranquil tone, though Picard thought he detected a very subtle barb in the woman's words.

But the thought was fleeting, and quickly dismissed as Picard turned to La Forge. "Have you narrowed down the possible launch window?" he asked. "Could the ship have been retrofitted with a modern warp core? And if so, what would its peak velocity be?"

All three officers seemed taken aback by the captain's sudden fervor. "Um . . . three hours at the most, and with upgraded engines and structural integrity, it could hit warp 6, maybe 7."

Picard smiled and nodded enthusiastically, then turned, heading for the bridge. "Sir?" Choudhury called behind him.

He paused before issuing his new orders to the helm, and turned back briefly. "You're right, Lieutenant," he told her. "It is a leap. But when you reach the limit of where small steps can take you, that is what must be done."

9

———

Beverly Crusher was not easily shaken. She had been a doctor for over thirty years, and in that time she'd had to deal with just about every type of medical emergency imaginable, and more than a few that at the time had been unimaginable. She'd lost more patients than she would ever care to count: to violent attacks, to strange, exotic alien diseases, and to pointless accidents.

But young Matthew's near death had unsettled her deeply. Here she was, on a Federation member world in the late twenty-fourth century, and she had nearly lost an infant to dysentery and dehydration—dehydration on a planet that was almost completely covered in water! This kind of thing had been eradicated three hundred years ago—easily eradicated, by simply ensuring that people had access to clean drinking water. There was no reason in the universe why this poor, harmless child should have come so close . . .

Crusher stopped herself, closed her eyes, and took a pair of deep breaths as she forced her mind to clear. Of course, it wasn't just the medical facts of the case that were affecting her. She opened her eyes again and looked at Peggy, slumped in one of the tableside chairs, a cold, untouched cup of tea in front of her. No parents, no husband—and now Crusher had to tear her away from her son.

She shook her head ruefully and clapped her med supply case shut. Miranda had gone down to the river that looped around the camp and discovered several dozen exotic microbes in the water. Crusher was able to isolate the contagion, produce a counteragent, and inoculate both mother and child. Though Matthew had reacted positively to the new drug, he had already suffered too much internal organ damage for the doctor to risk keeping him out of stasis. She told Peggy it was better to leave him up here on the runabout; that way, they could get him to the nearest starbase and a proper neonatal ICU just as soon as this fact-finding mission was wrapped up. Reluctantly, Peggy joined her on the transporter and beamed back down with her to the planet.

Moments later, they were standing just outside the hastily constructed plastiform building that served as the camp infirmary. It had been one of the first structures erected, before concerns about overtaxing the industrial replicators had arisen, and was far more solid looking than the rest of the camp. It was, frankly, little more than a gray and rather sad-looking hut.

Inside, Crusher was dismayed to find things were just as gray. Beyond the entryway was a small examination area surrounded by a thin curtain, and beyond, a ward housing two dozen cots and an array of outdated and nearly obsolete medical equipment, some of it as much as forty years old. One of those obsolete tools noticed their arrival from across the room and started walking their way. Crusher's eyes widened in shock at the sight of the sharp-nosed, high-foreheaded figure. "I don't believe it . . ." she muttered under her breath.

"Someone you know?" Peggy asked.

Before Crusher could answer, the figure was right there in front of her, smiling his artificial smile. "Good afternoon," said the Emergency Medical Hologram. "Would you please tell me the nature of your medical emergency?"

"A Mark III EMH?" Beverly blurted.

The hologram continued smiling, an act that made his chin all but disappear. "That's correct. I am a third-generation version of Doctor Lewis Zimmerman's life- and labor-saving holographic program," it explained unnecessarily. "I am fully qualified—"

"Yes, I know, I know," Crusher interrupted. She'd heard this spiel more than enough times before. "Aronnax Station didn't have a more updated version?"

"They did." The hologram maintained its cheerful expression—one of the many improvements over the previous models—though it retained the undertone of Zimmerman's arrogance as it spoke. "Aronnax Station currently has an EMH Mark IX running in its medical center. Prior to my current activation, my program had been lying dormant in Aronnax's surplus storage depot for four years, ten months, thirteen days."

Crusher grimaced. Although her attitude toward the medical holograms had moderated considerably over the last decade, having seen their value demonstrated in numerous practical situations, she had the feeling she was about to be reminded of the reasons she had been so slow to warm to the things. "I'm Doctor Beverly Crusher," she informed the hologram. "Report."

The EMH continued to smile vapidly, but its eyes narrowed at her slightly. "There is no Doctor Beverly Crusher assigned to Aronnax Station, or anywhere else on Pacifica. I require a positive identification before I can share patient information, so I must respectfully refuse your order."

"There's a Starfleet runabout, the *Genesee*, in orbit," she said, afraid she already knew what the response would be. "Interface with its computer; it'll verify my identity and authorities as a Starfleet medical officer."

The EHM barely paused before announcing, "I'm afraid I am unable to verify the identity of the vessel in orbit." His eyes were now thin slits with tiny black beads peering through.

She was afraid of this. The Mark III had been in service during the height of the Dominion War, and featured extremely stringent security protocols—a good thing if a Founder was trying to use it to gain access to private medical data in order to better impersonate someone; not so good if anyone with a legitimate and vital need to that information came looking for it. It was for this reason that the Mark IV had been rushed into use so soon after the end of the war.

Fortunately, it did retain one old feature from its preceding versions. "Computer, deactivate EMH."

"Now, wait a min—" the EMH started to object as the portable hologenerators fell silent without protest. Once it was gone, Crusher guided Peggy over to one of the few vacant cots. She lay down, all her will and strength sapped, and was out almost as soon as her head touched the pillow. Beverly studied the portable life-signs monitor beside her bed (of the same type she had first used in medical school), and was satisfied that, physically at least, the young woman was well.

"Are you a doctor? A *real* doctor?"

Crusher turned to face a tall, pale-eyed, dusky-skinned woman. She wore a small disk on her forehead that identified her as a Risian, and would have been stunningly gorgeous if not so disheveled and visibly exhausted. "That's right."

"Thank goodness. Please look at this man."

Crusher nodded and let the woman lead her

to a cot where she found a male S'ti'ach lying unconscious. His only visible injuries were to his arms, which were both wrapped in dingy bandages stained with dried brown blood. Yet the vital signs monitor at his bedside showed only nominal activity. "His name is Sasdren. The EMH couldn't tell what was wrong with him. He'd been giving him polyadrenaline . . ."

"Of course he did," Crusher grunted as she ran her tricorder over the head and torso of her diminutive, blue-furred patient. "But its effect diminished with each administration, so he started upping the dosage."

The Risian nodded. "Yes."

Crusher nodded as well. Federation interaction with the S'ti'ach was minimal until just a few years ago; they wouldn't even have been included in the Mark III's database. Crusher set her tricorder aside and opened her medkit, withdrawing a delta-wave inducer. She placed it carefully on Sasdren's smaller-than-average forehead, and moments after he drifted off into deep sleep, his life signs began to climb.

"Oh, my," the Risian woman commented as she watched the patient's seemingly miraculous rallying. "How did you do that?"

"The S'ti'ach have remarkable natural healing powers. When injured, they can put themselves into a coma-like state, similar to a Vulcan healing trance, and redirect all their metabolic energy toward repairing the physical wounds."

"But if it's natural, why wasn't he healing himself?"

"Because he didn't want to." Crusher lifted the bandages, revealing, as she suspected, deep brown gouges in the S'ti'ach's blue arm, which without doubt had been made by his own claws, trying to slice the brachial arteries. "The delta-wave inducer puts him in a deeper state of sleep, so that his subconscious mind can't interfere with his autoimmune functions." She wondered what had happened to him during the Borg attack and the evacuations that could have driven him to this. Then she decided she really didn't want to know.

The doctor looked up from her patient to the Risian. "Forgive my manners," she said, extending her hand. "Doctor Beverly Crusher."

"Arandis," the woman said, taking Crusher's hand and allowing herself a small sliver of a smile that did nothing to dispel the sorrow on the rest of her face.

"Have you been here helping in the infirmary for long?"

She thought about that. "A few days . . . a week, maybe? It makes me feel useful. Like I'm helping."

"There's plenty of help needed here, it seems," Crusher said as she looked around the ward, frowning. "Have you seen many cases of people getting sick after drinking from the river?"

"Why, yes," Arandis said.

Crusher nodded, then loaded her hypospray

with a fresh ampoule of the new antibiotic. "All right," she said, holding up the instrument and motioning for Arandis to lead the way. "Let's help these people."

Byxthar stood on the edge of the makeshift soccer field, watching several dozen children chasing a ball up and down its length. They weren't playing by any standard set of rules, so far as she could tell. She wasn't entirely certain that there were even teams, or if each individual was deciding on their own which goal to defend—some seemed to change their minds from one minute to the next. But they were all, without exception, enjoying themselves. The resiliency of children never ceased to amaze her. No matter what happened around them, no matter their cultures, species, or the circumstances of their displacement, almost nothing seemed to dull a child's desire to get up and play with others.

"You're one of the Starfleeters, aren't you?"

Byxthar started, having tuned out the crowd around her and not having noticed the approach of the young human man with the striped beach towel over his shoulder now standing beside her. "Hmm? What? No." She gestured to her plain dark civilian suit. "Do I look like I'm in Starfleet?" she asked with a smile.

The man narrowed his bleary eyes at her. "Yeah . . . you ain't got filth all over you. Plus, you came here with the new 'Fleeters, the redhead and the Tellarite and the one with the mustache."

Byxthar tried to control her reaction. She had wanted to observe the interactions of the various refugee groups without drawing any undue attention to herself. "I'm not in Starfleet. I'm just here checking on conditions for the government."

"What, undercover?" the man asked.

Byxthar grimaced. "In a way."

"And?"

Byxthar stared at the man, not understanding his query. She found she could not hear anything coherent in his thoughts, either; more a jumble of half-formed thoughts and unvoiced emotion, somewhat muted by a dull throbbing pain. The only impression to come through clearly was his almost physical need for alcohol. Seeing her incomprehension, the man turned and pointed behind them with his chin. "How do the conditions check out?"

Byxthar turned away from the soccer game to look at the camp proper. "And . . ." Despite her efforts, a low murmur of the shock and depression and fear that emanated from the collective minds of the refugees seeped through her psionic shielding. "And they're not ideal . . . but they could be far worse."

The man said nothing, gave no response at all. After a moment, Byxthar turned away from him and back to the children.

"I didn't vote for Bacco."

"Oh." Byxthar couldn't tell what had prompted

that comment, and she certainly didn't want to get pulled into a political debate.

"Didn't vote at all, if you want to know the truth." He rubbed a hand across his whisker-stubbled chin. "Never have; never gave a damn. Just like them," he said, indicating the children on the field with a tilt of his head. "Not a care in the universe. What's it matter if Bacco or Zife or who-ever ended up running the government? It's still the same Federation, right? We go on living the same lives we always lived, never worrying about anything, never wanting for anything, knowing nothing's going to change.

"Then it does change," he said, and a shiver ran through his body. "And then where's the Federation? Then what does the Federation do?" He sneered at her. "It checks on conditions. It says, things could be far worse. Thank you, Federation! Aren't we lucky, then?"

"I . . . didn't mean to minimize . . ."

But the young man had already turned and started walking away, straight across the soccer field, interrupting the flow of the game, but only briefly. Once the trespasser was out of the way, play continued as if it had never stopped. Byxthar watched him as he disappeared over a small rise beyond, then sighed and tried to focus her perceptions again on the simple joy of kicking a ball back and forth in the grass.

• • •

Gliv grunted triumphantly and extracted the aberrant isolinear chip from its slot inside the replicator. He pulled his head and arm out, and turned to show it to Amsta-Iber. "Look at that," Gliv said. "The optical substrate has been completely decrystallized."

The Grazerite scientist, standing back and peering over his shoulder, shook his head at him. "I don't know what that means."

"It means you're overworking this poor machine," Gliv answered as he tossed the defective chip into his tool case and then plugged a new one into his tricorder. The handheld device ran its reconfiguration routine, turning the new chip into a clone of the previously scanned original. "If you keep abusing it as you have, you shouldn't be surprised when it decides to stop working."

"You make it sound as if it's a living thing with its own will," Amsta-Iber snuffed.

"Well, that's silly," Gliv answered the Grazerite. "Isn't it?" he then asked the replicator. "Yes, of course it is." That would have at least gotten a giggle from one of his human colleagues back on Luna, but from Amsta-Iber, nothing. Gliv didn't understand why human-style humor seemed to be such a difficult concept for most other races to grasp. He'd come across it at an early age, in the form of a flatvid recording of a human named Groucho Marx who issued subtle and clever insults like the most sophisticated Tellarite. When he joined Starfleet Academy, his human classmates introduced him to the full spectrum of Earth humor, from wordplay to slapstick, and all of its greatest practitioners.

What did get a reaction was when he replaced the chip and the replicator came back on line. "There," he said as he snapped the rear panel back into place. He stepped back to make room for the refugees already waiting in line for food. "It'll work for now, but really, we should reconfigure the camp layout if you want to minimize future problems."

"Reconfigure how?" Amsta-Iber asked, falling in step with the engineer.

"Well, you have your food replicators here, and you have your latrines all the way over there," Gliv said, gesturing to the emergency field 'freshers set up beyond the edge of the camp shelters.

Amsta-Iber stared at him in complete incomprehension. "Yes . . . ?"

Gliv couldn't help but grin now. "Well, the emergency field replicator can use a broad variety of organic base material, other than standard organic particulate suspension, from which to replicate menu items."

Amsta-Iber nodded. "Yes. We ran out of raw food stock fairly quickly, and have been resupplying the replicators' reserves with roots and grasses and such."

"Which it can use on a short-term emergency basis," Gliv said, "but it requires greater power consumption to transmute those complex molecules. However, you do have a source of organic matter that can be far more efficiently converted by the replicators." He again pointed to the latrines.

The Grazerite curled his cleft lip at Gliv. "Your attempts at humor are becoming annoying," he said.

The Tellarite laughed in spite of himself. "You're a Starfleet scientist. You must know that waste recycling and food replication systems are interconnected this way in all our ships and bases."

The meteorologist had no immediate answer, but just continued to give Gliv a look of extreme distaste. "Yes," he finally responded, "but one never has to think about it. And we certainly can't put the 'freshers in such close proximity to our food source!"

Gliv shook his head again. "The Mark VII emergency portable refreshers are airtight, watertight, automatically sterilize, and break down every bit of solid, liquid, and gaseous waste matter into safe, inert—"

"I know all this," Amsta-Iber snapped, "but you can't simply ignore centuries-old taboos shared by practically every civilized race to ever advance into space."

Gliv threw his arms up. "Fine! I'm only trying to offer short-term advice to help you avoid long-term disaster. Feel free to ignore it."

The Grazerite glowered at him for a moment, but then his expression turned to one of concern. "Do you really anticipate that all these people are going to be here long-term?"

Gliv followed Amsta-Iber's gaze, looking back at the long lines of hungry, homeless people. "I certainly hope these people are only here temporarily," Gliv said. Though he himself had spent the last eighteen months "temporarily" stationed on Luna, analyzing and making repairs to the over-three-hundred-year-old atmospheric domes that had housed humans' first off-Earth settlements. It wasn't particularly challenging work, but he had been perfectly willing to "pay his dues," as his C.O. put it, before a better posting came along. Trouble was, the dues he'd paid never seemed quite adequate. "But I do not know how long they could be here."

The two men stood and said nothing for a moment, until the silence became unbearable to the Tellarite.

"Say, ever hear the one about the human, the Klingon, and the Ferengi . . . ?"

As she finished up her preliminary survey of the iy'Dewra'ni encampment, Miranda Kadohata's shock over what they had found turned to anger.

Despite her initial reaction, she knew this was nowhere near as bad as what she would have found in similar camps on Earth in the wake of its many wars. These people had food replicators, sanitary waste disposal, and access to medicines undreamt of centuries ago. The cloth shelters, though spartan and not especially spacious, were far sturdier than they looked. All the tents were equipped with a battery-powered lighting system and a modular heating and cooling unit for those species who did not find Pacifica's balmy climes so pleasant as humans did. They weren't the kind of accommodations most visitors to Pacifica's resorts expected, but they were not all that uncomfortable.

But still, as she walked along the increasingly muddied footpaths of the tent city, she couldn't help but think that a place like this just should not exist in the Federation. It was beneath what they, as a society, were capable of. Even taking into account how little warning they had had ahead of the Borg's devastating assault (there had been scattered attacks for weeks, yes, but nothing that predicted the mass invasion at the Azure Nebula), how quickly the Selkies had had to react to the sudden influx of people in need, or how temporary the current situation was supposed to be—all she was seeing here were stopgap measures.

And the people saw it, too. At the start of her inspection, she was rushed by streams of excited and adulatory exiles, who noticed the uniform and immediately assumed that their rescuers had come at last. When Kadohata had to tell them that she was only part of a small advance group, and that they would do whatever they could for right now, she felt guilty for having built up and then dashed their hopes. They were like lost souls in purgatory waiting to be delivered to paradise—or, perhaps more fittingly, caught in a state of limbo.

She headed back to the administrative building, but paused to join a small crowd listening to a quartet of Damiani singing what sounded like a Bajoran hymn, in lovely four-part harmony. She almost allowed herself to smile and enjoy the performance, but her combadge emitted a chirp. *"Dillingham to Kadohata. Could you come back down here to the river, Commander?"*

She stifled a sigh and tapped the device on her chest. "On my way." As it turned out, a number of refugees, impatient with the lines at the food replicators, had found the same path down to the riverbank, where they had gotten their water and then, to varying degrees, had gotten sick. As she had gathered the specimen scans for Doctor Crusher, Dillingham had confronted one of the Selkie law enforcers. She had left him there two hours earlier, quoting obscure Federation regulations about Pacifica's legal obligations to the refugees' health and safety.

Back at the river, Kadohata found Dillingham now being confronted by a different official. By the cut of his uniform, she assumed that this was a senior member of local law enforcement, and probably not inclined to defer to the civilian lawyer. "Hullo," she said as she approached. "I'm Commander Miranda Kadohata. What's all this, then?"

The Selkie stepped forward, extending his hand and giving her a tight smile. "Commander. Commandant Thwa Minha, Pacifica Security, iy'Dewra'ni Division." He stood a full head taller than Kadohata, and when she accepted his hand, it wrapped tightly around her fingers—enough to be uncomfortable, but not so hard that she could say that it was intentional. "Commander, I've heard about the rash of illness among the refugees. Am I right to understand the cause has been found and taken care of?"

"Yes," Kadohata said, "our doctor was able to find a treatment. Thank you for your concern, Commandant."

"Of course," he said. "Visitors have been drawn to the waters of Pacifica for ages; it's terrible that these particular waters have sickened anyone. And, naturally, we all want to prevent any further illnesses caused by off-worlders being exposed to the water from this river."

Between Minha's silky tone and the sudden tension in Dillingham's jaw, Kadohata deduced that they were finally about to get to the problem at hand. "Yes?"

"And the simplest solution to that end is to erect a barrier fence around the perimeter—"

"Which you cannot do!" Dillingham interrupted in a low, frustrated tone. He looked to Kadohata and explained, "There can be no fences, no energy barriers, nothing to suggest an enclosure. Article 109, section forty-se—"

Minha made a strange, subvocal sound that clearly indicated his own irritation. "Do you have the legal citations regulating the use of waste extraction memorized, too, Mister Dillingham?"

"This is supposed to be a sanctuary, not a prison!" Dillingham said heatedly. He was a mild, professorial-looking man, but Kadohata was getting the feeling that was a façade over a volcanic temperament. "Putting up a fence creates the wrong image."

"The fence would be to protect them," Minha said, evidently repeating a previously stated point. "From drinking unsafe water, from slipping down the steeper parts of the riverbank upstream. We do agree that *protection*—of lives, of health, of rights—is our shared primary goal, don't we?"

Dillingham shook his head. "Your concern is protecting the native residents against the irrational fear that these refugees—"

"There is nothing irrational—"

"Commandant," Kadohata interrupted, raising her voice only enough to quiet both men. "How would you propose to have this . . . safety barrier constructed and put up?"

Dillingham looked at her aghast, while Minha looked confused. "The components would be manufactured by industrial replicators, of course. Then we'd have contract laborers put them up."

Kadohata nodded. "I ask because the replicators in the camp are being overtaxed, and we could certainly use all the extra sets of hands we can get."

Minha gave her the first genuine smile she'd seen from him. "I'm sure something can be arranged with the nearby manufacturing concerns. As I said, we all are concerned about your people and—"

"*Our* people, Commandant," Kadohata corrected him sharply. "These are fellow Federation citizens, remember. And you'll keep that in mind, I'm sure, as you determine the exact form that this barrier eventually takes."

"Commander," Dillingham said in an urgent low voice, "you cannot permit this. It's a violation of these people's dignity. Any kind of enclosure that suggests these people have been penned in would be potentially psychologically damaging to the people here."

Kadohata stared at him for a moment, then turned to the Selkie. "Thank you, Commandant." She then took the lawyer by the elbow and started leading him away. "You've spent two hours here, prattling on about regulations and statutes and the harm that might be done to these people. You haven't actually seen the camp yet, have you?"

"I saw it," he answered, bewildered. "When we beamed down."

Kadohata sighed and pulled him along faster. "Come," she said as they approached the edge of the tent city. "Let's introduce you to the people you're defending."

10

———————

A burst of static came over the bridge audio receivers, and then a voice cut through the background noise: *"This is the* Libra, Enterprise. *We read you loud and clear!"* Whoops and cheers were heard in the background over the scratchy audio-only transmission from the once lost Denevan freighter.

The *Enterprise* bridge was a bit more restrained, but a palpable feeling of relief and triumph engulfed them at this confirmation that this would be a rescue, and not a recovery of remains. Jasminder Choudhury all but laughed aloud, and quickly swiped her hand over her eyes, pushing away the tears of joy.

Captain Picard, standing at the center of the bridge before his chair, turned to share a broad smile with her and with the rest of the bridge crew, then raised his head slightly as he again addressed the comm. "What is your status, *Libra*?"

"We had to eject our antimatter stores three days

out of Deneva," reported the captain, a woman who identified herself as General Katherine Seton. *"We were en route to Ingraham B. We've just been limping along on impulse and trying to keep everyone as calm and comfortable as possible. Fortunately, Plan 2757 allowed for a long wait."*

It was truly impressive how much thought and preparation the Denevan government had put into their evacuation plan, particularly to Choudhury. In her family, the only time politics ever came up was when her father and Uncle Narayana railed against the incompetence of the politicians in Lacon City.

"It won't be much longer. Lieutenant Faur," Picard said to the young woman at the conn, "how long until we can rendezvous with the *Libra*?"

Faur consulted her console and answered, "One hour, twenty-one minutes, sir."

"Just enough time to bake a cake," Seton quipped.

"We'll be able to replenish your antimatter and make whatever other repairs might be necessary to get you back under your own power," Picard said. "Do you require any medical or other assistance?"

"We've had a handful of injuries since leaving, plus two births. They're being taken care of, but I'd rather they were in a real, fully equipped sickbay."

"Of course," Picard said, then looked to Worf. He nodded in response, then tapped his combadge and spoke quickly to Doctor Tropp in sickbay.

"Otherwise, we're managing," Seton continued.

"Though I know I can't be the only one looking forward to getting outside again."

"And . . . how many others are there?" Picard asked.

"Two thousand, seven hundred and fourteen," came the answer. Choudhury gasped softly in surprise. Over twenty-seven hundred saved. It was by far the best news she'd heard since the attack on her home, yet, at the same time, she couldn't help but reflect on how very, very small that number was compared to the planet's total population.

"We'll do all we can to ensure their ordeal is brought to a swift conclusion," the captain promised.

"May the Great Bird bless you, Captain Picard," Seton replied. *"We look forward to seeing you. Libra out."*

The signal terminated, and Picard paused, savoring this brief, bright moment in what had been a very dark few days. Then he said to Worf, "Contact Commander La Forge. Have him assemble an engineering team to board the *Libra*." He then turned toward the bridge's rear stations. "Lieutenants Choudhury, Chen, with me, please," directed the captain before heading for his ready room.

Choudhury looked over at T'Ryssa Chen at the auxiliary science station, an incongruous look of surprise on her Vulcan face. She turned from Picard to the security chief with a look that seemed to ask, *What did I do wrong* this *time?* Choudhury just gave her a shrug before turning to follow after the captain.

Picard waited until Chen, marching double-time, caught up behind the long-legged Choudhury and then gestured for both of them to have a seat on the small couch by the door. The captain himself remained standing, pacing a bit. After a moment he said, "It occurs to me that the *Libra* poses a rather unique situation. This is the largest group of evacuees we've encountered thus far— almost a small colony unto themselves. Given this, it's my opinion that once we rendezvous with the *Libra,* the away team should be led by the *Enterprise*'s diplomatic and contact specialist."

Choudhury raised her eyebrows in surprise, though it was nowhere near the surprise Chen herself showed, once it dawned on her that the captain was talking about her. "What? Me?" she finally stammered. "But . . . this isn't a first contact. Denevans are humans . . . aren't you?" she asked, turning to Choudhury. "Well, I mean, I know *you* are," she added, backpedaling furiously, "though that doesn't mean *all* Denevans are. I mean, I'm the last one who should be pigeonholing people by species, right?" she added, flicking at the point of her tapered right ear.

"Lieutenant Chen—" Picard said, his eyes rolling back just slightly.

"Sorry, sir," she said. "It's just . . . leading an away team! I'm just so honored. It's like I've just been awarded—" Chen then noticed the stern glare Picard was giving her and clamped her mouth shut, bringing her rush of blather to an instant halt.

After a moment, she let out the breath she was holding and said, "Thank you, Captain, sir. I won't disappoint you."

Choudhury looked from one to the other with a tiny bemused smile. Chen was an "odd duck," as her great-grandfather used to say. She had gotten to work closely with the younger woman just once since joining the *Enterprise*, teaching her meditation techniques during their encounter with the "Noh Angel" stellar cluster entities. To her regret, though, Chen balked at the suggestion that their lessons continue beyond the end of that mission, insisting she was more comfortable with the way she had always dealt with her turbulent mix of human and Vulcan emotionalism—that is, just letting them all out.

"See that you don't," Picard told her. "I'm giving you an opportunity to prove what you are capable of, Lieutenant. Do not treat this matter lightly simply because these are Federation citizens. It would be truly unfortunate if you were to cause them to renounce their citizenship," he added, letting the slightest hint of a smile show through his stern visage.

Chen, perhaps out of an abundance of caution, refrained from smiling back. "Aye, sir."

Picard nodded. "Dismissed, Lieutenant." Chen sprang from her seat and bounded out of the ready room like an eager puppy, and Picard smiled after her. It was an interesting dynamic, Choudhury noted: Picard brought out the more disciplined side of Chen, while the lieutenant seemed to temper the stuffier aspects of the captain's personality.

Once the doors closed, Choudhury told the captain, "We Denevans are a pretty tolerant lot, sir. I wouldn't worry about her doing too much damage."

Picard chuckled once as he took a seat opposite her. "No, I'm not," he assured her. "We just may not be seeing many first contact situations in the near future, and I want to ensure that the growth she's shown in the last several months isn't allowed to stagnate. At any rate, I know you'll keep a careful eye on her."

Choudhury felt her heart being seized inside her chest. "Sir?"

Picard looked at her with a confused expression. "The reason I had called you both in here was because I intended to have both of you as part of the away team. Naturally, I assumed you would want to be there to greet them."

Choudhury tried to quickly find her center and school her expression. "Well, that would be Lieutenant Chen's decision as team leader, wouldn't it?"

"Well, yes . . ." the captain said, still confused.

"Frankly, I tend to agree with you, sir," she continued. "I would think this an ideal assignment for one of my junior officers."

Picard said nothing, but studied her with his hawk-eyed stare. "Are you concerned that you will be seen as taking advantage of your position in order to interject yourself into this mission?"

"No, sir," Choudhury said without any further elaboration.

Picard continued to stare at her skeptically. "Very well, then," he finally said. "Make whatever arrangements for security assignments you feel best with Chen."

"Yes, sir," she said, rising, and headed out of the ready room before he could ask any more discomforting questions. It simply wouldn't do for her commanding officer to learn what mixed feelings she had about what they would find once they rendezvoused with this ship—or, more precisely, what she would not find aboard.

Lieutenant Trys Chen walked into the transporter room to find the rest of the away team—*my team,* she repeated to herself just to feel that shiver of pride run up her spine again—already gathered and ready. Geordi La Forge had one of his junior engineers, Ensign Maureen Granados, and the Andorian intern, Doctor th'Shelas, was accompanied by Nurse Mimouni. The team was rounded out by a single security officer, Rennan Konya. Chen was still curious as to why Jazz had begged off this assignment, but since that meant she was getting her boyfriend as the team's security officer instead, she couldn't complain. She smiled broadly at them all and said, "All right, people, are we ready to get this boarding party started?"

They responded with nods, plus one "Ready,

Lieutenant" from Rennan. Chen resisted the urge to give him an extra little wink, and gestured for the team to step up to the elevated transporter pads.

As her team took their places, La Forge hung back from the rest and sidled up beside her. "You know," he whispered, "it's usually bad form for the team leader to be the last to show up for the start of a mission."

Chen turned and stared at the commander. He was still smiling, but his circuit-lined eyes conveyed the authority he put behind his words. "What, so you're my chaperone?" she asked, somehow keeping her voice at the same low volume he had used.

"More like your backup support." Both his eyes and smile turned a bit friendlier as he said that, which helped to stop the protest rising in Chen's throat. She couldn't really blame Geordi or the captain for leaving the training wheels on, and she was still nominally the team leader.

"Thanks," she said. "I'll remember that if there's a next time."

La Forge just nodded, and allowed her to lead him up onto the transporter. As the uncomfortable sensation of having her atoms taken apart and put back together subsided, Chen found herself on the bridge of the *S.S. Libra*. If she hadn't known beforehand that the freighter was a museum piece, she might have worried she'd been transported through a temporal field at the same time. Every piece of equipment screamed of twenty-second-century technology and design.

The *Libra* bridge had a crew of four: three in military uniforms, plus a craggy-faced, dark-skinned man in a civilian suit. Once the *Enterprise* team had fully materialized, the tall, ash blond woman in the center seat stood and stepped forward. "Welcome aboard," she said, smiling broadly. "General Katherine Seton, Deneva Defense."

Chen gave La Forge a quick sideways glance, then stepped forward herself. "Lieutenant T'Ryssa Chen, *U.S.S. Enterprise*," she said, raising her right arm.

The general apparently misinterpreted the move, as she quickly lifted her own right hand above her shoulder and spread her fingers. "Peace and long life, Lieutenant."

"Uh . . . yeah, and you, too," Chen replied, lifting and dropping her hand in a single motion, hoping no one noticed that she wasn't able to actually form the V-shape. She tossed her head, trying to inconspicuously get her hair to fall over her uncovered left ear.

The general turned and gestured to the civilian. "And this is Gar Tiernan, Vice President of Deneva."

Chen made sure her hand was properly positioned so that Tiernan was forced to shake it. "Mister Vice President, sir."

Tiernan took it and said, "Any word yet on the passengers beamed to your sickbay?"

Chen turned and stepped to one side. "Doctor th'Shelas?"

"The newborns and their mothers are all in perfect health," the doctor reported. "The other injured passengers you beamed over have been treated and should make quick and complete recoveries."

The Denevans all smiled at hearing that. "Excellent," the general replied.

This really is going excellently, isn't it? Chen nodded back, and sneaked a quick, self-satisfied smile at Commander La Forge as she turned to present the rest of the away team. "This is Nurse Antoinette Mimouni. She and the doctor are here to check on the rest of your not-quite-such-emergency medical cases. Chief engineer Geordi La Forge and Ensign Maureen Granados—they'll be helping you get back under way to Ingraham B—"

"Ingraham B?" The entire group seemed to be caught by surprise at that, but it was Vice President Tiernan who asked, "Why would we continue on to Ingraham B instead of heading back to Deneva?"

"Well, because Deneva—" Chen started to answer, and then quickly caught hold of her runaway tongue as realization dawned. "You don't know."

Seton's eyes widened in concern. "Know? Know what?"

Chen cursed her tongue for slipping loose again so quickly. The Denevans all stared at her with expressions of worry and expectation, repeating the general's question. Chen turned to La Forge, who obviously was no more eager to answer the Denevans' question than she was. All the same, he stepped forward, putting himself between Chen and Seton, and began to explain what had happened when the Borg reached their home planet.

Chen couldn't help but turn away from their reactions as she fell back with the rest of her former team.

The dark gray orb at the center of the starscape was unrecognizable—just another dead world, one of the almost infinite number of planetary masses on which life had never found a foothold.

Or so it had seemed, at least until the probe making the recording reached orbit and pierced the dust-filled atmosphere. Enhanced visual sensors cut through the layers of thick toxic smoke, bringing forth every detail of the planet's surface with horrific clarity. Then there was no mistaking what world this was: there was the distinctive western coastline of the Iapetus Ocean, and the Summer Islands just across the Bealtaine Strait. And on the south shore of the largest island, where the capital, Lacon City, had once stood, there was nothing but an ugly black scab of molten glass and metal.

Vice President Garson Tiernan of the planet Deneva—now presumably President Tiernan of the Denevan Diaspora—sat in the darkened observation lounge, his chair turned to the wall-mounted screen, while Jean-Luc Picard sat in silent reverence across the table from him. Together, they watched for a seventh time as the rest of the world's familiar geography rolled past, all signs of human habitation on every continent reduced to nothing but blemishes on the scorched terrain. As the probe descended for a lower-altitude scan on its second orbit, the image started to break up, the effect of residual radiation in the aftermath of the attack. By the time it crossed the terminator to Deneva's nighttime side, the screen went completely black as the probe transmitter was overwhelmed and failed.

After a brief, still moment, Tiernan hit the control embedded in the conference table's surface and started the visual recording again. "There's nothing to be gained by torturing yourself like this, Mister Tiernan," Picard said sympathetically.

The vice president did not even acknowledge that he had heard him, instead fixing all his concentration on the images flashing before him. Tiernan had been unable to watch the full recording the first four times without rejecting the truth of what he was seeing, or turning his head away, or stopping to vomit. The fifth time through he managed to watch the whole horrible record from start to finish, and had demanded to see it a sixth time. "I owe it to them, Captain," he had said in a strained voice. "I owe it to those people down there to bear witness to what happened here, to brand these images into my memory." The probe completed its circumnavigation again minutes later, and before the screen had time to darken, Tiernan had restarted it a ninth time.

At last, Picard had to lean forward and hit his own control panel, blanking the screen and bringing the room lights back up. "Sir, with all respect to the deceased, you are now the presumptive leader of the *survivors* of Deneva. That these people have a leader was the very reason, as I understand it, that you were included in the Plan 2757 evacuation. And while you have my deepest sympathies, there are pressing matters at hand that need to be addressed."

The Denevan pivoted his chair toward Picard. He seemed to have physically deflated since first being escorted into the lounge, and his face looked as if it was threatening to slide right off his skull. "You're right, Captain," he said, grabbing onto the chair's armrests and pulling himself upright. "Do we know how many other Denevans managed to escape safely?"

"The current estimates are just over one million," Picard said.

"No . . ." Tiernan said with a shudder.

"That so many were saved is a testament to the Denevan government's organization and planning."

"So many, you say—that's less than one-tenth of one percent . . ." Tiernan dropped his head for a moment, making an effort to compose himself. "Focus on the living," he mumbled to himself, then raised his head again. "How are the repairs on the *Libra* coming?"

"You should be back under way within the hour," Picard assured him, just as the comm signal chimed. "Excuse me," he said before tapping his combadge. "Picard."

"Captain," said Ensign Šmrhová, the officer currently at tactical, *"we're receiving a message from the Federation Council offices on Earth. Councillor Lynda Foley of Deneva."*

Hearing this, Tiernan felt some of the darkness surrounding him lift. "Please pipe it in here, Ensign," Picard said, and moments later, the face of a dark-haired woman of indeterminate age appeared on the screen.

"Lynda!" Tiernan said, getting up out of his chair and moving toward the viewer as if about to embrace her. "It is so good to see you!"

"Not half as good as it is to see you, Gar!" the councillor replied, her cheeks dimpling deeply as she smiled. *"And Captain Picard, thank you so much for finding these lost sheep of ours."*

"No thanks are necessary, Councillor," he told her, smiling.

The councillor's expression turned more somber as she looked back to Tiernan and asked, *"President Cordaro?"*

Tiernan's expression mirrored Foley's. "Stubborn to the end. Sent her entire staff and security detail home to their families, but refused to be budged from her desk."

Picard stood at that point, saying, "I assume, Madam Councillor, that you two have quite a bit to discuss. If you would excuse me, then . . ."

With the leave of both Denevans, Picard walked out onto the bridge, only to find Lieutenant Chen waiting patiently for him at the lounge door. "Sir, I wanted to tell you again how sorry I am for the way things went," she said forlornly once the doors slid closed behind him. "Seems like I'm capable of fouling up a contact mission with humans, after all."

"Nonsense," Picard chided her. "I shouldn't have put you in such an untenable position to begin with." Picard shook his head ruefully. He should have relayed the information himself during their initial contact with the *Libra*, but, caught up as he was in the moment of triumph, the calamity that preceded it was banished from his thoughts. "It's never easy to relate such tragic news."

"Almost makes you feel guilty."

Picard's right eyebrow arched upward. "Beg pardon?"

"No, not you, specifically, sir," Chen said. "I meant . . . we came through the war pretty okay. We didn't lose homes or family members. Hell, I even ended up gaining in that department." Picard did not know what that comment meant, or why there was such apparent bitterness behind it. "But these people—where do they go now? What do you do when you lose everything like that?"

" 'Let me embrace thee, sour adversity, for wise

men say it is the wisest course,'" Picard said. "Shakespeare," he added for Chen's benefit.

She gave him a small smile. "Yes, sir. The 'thee' kinda gave that away."

Picard returned the tight smile, then said, "I have no doubt these people, as determined to survive as they are, will find a way to embrace this tragedy, and become all the stronger for it."

"So the rest of them who were killed on Deneva weren't determined enough?"

Picard answered the young woman with an angry glare, then looked across the bridge toward the tactical station. He was slightly relieved to see Ensign Šmrhová currently manning Choudhury's station, though that did not alleviate his outrage at Chen's thoughtless comment.

To her credit, she immediately looked abashed. "No! I know that's not what you were saying, Captain," she said quickly, keeping her voice low enough for just Picard to hear. "I was just wondering aloud, you know—where's the sense in all this? Why these people, not those people? Why us, not them? At the risk of sounding like a cliché," she said with a sardonic laugh, "it is not logical."

Picard sighed. "Far greater philosophers than I have attempted to answer that question over the ages," he said, shaking his head. "Why do bad things happen to good people? I don't know. I doubt the answer to that question can be knowable. We can only try and take solace in the fact that the enemy who caused this calamity is gone now, and do all that we can to help those who have suffered."

Chen was about to say something in response, but before she could, the conference room doors slid open. "Captain Picard . . . Lieutenant," Tiernan said, stopping short when he saw the two *Enterprise* officers standing in his way. He looked fully revived, the void Picard had seen earlier in his eyes now filled with renewed purpose. "Captain, what is your itinerary once the *Libra* repairs are finished and she's back under way?"

Picard quickly shook off his surprise at the Denevan leader's sudden transformation and said, "We're on a rescue and recovery mission. We don't have an itinerary as such, but—"

"Then I need to ask that you take me to Earth," Tiernan interrupted. "I need to meet with President Bacco, and as soon as possible."

"Why?" Chen asked, also clearly taken aback by his unexpectedly elevated mood.

"I was just shown her postwar address," he explained. "'We will rebuild these worlds,' she said. That's my primary obligation now: to make certain that the promise made to my people is kept."

Picard pursed his lips as he recalled his recent conversation with President Bacco, about her speech being "too inspiring." He vacillated a moment as he considered the remarkable revitalizing effect the Federation president's words had on Tiernan, then told him, "Mister President, I'm sure you understand that it will be some time before the Federation can take on a project of such magnitude as re-terraforming Deneva. The immediate concern has to be for our displaced citizens, like those on the *Libra*—"

"Well, yes, of course," Tiernan said. "But Ingraham B was only ever meant to serve as a temporary refuge. These people are going to need a planet to go back home to, after all."

Picard said nothing; it was not his place, after all, to tell planetary leaders how to lead. "Very well. As soon as the *Libra* is back under way, we will set course for Earth. Lieutenant Chen, would you be kind enough to escort President Tiernan to VIP quarters?"

Tiernan grinned gratefully. "Thank you, Captain," he said before following Chen into the turbolift. Picard returned the man's smile, though he was fairly certain that he was doing him no favors by accommodating his appeal.

Worf stood at the center of the bridge, hands folded behind his back, watching as the exterior running lights on the *Libra* were reilluminated, one by one. And as he watched the ship come back to life, he allowed himself a rare smile.

Today is a good day to live.

There had been too little glory in the recent war against the Borg. His fellow Starfleet officers and Klingon warriors—and, he had to concede, even the Romulans—had done battle against the invaders with great honor, and there were some victories, such as at Troyius and Ardana. But many of the dead had been children, or elderly, or infirm, slaughtered without a chance of defending themselves. A Klingon did not shrink from death, but being witness to a purposeless slaughter of this magnitude would have given even Kahless himself pause.

The *Libra* recovery, though, was a great triumph in the face of all else. The Denevans' foresight and their willingness to sacrifice in order that some few might survive brought their entire people honor. Their feat, and that of the outmoded, centuries-old freighter, was one worthy of song.

"Number One?" Worf turned and noticed that the captain had finished his conversation with Lieutenant Chen and the Denevan vice president, and was now moving around to the starboard side of the bridge. "Would you join me, please?" he said.

Worf nodded, turned the conn over to Rosado, and fell in step behind Picard as he entered the ready room. He was gratified to see that the *K'jtma* goblet had been given a prominent placement in the captain's personal refuge. Picard went directly to the replicator, and as he manually keyed in a request, he said over his shoulder, "I haven't yet commended you, Number One, for the remarkable deduction you made, which led us to the *Libra*."

"Thank you, sir. But I was not the only one—"

"No, but it was your instincts," the captain said, turning back to him with two identical metal cups in his hands. "You're the one who questioned that single reference, and that's what brought us to the brightest moment of our current mission." Worf caught the unmistakable whiff of bloodwine as Picard handed one of the cups to him and raised the other. "*Qapla*, Worf."

Worf smiled and returned the salute. "*Qapla!*" Replicated bloodwine was never very good, but this drink he shared with his captain was more than acceptable.

Picard gestured for him to take a seat on the sofa, and Picard sat in one of the matching chairs set at an angle to him. Once they were both settled, the captain crossed his legs and said, "I don't suppose you've had any other brilliant insights as to where we might find more exiles in distress?"

"No, sir. Though Lieutenant Elfiki did raise the possibility that some evacuation ships may have attempted to take refuge in the Paulson Nebula, and may still be there."

The captain nodded thoughtfully. The Paulson Nebula was rich in sensor-resistant elements, and as it was normally uninhabited, the Borg theoretically would have ignored it during their genocidal rampage. "Do we have any solid indication that there are in fact any ships hiding there?"

"No, sir. Although, given the close proximity of the Paulson Nebula to the Azure Nebula, the data we have is understandably limited."

"It's certainly worth investigating," Picard said, and then sighed. "However, we have been asked by President Tiernan to transport him back to Earth."

"He doesn't intend to continue on with his people to Ingraham B?"

"No. He apparently intends to petition President Bacco for an expedited timetable for the restoration of Deneva."

Worf's eyes widened in surprise, as the memories of walking on that devastated planet with Jasminder arose unbidden in his mind. He had to take another swallow of bloodwine to push back the vividly recalled taste and smell of ash in the Denevan air. "That would seem a poor use of his energies," Worf said levelly. "Under the best circumstances, it takes decades to terraform a planet. The conditions on Deneva . . . he must realize the challenge that restoring it to even a fraction of its former state would present."

Picard sighed. "No, Number One. I don't believe he does. He's not a planetologist or a terraformer; he's a politician."

Worf responded to this with a single dry chuckle. As an ambassador, he had dealt with more than his share of governmental officials who demanded results without any understanding of—or interest in—how those results could be reached. Worf sometimes thought they believed there was a button on their desk, which needed only to be pressed, causing all their problems to be automatically fixed.

"I'd appreciate any suggestions you might have,

Number One, on how we might best broach this matter with Mister Tiernan," Picard said, leaning forward in his chair. "Your experience in your previous role, I suspect, may provide some fresh perspective."

Worf's eyes widened. "Sir . . . I'm honored that you feel I can offer any unique contributions."

"No need for false modesty, Worf," Picard said, smiling.

"There is nothing false about it, sir," Worf answered with utter seriousness. "You are far more accomplished as a diplomat than I. I do not believe, in my four years in the position, there was a single situation I faced where I did not ask myself, 'What would Captain Picard do?'"

Picard grinned and shook his head. "I've always considered myself an explorer first. And I've always had the option, when dealing with politicians, of simply beaming back aboard ship and leaving them behind as soon as my specific mission was complete. You didn't have that luxury during your time in the embassy."

"No, I did not," Worf said in a low rumble, remembering more than a few of the governmental officials he'd dealt with whom he would have liked to escape at warp speed.

Before he could say anything, though, he was interrupted by the beep of the comm, and the voice of Ensign Šmrhová saying, *"Bridge to Captain Picard. You have a priority message coming in from Starfleet Command."*

"In here, Lieutenant." Picard moved around behind his desk and activated his desktop monitor. Worf followed, positioning himself at the edge of the captain's desk, where he could see the image of Admiral Akaar as it appeared on the comm screen. "Admiral," Picard said in greeting.

"Captain Picard, the Enterprise *is needed at Alpha Centauri III immediately,"* the craggy-faced Capellan said without preamble.

"Alpha Centauri?" Picard asked. "Why? What's happened?"

"There's rioting in the streets of the capital," the admiral said, his paled face almost the same color as his long white hair. *"There are reports of violence, fires, even looting!"*

On Alpha Centauri? Worf wanted to exclaim, though he had enough self-control not to question the admiral aloud. Alpha Centauri was one of the five founding worlds of the Federation; the idea of such things happening there was only slightly less unthinkable than having them happen on Earth. Worf exchanged a look with the captain, and saw a look of disbelief he was certain matched his own.

"There are conflicting accounts—the protests were started either by the refugee groups placed there, or by residents protesting the refugees' presence," Akaar continued, also plainly staggered by the news. *"Local law enforcement is doing what they can—"*

But the captain was looking away from the admiral's image now, raising his head slightly and calling, "Picard to bridge. Set course for the Alpha Centauri system and engage at maximum warp!"

The admiral, rather than being annoyed at being interrupted, simply gave the captain a curt nod. "*Godspeed,* Enterprise," he said, and ended the transmission.

"Alpha Centauri . . ." Picard put his hands forward on his desk, as if supporting a huge weight across his shoulders. Worf waited respectfully as Picard stood like that for a moment, and the first officer wondered if the captain's spirit, so recently renewed by the Caeliar, had been broken.

Then Picard shook his head, straightened up, and turned to Worf with a fire of determination in his eyes. "We've lost too many worlds already, Number One," he said, as he started to move toward the bridge. "We will not allow another to fall."

11

Two full moons had risen over Pacifica, casting an ethereal glow over the iy'Dewra'ni camp. Beverly Crusher leaned wearily against the doorjamb of the infirmary building's entry, breathing in the cool night air and marveling at how peaceful and serene the place seemed at that moment.

It certainly hadn't been peaceful or serene for most of her day. She was able to release the majority of the infirmary's patients after administering her new inoculation. But once word had gotten out that "a real flesh and blood doctor" was now at the infirmary, the line of people with minor ailments and injuries wrapped around the building. She understood the reservations people had about the EMH, and she realized that most people outside of Starfleet had never encountered one before. But she'd been surprised by how many civilians flat-out refused to deal with the computerized holo-gram, opting instead to suffer in silence.

Fortunately, she had Arandis, who continued to be a great help, administering treatment to the simpler cases—including a lot more who had picked up the waterborne microbe—and just generally projecting her good nature unto the tired and irritable patients as they filed in and out. The Risians were legendary for their generous, giving natures, and Arandis was proof of that, working herself beyond the point of exhaustion and finally falling asleep sitting upright in a chair in the corner of the infirmary.

Crusher's gaze rose from the camp up to the larger of the two moons, and then beyond. *I wonder where Jean-Luc is right now,* she thought, as she absently rubbed the curve of her belly.

"Bev? You're still here?"

Crusher brought her head back down as Miranda Kadohata approached, dragging a small antigrav sled behind her. Her dark hair was a mess, flying in all directions. The knees of her uniform pants were caked with mud, as were the cuffs of her shirt. Still, she favored Crusher with a smile. "I'm still here," the doctor confirmed. "You look pretty pleased with yourself."

Kadohata nodded as she walked past Crusher into the infirmary, went to the small storage unit in the corner, and grabbed one of the small squeezebulbs of water there. "Commandant Minha came through with that extra industrial replicator," she said. "We've got it up and running, and made some safety fixes to the family section of camp." Her smile faded a fraction then. "So many of these children were put on their ships without either parent . . ." She shook her head and trailed off as she drank deeply.

Crusher could think of nothing to say to that. She knew Miranda had talked at length with her husband earlier, and things seemed to have been patched up somewhat. Still, she understood that being apart from her loved ones was never going to be easy. Her thoughts started to drift again . . .

"Bev!"

Crusher's head jerked up and she refocused on the woman talking to her. "Bev, you're exhausted. Go back to the ship and get some rest."

The doctor shook her head. "I have patients to look after," she said as she headed back into the ward.

"Not so many anymore," Kadohata noted as she followed Crusher. "What about that Risian woman who was . . . Oh," she said when she spotted the sleeping Arandis. "Still, you need your sleep too, love. Especially in your state."

Crusher tilted her head and raised one eyebrow. "I don't remember you slowing down when you were three months along, during the Delta Sigma IV mission," she said. "And that was when a *doctor* was telling you to."

"A wise and brilliant doctor, whose advice I wish I had taken," Kadohata answered.

"Miranda . . ." Crusher started, but as much as she hated to admit it to herself, she wasn't twenty-four anymore. She was discovering she could not shake off the fatigue and other effects of this pregnancy like she had her first time. Finally, she sagged and said, "You won't hesitate to call if there's any trouble whatsoever," making it more of an order than a request.

"Medical trouble," Kadohata countered.

"Fair enough," Crusher said, suddenly unable to resist the call of a nice soft bunk. She felt a quick flash of guilt, knowing everyone else in the camp was sleeping on thinly padded cots and sleeping mats, but it wasn't enough to stay her hand as she tapped her combadge. "Crusher to *Genesee*. One to beam up."

She was greeted, when she rematerialized on the runabout's transporter pad, by the sounds of a shouting match in progress in the living area. Crusher made her way astern and found Dillingham, Byxthar, and Gliv sitting around the table, which was strewn with the remains of a full dinner. "What's going on here?" she demanded.

"Ah, Doctor-Commander," Byxthar said as all three turned toward the doorway. "You'll be able to help settle this."

"Settle what?" she asked warily.

"We were discussing the reports we each plan to make to Director Barash," Byxthar answered, facing Crusher but directing her eyes at Dillingham. "The professional, comprehensive reports expected from a team of experts . . ."

The human gave her an acid look back. "And while you're working on your next book—oh, excuse me, your 'comprehensive report'—these people are living in the equivalent of a prisoner-of-war camp!"

"Hyperbole doesn't help your case, Counselor," Byxthar said with a belittling sneer.

"A POW camp would be better planned and built," Gliv countered. "We'd be violating the Seldonis IV Convention if we did have prisoners of war here."

Crusher pinched the bridge of her nose. "Excuse me," she said, loud enough to silence the others. "But just what, exactly, is it you're arguing?"

"We've reached the limit of what we can do here for these people," Dillingham answered, wearing a sour expression. "I know Director Barash didn't set any timetables for submitting our findings—"

"Because he didn't want to put restrictions on how we did our jobs," the sociologist interrupted.

"—but I'm afraid the longer we draw out this fact-finding mission," Dillingham said, talking over his fellow team member, "the longer we delay any real help coming."

"I'm sorry?" Crusher said, her tiredness suddenly banished by a surge of indignation. "*Real* help? What is it that we're here to do?"

Dillingham turned instantly apologetic. "I certainly didn't mean . . . I know you were in the infirmary all day, and Gliv here was busy with his repairs. But all I can do is make my suggestions and file briefs—which I do plan to do regarding Kadohata and this fence issue—"

Crusher had no idea what the "fence issue" was,

nor did she care. "What do you mean, that's all you can do? How can you look at what's going on down there—you compare it to a prison camp—and then come back up here, have a nice big supper, and say, 'There's nothing I can do'? I'm sure Gliv would have appreciated an extra pair of hands."

"To be serious, sir," Gliv said, eliciting surprised looks from the other two, "these people's basic needs are just barely being met. We would need a full team of engineers and a starship in support to fix all that needs fixing. One pair of hands wouldn't make much difference."

"Not much, but some, right?" Crusher challenged him. "You're not arguing that we should do nothing, are you, Ensign?"

The young Tellarite at least had the good sense to look shamed. But then Byxthar rose to his defense. "Begging your pardon, Doctor-Commander, but we weren't sent here to fix the camp by ourselves." She stood up from the table, and circled around to face Crusher directly. "I do admire you Starfleet officers, rolling up your sleeves and jumping in the minute you see something that needs doing. But, I've been dealing with refugee issues for a long time, and the one thing I can tell you is, you need to keep your detachment." Byxthar fixed Crusher with something akin to empathy for her. "Our only job is to gather information for Director Barash; *he'll* take care of what has to be done next. It's not our responsibility."

Crusher stared daggers at her, and tried to get

control of her thoughts before the Betazoid woman picked up something that went too far over the line. But she was interrupted by a loud double tone from the comm, and then the voice of Miranda Kadohata calling from the surface.

The doctor hit her combadge. "Crusher here. What is it, Miranda?"

"Bev, sorry, but it's the Risian woman. Arandis. She's gone into some kind of convulsions."

Crusher cursed silently. "Is she still breathing?" she asked Kadohata, and at the same time pointed to Gliv. With a gesture, she sent him scurrying to the runabout's cockpit and transporter controls.

"Yes. I got her flat on the floor . . ."

"Good. Just stand clear, we're beaming her up," she said to Kadohata, then called forward, "Gliv, whenever you're ready!"

"I'm bringing her right back there to you, Doctor," the ensign said through the intracraft comm. *"Energizing."*

The three moved back against the bulkheads to make room for the woman, who arrived shaking and writhing on the deck. Crusher knelt over her with her tricorder, and then cursed aloud. Dillingham and Byxthar stood by mutely as she muttered a few more profanities in frustration and pressed a hypospray to Arandis's neck. Her convulsions instantly subsided, and her entire body went lax.

"What happened?" Dillingham was the first to ask.

"The microbe has mutated," Crusher growled.

– 251 –

Which, depending on when it mutated and how it had spread, could mean that most of the inoculations she'd administered to the rest of the camp would prove completely ineffective. She rubbed her face, and then looked up to the two other team members. "Put her in one of the open bunks," she said, pointing to the small private cabins that abutted the living area.

"In one of *our* bunks?"

Crusher spun on Byxthar. "Listen to me: I command this mission team. Your job is what I tell you it is! If you want to file a grievance when we get back," she added as she included Dillingham, "feel free, but for now, do as I say!" Crusher headed for the front of the ship, leaving Dillingham and Byxthar to care for the unconscious woman.

Gliv turned as she entered. "Is everything all right, Commander?"

Crusher didn't answer, but simply stepped around the engineer and slipped into the pilot's seat. Without a word, she disengaged the autopilot, and then keyed a deceleration command sequence into the control panel.

"Doctor?" the ensign said, jumping up out of his chair, and stopping short right behind the commander's. "Sir, what are you doing?"

"The mission has changed, Ensign," she said. For a moment, her thoughts went to baby Matthew and the other patients in the infirmary who needed more help than she could provide with her current resources. But they weren't in immediate danger;

not as much as the rest of the camp was without a serious show of support. "Looks like we're going to be here awhile," she said, adjusting the pitch of the ship as it dropped into Pacifica's upper atmosphere. "We might as well make ourselves at home."

Worf approached Jasminder Choudhury's quarters and rang the signal chime, then after a brief wait, rang it a second time. After ringing it a third, Choudhury answered the door with tears in her puffed and reddened eyes. "Lieutenant," he said, "may I speak with you?"

"Worf," she said. "Could this possibly wait? I'm—"

He didn't wait for her to finish making her excuse, but simply walked through the open doorway, forcing her to step back. The lights were dimmed, and the portals looking out into space beyond the ship were set to opaqueness. He paused to consider the small holo on her workstation desk—an image of Choudhury standing with her father beside a majestic old oak tree the two had planted together decades earlier. It was the same image she had shown him when they had first learned of the destruction of her family's homeworld, using it to illustrate the bond she shared with her family and home. He heard the door slide closed behind him, and then Jasminder came around in front of him, defiance on her face. "What is it, Worf?"

"Lieutenant Konya is currently in the holodeck, running urban pacification drills with your security team in preparation for our arrival at Alpha Centauri. Why are you not doing so?" he asked.

"Rennan is perfectly capable," she said in response.

Worf fixed her with one of his penetrating Klingon glares. "Of course he is. But that does not answer my question. You are chief of security."

"And I delegated the responsibility to him, as is my prerogative." She stood her ground, showing no sign of feeling intimidated by the larger man.

"You also delegated the responsibility for the *Libra* boarding party team's security," Worf noted, causing the woman to noticeably stiffen. "I'm curious as to why."

"Do I need to explain all my decisions to you, Commander?" she retorted, stressing his rank.

"Only the ones I ask an explanation for, *Lieutenant,*" he shot back, instinctively responding to the challenge to his authority. Worf knew, though, that this insolence was only a defensive front, hiding a deeper issue. He blew out a short breath to purge his anger, and continued in a more moderate tone, "Your decisions since the discovery of the *Libra* and Plan 2757 especially beg elaboration."

A look of naked anger blossomed across Jasminder's normally bright and peaceful face. "Why? Because you would have done things differently when you were security chief?"

He refused to acknowledge her aggressive stance

this time. Worf searched her eyes, trying to find something beneath the surface of her fury. "Your parents could have been on that ship."

Jasminder reacted as if she had been slapped. "Or your sisters, or their children, on any of those Denevan evacuation ships," Worf continued. "I know how you honor your family, yet you behave as if you were afraid to find them." He tried to keep his tone flat, but he heard the note of accusation and disbelief coming through in his voice.

"Afraid to find them?" Jasminder shouted back, her face flushing. "You son of a bitch, you think I was afraid, that I would so *dread* finding my family alive?" Tears started streaming freely down her face again. "I would give anything if I thought I'd ever see them again, damn you. But *I won't!*"

"You cannot know—"

"I *do* know!" she cut him off. "I know my family, Worf. They would never have taken a spot on any of the evacuation ships if it meant that by doing so, another person was left behind." Her anger then seemed to burn itself out, like an ember thrown from a fire. She turned away, and dropped onto the sofa in her cabin's living area. "Every one of those people we found represents someone my father and mother sacrificed themselves for," she said, her head dropping in shame. "And why them? I know that makes me a horrible person for thinking it, but why do they get to live? What makes them any more worthy?"

Worf crossed the room and seated himself on

the opposite side of the sofa. "They honored themselves and you with their selfless act," he told her.

"Yes, they died with honor," she said sourly. "And with good karma, and in a state of grace, and whatever other ways you can choose to soften it, and none of them change the fact that they're gone."

"Of course it does not. There is nothing soft in death, which you well know." Worf's mind flashed briefly back to the hazy jumble of disconnected memories of the Khitomer outpost collapsing around him, the smell of blood and the screams of pain. "To say one died well, however it's phrased, is to acknowledge the way they lived their life, and to recognize that we have the duty to live life as well as they did before death comes for us."

He couldn't be certain whether his words were having any impact. She sat with her head down, and a thick lock of her black hair, which had worked free of her ponytail, fell over the right side of her face. Worf found himself fighting the urge to reach out and gently brush it back. "Your parents gave their lives for others, just as you joined Starfleet to protect others, even at the risk of your own life. You owe it to them and to their memories to continue to do so."

Jasminder kept her eyes downcast, though at least she was no longer crying. Worf sat with her a moment longer until, deciding nothing more would be said, rose and headed for the door.

"Worf?"

He stopped and turned back to see her lift her head and push the loose tresses back behind her ear. "Worf . . ." she repeated, and then seemed to be considering a list of things she wanted to say to him, before settling on "Thank you, Worf," with a wan smile.

He took that as a very good sign, and smiled back before exiting.

Trys Chen squatted on her haunches and looked at the newborn child in the sickbay nursery through the side of his transparent crib. "He's kind of an ugly baby, isn't he?"

Doctor Tropp crossed his arms over his chest and fixed her with an exaggerated scowl. "You know what, Lieutenant? I suspect that the majority of the seemingly thoughtless, socially inappropriate comments you make are wholly intentional, simply to get a reaction out of your audience."

Chen looked up and briefly met the Denobulan's eyes, then turned back to the child. "Seriously, look how scrunched his face is. You sure he's all right?"

"He's fine," Tropp sighed, taking her by the elbow and helping her to her feet. "All the *Libra* patients are fine. Your concern is laudable, but unnecessary."

Chen nodded, but continued to study both the little boy, and the prettier baby girl in the crib next to his. "These guys are never going to understand how much everyone else around them has lost. As far as they're concerned, the way things are now is the way they've always been."

Tropp considered that, and nodded. "One might almost envy them that."

Chen thought about that as she left sickbay and headed back to her quarters. She had taken it upon herself to tell the Denevans who had been transferred to sickbay that, thanks to their new president, they wouldn't be going straight to Ingraham B. They'd taken that news pretty well, but only because most of them were still trying to get over the earlier news about not returning to Deneva.

As she entered her cabin, she noticed an icon flashing on her computer monitor. "Computer, play back messages," she said, as she kicked her boots carelessly across the room and against the outer bulkhead.

The computer chirped like a robotic parakeet, and then informed her, *"Response protocol activated. Initiating transmission to Starfleet Headquarters, Earth."*

"What the hell?" Chen asked the disembodied voice, and then went over to study her monitor screen. She had no time to read the informational text that appeared below the Starfleet emblem on the screen before it disappeared, to be replaced by the image of a female Gallamite with two solid pips on her collar. *"Lieutenant T'Ryssa Chen?"*

"Yeah. Who wants to know?"

"My name is Lieutenant Joham," she answered,

then asked, *"Is your mother Lieutenant Com-mander Antigone Chen?"*

"Uh . . . yes?" Red Alert klaxons went off in her head. She'd been in and around Starfleet long enough to recognize this script, but she knew it couldn't be . . .

"I regret to inform you that Antigone Chen, serial number GB-018-494, was killed in the line of duty on stardate 58119."

"No. No, this is a mistake," Chen said, even as she realized that Joham must have heard the same denial from practically every family member she contacted. In this case, though, it was true. "My mother is a science officer on the *U.S.S. Wounded Knee.* They were out toward Berengaria during the war; the Borg never came near them."

A mortified expression crossed the Gallamite's face, and she lowered her head, giving Chen a per-fect view of the brain inside her transparent skull. Chen inhaled, not realizing that she had stopped breathing. Joham would check her records, find that someone had transposed digits in the serial number or some equally stupid mistake, and apologize for scaring the hell out of her. For all the issues between her and her mother, despite all the times she'd denied caring about the woman . . .

"Lieutenant Commander Antigone Chen trans-ferred from the Wounded Knee *to the* Grace Hop-per *on stardate 57809. That vessel was destroyed, and all hands lost, while engaged in combat with the Borg in the Zeta Fornacis system."* The lieuten-

ant was now looking up, straight into Chen's eyes, completely confident in what she was saying. *"The president and the commander in chief of Starfleet offer their condolences."*

"No!" Chen shouted. "No, this is a sick, sick joke . . ."

"I assure you it's not a joke, Lieutenant," the Gallamite said.

"It has to be!" Chen insisted. "If my mother had been killed by the Borg, I would have been notified weeks ago!"

"Your mother had listed her parents, Xun Chen and Ismene Zavos, as her next of kin on her initial Starfleet application, and failed to update that information following their deaths three years ago."

I had grandparents, Chen thought. Which shouldn't have been a revelation, but Antigone had never talked about her own parents. And now they were dead. A grandmother and a grandfather she never knew.

And a mother she barely knew any better. Also dead.

Joham went on about how they'd searched for Antigone's other relations, but Chen wasn't listening anymore. She continued not listening until Lieutenant Joham signed off and the monitor went black. She just sat stock-still as she stared into space, and had anyone been watching, they would have easily mistaken this as a display of perfect Vulcan emotional control.

Until, of course, she hurled the computer monitor against the nearest bulkhead.

12

For nearly three decades, Meron Byxthar had been studying the sociological aspects of the lives of refugees. But until now, she had never truly understood what it was like to be caught in a place with no reasonable hope of ever returning home.

The Betazoid stood at the edge of the camp as the sun peeked over the horizon and glinted off the bright white hull of the *Genesee* where it sat grounded at the entrance to the camp, right beside the infirmary. The two food replicators had been ripped out of the cabin, and now sat up against the starboard nacelle, where early-rising refugees were lined up for their morning meals. On the other side, along the port nacelle, Ensign Gliv had moved the portable 'freshers, for some reason also connecting them directly to the ship's auxiliary ports. And from the ship's stern, a thick cable ran into the administration shack, the impulse engines now replacing the emergency generators that had been powering the camp's equipment.

The ship was now irrevocably a part of the iy'Dewra'ni camp, never to fly again.

Which meant she was just as stuck here as everyone else in this forsaken place.

"Doctor Byxthar!"

She jumped, so caught up in her thoughts that she hadn't even sensed Amsta-Iber come up behind her. "Doctor, I just wanted to express to you again what it means to me that you and your team have made this firm commitment to dealing with the crisis here."

"Don't thank me," Byxthar said witheringly.

The Grazerite reacted in surprise. *She was more pleasant when the refugees were hopeless and miserable,* she heard him think, and it was all she could do to keep from lashing out at him. How dare he make her out to be such a heartless monster?

She turned away from him, looking again at the grounded ship and at the scores of people surrounding it. She let her psionic senses open just a bit wider, not believing the hopelessness and misery had really abated as Amsta-Iber had implied, but checking anyway.

I am not a heartless monster, she told herself, as an upsurge of renewed optimism washed through her senses.

•   •   •

Arandis's eyelids fluttered and opened just enough to cause her to wince against the light. "Good morning," Doctor Crusher said, smiling down at her as she snapped her tricorder shut. "How are you feeling?"

The Risian woman rolled her head one way, then the other. "Where am I?" she rasped weakly.

"You're on our runabout."

Her eyes met Crusher's. "Going home?"

The doctor's smile faltered slightly. "Not just yet."

A shadow seemed to pass behind the woman's eyes, but she blinked and shook her head as if willing dark memories away again. "What happened?" she asked.

"You passed out," Crusher told her. "You were infected by a mutated microbe, but it's gone now."

Arandis took that in. "Tired," she said.

Crusher nodded and gave her a kind but stern glare. "Yes, well, you were pushing yourself pretty hard all day. You should have said something if you were feeling sick or feverish."

The Risian sighed. "It's our nature to give."

"Well, you're going to have to get used to doing a little taking for now," Crusher said, patting her hand before turning and leaving the private cabin. As she passed through the living area, her eyes went to the now-open alcove where the food replicator had been, and mused about how much she would have loved a double-strength French roast right then. Stifling a yawn, she stepped out of the runabout, drawing the attention of the refugees lined up to access the newly set-up replicators. At first, she thought she just imagined they looked a little brighter this morning, a little less dejected than they had the previous day.

"Thank you, Starfleet!" an unseen man shouted from the multitude. This sparked a wave of cheers and exclamations of gratitude. Crusher acknowledged them with a modest wave as she walked from the runabout to the infirmary.

Miranda Kadohata, drawn by the shouting outside, met Crusher at the infirmary's entrance. "Beverly," she said, frowning at her. Her black bangs hung limply over her eyes, which were underscored with dark crescents. "That was nowhere near eight hours."

"Uh-huh," the doctor answered as she squeezed past her.

"Bev, love, you were up how long last night chasing down these mutations?" the second officer asked, arms crossed over her chest.

"Aren't there other places in the camp you can make yourself useful?" Crusher asked, only slightly joking. She was beginning to seriously regret her suggestion to Jean-Luc of having Miranda along as a chaperone. She knew Miranda's intentions were nothing but good, but there was only so much mothering she could take.

"I like it here just fine," she said, her expression changing subtly. "In the middle of things."

Crusher studied her out of the corner of one

eye. "Peggy stayed in the family section during the night, I take it?" she asked. She had checked on Matthew just before looking in on Arandis; his condition had not changed while in the stasis chamber, which was all she could hope for right now.

Kadohata nodded again, and Crusher saw the same tiny tightness again at the corners of her eyes. As a mother herself, she could tell Miranda was having mixed feelings, here caring for the children of strangers, when her own were light-years away. It was what they did as Starfleet officers, though that didn't make it any easier.

Taking in the ward, she noticed one bed missing its occupant. "Where's Sasdren?" she asked, crossing to the vacant cot.

"He's scarpered. Insisted on discharging himself," Kadohata said with a sigh; Crusher wasn't sure if it was meant for the patient or for her and her stubborn insistence on doing her job. "He said he was fully recovered, and the tricorder said the same thing." Kadohata handed Crusher that tricorder then, and the doctor saw, indeed, that the S'ti'ach's physical injuries had completely healed. Crusher was far less certain about any other wounds he'd suffered.

The doctor shook her head. "Well, it's not as if we could have kept him here against his will." She only hoped he didn't try to repeat what had put him in the infirmary in the first place.

Kadohata put a comforting hand on her shoulder.

"You can't let yourself worry about what might happen next," she said, as if reading her mind. "You did your best by him. You've done so much good here . . ."

"Hardly feels like I've done anything," Crusher said. She dropped onto Sasdren's empty bed, suddenly feeling as if the full weight of this world was settling on her shoulders.

Kadohata gave her an incredulous smile. "Are you kidding? Did you hear the people out there just now?"

Crusher chuckled and let her eyes slip closed, and the roar of the approving crowd came back to her memory . . .

Then the curtain fell, muffling the sound of applause from the audience. The lights came back up on the stage, and Beverly and her fellow cast members all hugged and congratulated one another on a successful opening night performance. Though she'd questioned how well a four-hundred-year-old adaptation of an eight-hundred-year-old Shakespearean comedy would play in 2357, the St. Louis Theater League's production of *Kiss Me, Kate* seemed, from their vantage point, to be a hit. It had been an amazing, terrifying, exhilarating experience, her first time dancing in a public forum, as well as her first time ever in a full-scale theatrical production. As thrilling as it had been competing in the All-City Dance Competition earlier in the year, this experience had been at a whole other level.

The adrenaline dissipated by the time she'd changed out of her costume and stepped out the stage door into the warm, muggy Missouri summer night. The other chorus dancers were off to the nearby bar to continue their post-show celebration, but she had clinic hours in the morning, not to mention a babysitter with a curfew. But as she was bidding them good night, she was stopped cold by the sight of an old, familiar face, waiting for her under a streetlight by the curb. "Walker? Walker Keel?"

The tall, distinguished-looking older man crossed the sidewalk to give her a big hug. "Beverly. It's good to see you."

"You, too! Walker, how long has it been?"

"Too long," he answered, and his smile faded away. "I'm sorry I couldn't make it for Jack's funeral," he said in a subdued tone.

Beverly took a small sharp breath and forced a smile for her friend, the Starfleet captain. "I know." She'd been out of uniform for three years, but she hadn't forgotten how duty took precedence over all. The *Horatio* had been assigned to the Tzenkethi border at the time, and Walker had sent her a very touching condolence message. He had known Jack longer than anyone she knew—he had been the one who introduced the two of them—and Beverly believed that, if not for the risk of a major interstellar incident, he would have been back on Earth to pay his respects in person in a heartbeat. "What are you doing here now?" she asked.

"Are you kidding? I love Cole Porter." Beverly gave him a playful swat on the arm, and Walker smiled again, bringing out a bunch of new lines on his craggily handsome face. "No, seriously—the *Horatio* is undergoing a major refit at Utopia Planitia, so I decided to look up some old friends back here on Earth. Have you had dinner yet?"

"I . . . well, no," she answered. She'd had a light meal before the show, and was planning to have a little something when she got back home. But she couldn't refuse her old friend, and so they made their way to a small, warmly lit steakhouse a few blocks from the theater.

"I gotta tell you, Bev," Keel said, sipping at his drink, "you impressed the hell out of me up there tonight. I never knew you could dance like that."

"Neither did I," she said with a laugh. "I saw a notice at the local community center for dance lessons, and decided on a whim to give it a try. But I love it. It's really amazing to discover that you have this hidden talent, and to be able to bring it out, develop it . . . it's very rewarding."

Walker nodded as he studied Crusher's face intently. "More so than medicine?"

"Well, I'm not about to give up my practice to dance full-time," Beverly said. Her partnership with Doctor Tina Halloway was a good one. It allowed her to keep regular hours and gave her plenty of personal time to spend with Wesley, as well as her own pursuits. "I've known I was going to be a doctor since I was a girl; that hasn't changed. But I can do both."

"The Dancing Doctor," Walker said with a small laugh. "But having a private practice on Earth—especially so far removed from San Francisco or Paris—has got to be a huge change from running a starbase infirmary."

"Oh, yes, that's for sure." Beverly nodded. "It's a rare week when I see anything more serious than a case of indigestion. Speaking of which," she said as the waitress approached with their dishes. She set a chicken Caesar salad in front of Beverly, and for Captain Keel, a charbroiled sirloin with baked potato and broccoli. He attacked with his knife and fork, carving out a bite-sized chunk of beef, popped it in his mouth, and moaned in mild ecstasy as he slowly chewed. "Oh, you can't get that from a Starfleet replicator . . ."

Beverly chuckled at his exaggerated pleasure as she speared a forkful of greens for herself. Her salad didn't elicit the same reaction as Walker's steak, but it was still quite good.

"Do you ever miss it?"

Beverly swallowed. "Starfleet? No," she answered quickly. "No, I have no regrets about leaving. I have a good life here, and I've been able to give Wesley a nice, stable environment to grow up in."

Walker raised an eyebrow at her. "Come on now, Bev. Remember who you're talking to. Or have you forgotten about the *Prague*?"

WILLIAM LEISNER

Beverly didn't answer, though of course she hadn't forgotten her time aboard that tiny ship during her fourth year in the Academy's pre-med program. Walker had been a lieutenant commander, assigned as an officer-observer during the *Prague*'s month-long cadet training cruise—Starbase 218, to Memory Alpha, and then back to Earth. Under the watchful eyes of Keel and a dozen other supervisory officers, the command, engineering, and security staffs were being fully run by third- and fourth-year cadets. In sickbay, though, the *Prague* had a full medical staff, who the pre-med students were expected to simply observe over the course of the mission. It was a bit frustrating for Beverly, who had essentially been practicing medicine since she was fifteen, caring for the survivors of the Kevrata ship crash on Arvada III.

The frustration got pushed aside immediately when the *Prague* found itself in its own crisis situation. En route back to Earth on the last leg of the mission, they hit an uncharted tetryon field, taking out warp drive and knocking most of the crew against the decks and bulkheads in the process. There had been no fatalities—thanks in no small part to Crusher, who kept a level head and didn't hesitate to jump in and lend her assistance in the crisis.

"You enjoyed that," Keel told her now, with a knowing grin. "Being in the action. Being there to help when things go south, and being able to make a positive difference."

"That was years ago . . . before Jack." She felt that small dark void open up in her chest again at the thought of her late husband. The pain wasn't fully gone yet—she suspected it never would be, entirely—but she had come to accept her loss, and had gotten on with her life, a life she was happy with. "I've got a son to think about now."

"And where is he tonight?"

"At home, with a sitter."

"Mmm-hmm," Keel said.

Beverly scowled. "And it's just one quick tram ride there, so I can kiss him good night every night, and be there to see him off to school every morning. Something I couldn't have done in Starfleet."

"You two could have stayed on Starbase 32," Walker noted.

Beverly shook her head. "Not if I wanted to move up, I couldn't."

"And you wanted that, didn't you? To move up, to better yourself."

Beverly stared at her salad. "I wanted what was best for my son."

"I know you did, but what about what was best for you?" Walker asked, pointing with his fork. Somehow, she found she didn't have an immediate answer for him. "I was really amazed by what I saw up on that stage tonight, Beverly," he said then, poking at his potato. "You know what I saw?"

"What?"

"Passion," Walker said, fixing his eyes on hers. "The kind of passion I remember seeing in you on the *Prague,* and then later, while you were stationed on Tau Ceti III. You were always a person who wanted to live life to the fullest, to make the most of every experience, to push yourself to the limit and test your abilities at every opportunity.

"I saw you channeling that passion through your dancing, and I couldn't help but think: she doesn't really give a damn about dancing. This is just a safety valve. You're so frustrated with the way you've stunted your medical career, you need this active, physically and mentally challenging activity to channel and release it."

"That's—" Beverly started to say, planning to deny all he said. But the truth of the matter was, having been reminded of the *Prague* and of Tau Ceti III, and even of Starbase 32, she wasn't sure he was so far off the mark. She had come to St. Louis, to the middle of the continent, to get as far away as possible from the unpredictability of that old life. But there was still a part of her that craved it. So instead of a denial, what Beverly said was, "Why are you telling me all this?"

"This refit the *Horatio* is undergoing?" Walker said. "It's primarily to the interior, the cabins. Creating family living space."

"Family space?"

"With the Federation growing faster, and missions running longer and traveling farther out, crews need the option to bring their families along. The *Galaxy-* and the *Nebula-* classes, when they launch in the next few years, will have fully integrated facilities for family support, but our retrofit should make for fairly decent accommodations." Walker leaned forward over the table. "I'd like to have you and your boy aboard, Beverly. Chief medical officer."

Beverly shook her head. "Walker, you know I can't. It'd be the same as trying to raise him on a starbase, except worse. The risks—"

"No, it's not as safe as life in St. Louis," Walker allowed. "But it's also far more rewarding than treating stomachaches and sore throats. With all respect to your partner, your patients, and your choreographer, you're squandering your talents and your passion here. You need to be out there in the middle of things, pushing the edge of the envelope, the one making waves instead of sitting here watching the little ripples hit the shore."

"So, I should be in the middle, and on the edge?" Beverly joked, though not taking anything her old friend was saying lightly.

He chuckled. "Analogies were never my strong suit." Then he said, "You know what I'm saying is true."

Beverly shook her head. "Walker, Wesley's already lost his father. I couldn't do this to him."

Keel said nothing at first, but fixed her in his powerful gaze. "Beverly . . . what if I were to suggest that you were hiding behind your son? Using him as an excuse to keep you from facing up to what Jack did?"

Beverly felt her face go hot. "What is that supposed to—?"

"Yes, there's risk in Starfleet," Walker interrupted. "Jack took a risk when he volunteered to go outside the ship and cut away that nacelle. He could have played it safe and let someone else do the job. He could have played it safe and transferred off the *Stargazer* when you had Wesley. But that's not the person he was," he reminded her. "That's not the person *you* are. And I'm going to wager the apple didn't fall very far from either tree."

Beverly let Walker Keel's words echo in her head long after they had finished their meal and parted ways, with the captain making her promise to think about his offer and wait two weeks before giving a definitive no. On the ride back home, as she watched the nondescript landscape of her adopted hometown roll past her window, she forced herself to reexamine the choices she'd made over the past three years, and the one before her now. As nice a place as St. Louis was, Walker was right: other than geographically, it was far from the center of anything. And while she liked and respected Tina Halloway, and knew she was doing good for her patients in private practice, she knew she was limiting herself.

But to return to Starfleet—could she really do that? More important, could she do that to Wes, not only risking their lives, but surrounding him with reminders of his father's death? Or maybe Walker was right, that by putting limits on her potential, she was doing the same to her son, in the name of protecting him.

Once she arrived home and sent the babysitter on her way, she tiptoed into her son's room. He was fast asleep, still grasping the padd he had been reading. Beverly sat on the edge of his bed and put a hand on his arm. "Wesley? It's Mom. Wake up; I need to talk to you about something." The boy mumbled in his sleep, and Beverly shook him a bit harder. . . .

"I need to speak with her," she—or someone—insisted again, and she repeated the hard shaking . . .

And Crusher bolted awake, nearly vaulting up off the infirmary cot. She blinked her bleary eyes and found herself looking straight into Commandant Minha's huge black eyes. "Doctor, I must speak with you," he demanded, while Miranda Kadohata, standing just behind him, overlapped, saying, "Sorry, Bev, he wouldn't take no—"

"Commandant," Crusher said as the last vestiges of her dream fell away. "What is it now?"

"My troops are falling ill. Because of *your* people."

Crusher closed her eyes again and moaned silently. "Right back in the middle of things," she muttered as she forced herself up out of bed.

• • •

The *Enterprise* dropped out of warp on the outskirts of Alpha Centauri's binary system, and pushed its way toward the worlds circling the primary star. Soon, Alpha Centauri III came into view, and Picard reflected on how utterly peaceful and quiet the white-and-blue orb appeared from this distance.

"Sir," Ensign Šmrhová reported from the tactical station, "I'm only picking up minimal civil and emergency response communications. No indications of any kind of widespread unrest or violence."

Picard turned and gave her a quizzical look. "Nothing?" From Akaar's report, he had feared they would arrive to find the capital in flames.

"Nothing, sir," Šmrhová confirmed. "I'm seeing some evidence of some recent large fires in New Samarkand, but none currently burning."

Picard turned his gaze to Worf. "An overreaction by the planetary leaders, perhaps?" the first officer suggested. "Tensions are still likely to be high."

The captain sighed. While he certainly hoped whatever trouble may have erupted here had been dealt with, he was not pleased by the idea of being called away from his primary objective on a pointless mission by a panicked government official. "Standard orbit," he ordered. "Hail the capital."

Šmrhová keyed the command into her tactical console, and after a moment reported, "We're receiving a response from the office of the planetary governor, George Barrile."

"On-screen," Picard said as he stood and straightened the front of his uniform.

The view of the planet was replaced by the image of a middle-aged human man with a head full of thick white hair. He sat at a desk before a large window, through which Picard recognized the familiar skyline of New Samarkand. *"Captain Jean-Luc Picard of the U.S.S. Enterprise,"* he said, flashing a wide yet insincere smile. *"I suppose I should be honored."*

Picard wasn't quite sure what to make of that comment, so he decided to overlook it for the moment. "Thank you, Governor Barrile. We stand ready to assist you in any way."

"Yes, well," the governor answered, *"the immediate crisis has already been brought under control. We had to arrest a number of our 'guests' and enact some stringent measures on the group as a whole to avoid repetition of such violence."*

Alarms started sounding at the back of Picard's mind. "What sort of stringent measures?"

"That's hardly your concern, Captain."

Picard stiffened at that, and the scowl on his face deepened. "In fact, it *is* my concern," he answered. "I was ordered here because of this outbreak of violence, and it's my duty—"

"Starfleet's duty is supposed to be to the people of the Federation," Barrile interrupted. *"Do you intend to take over this office and declare martial law, Captain?"*

Again, Picard was caught off balance by the

governor's astonishing question. "What?! No, of course not!"

"Then, as the duly elected leader of this system, I would suggest you show a bit more respect for me and the citizens I represent!"

"Governor," Picard said, fighting down the ire this self-important bureaucrat had provoked, "I certainly meant no disrespect either to you or the people of Alpha Centauri, and I apologize for whatever offense I may have given. However, I am confused by your apparent hostility to our presence."

"I apologize if I'm being less than cordial, Captain," Barrile said, sounding far from apologetic, *"but being civil doesn't seem to get results anymore."* He took a deep breath, then said, *"I believe it would be better if we were to continue this conversation face-to-face."*

Picard nodded. "I can beam down as—"

"With respect, Captain, I'd rather you didn't."

Picard clenched his jaw. "Then I invite you aboard the *Enterprise*. Five minutes from now?"

Barrile nodded, and cut transmission without any further niceties.

"Charming," Worf observed.

Picard almost chuckled, but he could not summon up sufficient amusement. "Have the governor escorted to the observation lounge when he arrives." He spent the next five minutes replaying the conversation in his mind, trying to pick out some indication of the source of the man's animosity. He was still as bewildered as ever when the conference room doors opened and Governor Barrile was escorted in by Ensign Šmrhová. "Welcome aboard, Governor," Picard said, smiling pleasantly, determined to start this encounter with a blank slate.

"Captain." The governor squeezed his hand firmly. Picard dismissed Šmrhová with a nod, and once the doors had closed behind her, the governor said, "Before we begin, I want you to know that I am aware of your role in ending the latest Borg incident, and for that you have the thanks of all of Alpha Centauri."

Picard nodded in appreciation of the conciliatory gesture. "Thank you, Governor. My role was not quite as the news reports portray it."

Barrile shook his head, dismissing that as irrelevant. "However, as you are currently the only high-ranking Starfleet officer in this system, the remonstrations we have will just have to go through you."

"What remonstrations?" Picard asked, gesturing for the governor to take a seat at the conference table.

Governor Barrile sat, folded his hands on the tabletop, and leaned forward. "We, the people of the Alpha Centauri system, were betrayed by the Federation and by Starfleet."

Both of Picard's eyebrows arched in disbelief. "What? What do you mean, betrayed?"

"You may not even be aware of this, given your

part in the war," Barrile allowed. "But, in the first hours of the invasion, Admiral Jellico sent out an order to the fleet. He told them that if Earth fell, then the war would be considered lost. Any remaining ships were instructed to save themselves, and abandon the rest of the Federation's remaining worlds to our fates."

Picard's face fell. "How did you learn this?" he asked in a strangled whisper.

"I have my sources, whom I trust implicitly," the governor said. Then, after a moment of studying Picard's expression, he added, "And you *were* aware of that order."

Picard said nothing; he certainly couldn't deny the charge. The order had come at the war's darkest hour. The armada blockading the Azure Nebula had been obliterated, and the Borg were devastating everything in their path. Despite a few scattered incidents of success, resistance had finally been accepted as futile.

It was almost a full minute before Picard felt ready to speak aloud. "Governor . . . I certainly understand your reaction. But . . . from a command point of view, once the seat of the Federation was gone, that would mean the end of the war."

"Like hell it would!" Barrile snapped. "We all know they weren't going to just stop there and declare victory, Picard. The Borg were intent on taking us all out. It's just that those of us on this side of the Sol system weren't considered important enough to defend! I have a list of at least thirty-five hundred Centaurian Starfleet officers and crewmen killed in this war. Men and women who sacrificed themselves in defense of a hundred other alien worlds and colonies. How do I tell their next of kin that when it came to defending them, Starfleet couldn't be bothered?"

Picard opened his mouth to reply, but the governor barreled right over him. "And now that the war is over? Not only are we being burdened with all these refugees, with no Federation support, but at the same time we're having our mining and manufacturing industries federalized. Paris is threatening to come in and take control of our topaline processors and factories, and ship it all to Vulcan, Andor, and Tellar! Where does it end?"

Picard waited to be sure Barrile had finished, and then pulled his own thoughts together. "Governor, I do appreciate your anger over Admiral Jellico's orders—although I would expect that, had events reached such a point, very few if any of my fellow captains would have ever obeyed such a directive, allowing billions to die to save themselves.

"Hypotheticals aside, the Alpha Centauri system did in fact emerge from this war unscathed, while the other worlds you mention took massive damage from the Borg—"

"Captain, the four ships we did have in system during the war were all called away to other duties just as this deluge of refugees started arriving—that's not a hypothetical. It took a riot to get a starship back here. How much are we supposed to give, when we can't expect anything in return?!"

"Sir, the Federation has just suffered the worst disaster in its entire history." Picard felt his temper starting to get the better of him, and fought to keep his voice level. "With all due respect, this is not the time to begrudge the needs of other worlds or dwell on other petty slights—"

"Dismiss them as petty if you like, Captain," Barrile said as he leaned back in his chair. "I can promise you, the people of Alpha Centauri won't consider them that way."

There was something in the governor's words that struck a warning tone. "I'm sorry?"

"As soon as the worst of this refugee situation is dealt with," the governor said, "I plan to announce a systemwide plebiscite to consider the question of secession from the United Federation of Planets."

Picard's jaw dropped. "You cannot be serious!" he said. "Alpha Centauri is one of the founding members of the Federation!"

"Yes, I'm aware of that, thank you," Barrile replied snidely. "But this isn't the twenty-second century anymore. The galaxy has changed drastically over the last two centuries."

The galaxy has changed drastically over the last two months, Picard kept himself from snapping back. As he tried to form a more appropriate response, he was interrupted by the voice of Worf over the comm. *"Bridge to Captain Picard."*

"Yes, Number One?"

"We are receiving a transmission from Doctor Crusher on Pacifica."

"Acknowledged," Picard said, then turned to Barrile and said, "I'll have to ask you to excuse me, Governor."

Barrile shrugged and said, "I don't know that we necessarily have anything more to discuss, Captain."

Again, Picard bit back the sharp retort he was tempted to make, and instead said, "I will try to be brief."

Seconds later, he stepped through the doors onto the bridge. "Put the message on the main viewer," he said as he moved to the spot directly in front of his chair.

A moment later, the gorgeous face of his wife appeared on the screen, and in an instant his frustration with the Centaurian governor was almost completely forgotten. "Doctor," he said, carefully maintaining their professional association while on the bridge, though he was sure his smile was far wider than it would have been for just any member of his crew.

"Captain," Beverly answered, briefly flashing her own brilliant smile, before dropping it and replacing it with a far grimmer look. *"The situation on Pacifica is becoming untenable. We've got a growing health crisis, the local authorities are being less than helpful, and Director Barash is telling me it could be another two weeks before he'll have another ship available for a relief mission."*

Picard matched her look of concern. "What do you need, Doctor?"

"We need to get as many people out of this camp as we can, and relocate them to a more suitable location—more open space, more available shelter. I also need my own sickbay."

Picard hesitated. His immediate responsibilities undeniably were here, dealing with Governor Barrile. Leaving now would mean running the risk that he would carry through with his threat of rebellion against the Federation, and in the brief time he'd spent with the man, he believed that threat was quite real. What's more, were he to decide to order a course to Pacifica, it would be believed—and not inaccurately so—that his decision was colored by his concern for his wife and their unborn son.

His indecision lasted all of one second. "Ensign Weinrib, lay in a course for Pacifica. Ensign Šmrhová, please escort Governor Barrile to the transporter room. Tell him . . ." A number of possible messages flitted through his mind before he continued, ". . . tell him duty calls."

Crusher smiled at him again. *"Now I remember why I fell in love with you."*

"Nonsense," Picard said, putting on his most stern and sober face. "I'm merely living up to my obligations as a Starfleet officer."

"Exactly," Crusher answered with a teasing glint in her eye. *"Thank you, Captain. Crusher out."*

Crusher's image disappeared, and at the same time, Picard heard the conference room door slide open.

He turned, and Governor Barrile gave him a silent curt nod as he followed Šmrhová into the turbolift. Worf moved up to Picard's side and asked, "Has the crisis on Alpha Centauri been fully resolved, sir?"

"No, Number One," Picard sighed. "No, it hasn't. Governor Barrile is unhappy with the way his worlds have been treated of late, and he is threatening to withdraw from the Federation."

"What?!" The entire bridge had reacted to that news, turning toward the captain with expressions ranging from shock to incredulity. But it was, unsurprisingly, Lieutenant Chen who had given full-throated articulation to her disbelief. "You can't be serious!"

Picard gave her a sharp look.

"I mean, *he* can't be serious," she revised herself. "You, sir, I'm sure are. Serious, that is."

Picard shook his head at the young woman and said, "Unfortunately, he is by all indications quite serious."

"But at such a time," Worf said in a low rumble that hinted at barely restrained fury, "when so much has been lost. Such a thing borders on treason."

"I doubt he even comprehends just how much we have lost," Picard replied. "The war against the Borg was a brief, distant event that never directly impacted them. He's focused on his system and his people; I think he simply doesn't understand how dire the current situation is for the entire Federation at large."

"Maybe he needs to be shown, sir." Picard turned

back to look at Chen. "Maybe he needs to see the horror and the death and the shit up close . . . have his nose rubbed in it, so he *does* understand," she said heatedly. Picard was somewhat taken aback by her impassioned statement; the novelty of seeing a cheerfully emotional expression on Chen's very Vulcan face had long worn off, but the animosity she now displayed was something brand-new.

"Lieutenant," Worf said to her in a warning tone.

"Sorry, sir," she replied, not looking a bit so. Her eyes met Picard's, and refused to look away.

Picard considered her silently for a long moment, and then tapped his combadge. "Picard to Transporter Room One."

"Luptowski here, sir."

"Has Governor Barrile beamed back down to the planet yet?"

"No, sir," came the reply.

Picard nodded. "Thank you, Ensign," he said, tapping his badge again. A grin crept across his face as he then turned toward the conn. "Lieutenant Weinrib, break orbit."

"Aye, sir," Weinrib said as the ship started to push away from the planet.

"Enter course for Pacifica," Picard said, settling back into his chair, "and engage."

Worf started to turn back to his seat as well, but paused just long enough to lean on the arm of the captain's chair and tell him, with a small smile, "You were right, sir. This is much better than being an ambassador."

13

A crew of Selkie workmen leapt from the high riverbank into the water below, splashing just upstream of a small raftlike watercraft carrying a load of metal poles. It was still well before high sun, but already hot, and the workers were obviously enjoying the brief relief of being back in the water, diving and jumping, instead of laboring on the land.

"Knock it off, you lollygaggers!" the crew supervisor, a female Selkie named Yyeta'a, shouted from above. "We're here until this job is done, and I for one would like to get home before my kids grow their spiny fins!" The men grumbled insults that they thought could not be heard from their distance, and clambered aboard the raft to gather more materials and start hauling them back up the banks.

Yyeta'a frowned as she silently watched their slow progress. The fact was, only half of her sixteen children were still that young, and furthermore, she was really in no great hurry to get back to them. She had been called up as part of the security reserves when the off-world refugees first started to deluge the off-world enclaves, and while there was nothing pleasant about being around all these poor people robbed of their homes by the Borg, it was at least an interesting change from the day-to-day tedium of motherhood.

"Excuse me?"

Yyeta'a turned quickly, leading with the point of her rifle, toward the human male who'd approached. His hands immediately shot up, empty palms exposed, and he took a step back. "Whoa, hey, didn't mean to scare you, there."

"You didn't," Yyeta'a told the alien, though between his unkempt sand-colored hair and rumpled clothing, he was a bit of a frightening sight. "You shouldn't be wandering away from camp."

"Yeah, I shouldn't be in a camp at all, but the Borg didn't see things that way," he said grimly. "What's going on here?"

"We're marking the borders of the camp."

"A cage, huh?" the human said, sounding oddly resigned.

"No," she answered. "Not a cage. Just . . ." She trailed off as she glanced back at the sections that had already been erected, and realized how apt the description really was.

"And I'd always heard the Pacificans were a hospitable people," the man said. "Especially the women."

Yyeta'a flinched. She knew full well what kind of Selkie women this human was talking about—the kind who bristled under the social restrictions put on women of childbearing age and who rebelled against it, leaving their children to visit the alien enclaves like Eden Beach, engaging in the kind of things no decent female in her fertile period would spend her time doing. "If that's the kind of hospitality you're looking for here, forget it," she said, clenching the rifle a little harder.

"It's not," the man said, so quickly that Yyeta'a wondered if she had been insulted. "I'm just . . . this isn't how I saw the rest of my life," he said, glancing off toward the completed barrier section. "Granted, I've never really thought too much about my future at all . . ."

Something about the man—whether it was the sadness in his small sunken eyes or the vulnerability that showed on his pale-fleshed alien face—made Yyeta'a set her training aside and lower her rifle. "This is just temporary, you know. Starfleet will send more ships soon, and things will be back to normal."

"How? Look at this place," he said, flailing his arms out around them both. "Look at us. If I had come to Pacifica three months ago instead, we wouldn't be meeting like this." Yyeta'a didn't mention that they wouldn't have met at all; this was the first time she'd ever been face-to-face with an off-worlder. He dropped his arms and hitched his shoulders. "This here, this is too far past normal.

Normal is done and over with, and this is what's left in its place."

Yyeta'a, almost forgetting the reason she was here, took a step closer to the alien and placed her one free hand on his arm. "Things will get better, and soon," she said.

"Thanks," he answered quietly, though he clearly didn't believe it. His skin was strangely warm, and covered with a light coat of fine hairs. As an adolescent, Yyeta'a had heard other girls talk about humans, saying that as land-dwellers, they had special pheromones that were particularly strong in the open air.

She wasn't thinking about that right now, or about the normal life and family she had waiting after this deployment ended. "It will. I'm sure of it."

The man met her eyes and he finally smiled, sending an indescribable jolt through her. But before either of them could say anything more, she was startled by the crashing clatter of a dozen metal poles being dropped behind her. "What the deep?" shouted one of the two workers who had finally reached the top of the riverbank with their load of fencing material.

Yyeta'a realized what this must have looked like, and immediately swung her phaser rifle upward. "Step away!" she shouted, as the muzzle connected with the underside of the human's chin, caught for a moment, and then tore a bright red gash in his pale flesh.

"Aauurrgghh!" he screamed incoherently, bringing a hand to his bleeding face. "What the hell?!" He reached out, and between her earlier mental fuzziness and shock at the sight of alien blood, Yyeta'a was unable to keep him from grabbing the rifle out of her hands. He flung it to the ground and took a menacing step toward her. "Damn you, you—"

He never completed that thought, because one of the workers had slipped around behind him at that point with a three-meter-long metal fence pole in his hands. It whistled through the air before connecting with the back of the human's skull, knocking him off his feet and sending him face-first into the turf.

By this point, the shouts of the workers and the human had attracted the attention of other nearby Selkie guards, as well as other refugees. Yyeta'a wasn't sure what exactly happened next, only that she could barely hear her own thoughts over the noise and bedlam that followed. She knew she should have retrieved her rifle and pushed the angered alien hordes back. But the man had fallen right on top of it, and as she knelt beside him, she found herself just stroking the strange, fine strands on his head. "I'm sorry," she whispered, just before a thrown rock—from which direction, she couldn't say—struck her on the side of the head. She staggered and fell beside the unconscious human, and just as her vision went black, she whispered another apology to her children.

WILLIAM LEISNER

• • •

Kadohata perked her head up at the alarmed shouts carrying up from the edge of camp, and heard a wave of growing panic moving her way, toward the main part of the camp. She and Peggy had gathered a group of small children around them, reading from *The Adventures of Flotter,* and the younger woman faltered as she noted Kadohata's look of alarm.

"Keep going; keep them all calm," Kadohata told her in an even tone that, despite its softness, carried authority. After getting a hesitant nod from Peggy, she got to her feet and started moving toward the disturbance. She moved at an even, unhurried pace, even though every muscle and nerve in her body urged her to break into an all-out run.

The commander wound her way through the tent city, and as she reached its outer edges, she found herself weaving through a growing crowd of curiosity seekers. She was about to urge them all back to their temporary homes, but forgot her intention once she saw the scene being played out before her: a mob of irate refugees screaming and shaking their fists at a defensive line of Selkie guards brandishing phaser rifles. She was relieved to see that they were not pointing their rifles at the civilians, but it was very small comfort, and subject to change too quickly for her taste. Just beyond the Selkies' line, and in front of a section of new fencing, she thought she saw several natives squatting down in a rough circle, about the size of a humanoid. It didn't take much imagination to guess what had sparked this current tense standoff.

Then the line of native guards parted, and Commandant Minha stepped through. He hesitated just a moment, seemingly caught by surprise by the number of non-Pacificans he found himself facing. He recovered instantly, though, and called out, "You people, get back to the camp. There's nothing here that concerns you."

A voice shouted, "They killed one of us! A human male!" An angry buzzing spread through the crowd. Kadohata noticed a few of the guards gripping their rifles a little tighter.

"Nobody is dead," Minha said. "We have a minor injury that is being taken care of—"

"One you caused!" the voice shouted over his.

By this point, Kadohata had worked her way through the mob and crossed the short distance separating the refugees from the troops. "What is going on here, Commandant?"

Minha glowered at her, then grabbed her elbow and leaned in close as if to whisper in her ear. "One of your people attempted to assault a member of my barrier-building team."

"We're back to 'my people' versus 'your people,' are we, Commandant?" Kadohata asked.

"Spare me the patriotic pabulum, Commander," Minha growled. "The fact of the matter is, if Starfleet was doing the job they were supposed to be doing here, matters never would have reached this point."

Kadohata shook her head. "I'm not interested in this juvenile finger-pointing," she told him, letting her fatigue seep through. "Whatever's come before, the facts now are that you have a platoon of armed guards here threatening to make an already tense situation much, much worse."

"Then pull these people back," Minha insisted.

"And them?" Kadohata retorted, pointing to the guards.

"Commander," Minha said, raising his voice to address the crowd at the same time, "you forget that you are guests on this world. You—"

"This is how you treat guests?" shouted an angry female voice from behind Kadohata. "You herd them into pens like animals, give them only the minimum they need to live, if that?" She was joined by a chorus of other unhappy voices, echoing and expanding upon her sentiments. As their volume and the emotions rose, the Selkie guards grew more uneasy.

Kadohata turned toward the increasingly restive crowd. "Please, everyone, I know you're all tired and frustrated, but this isn't helping."

"And when are we going to see some real help, Commander?" the same voice demanded. "How long are we supposed to tolerate this?" she asked, over a rising swell of supportive cheers from behind her.

Minha clearly had had enough at this point. He

turned to the guard closest to him and, in a near whisper, told her, "Fire a warning shot over their heads."

"No!" Kadohata shouted with enough force to startle the young woman Minha had given the order to, and make her hesitate long enough for the commander to tell the commandant, "What is it you're warning them of? That you can shoot down a crowd of traumatized and unarmed people if you want to? Is that the message—"

But Minha wasn't listening. "Private!" he snapped at the female guard, and she quickly raised her weapon and pressed the firing stud. A phaser beam shot into the sky, drowning out every other sound on the field with its distinctive high-pitched whine. The mob screamed, many of them either fleeing or throwing themselves shaking on the ground.

Almost instinctively, Miranda reached out for the still extended phaser rifle and, using a move she had learned in Commander Worf's *mok'bara* class, wrenched it out of the guard's hands. She now held the weapon . . .

. . . and she found herself facing over thirty Selkies drawing their own weapons on her. Those refugees remaining and on their feet looked desperate enough and ready to charge the natives, the odds be damned. *Please, don't let me have started another bloody war,* she silently begged the universe. . . .

• • •

"Hold your fire!"

Jasminder Choudhury, operating on almost pure instinct and adrenaline, ran down from the top of the small rise where the transporter had put her team down, moving directly between the line of uniformed Selkies and the crowd of nonnatives. The *Enterprise* had just established orbit and was in the process of beaming Doctor Crusher's most critical patients to sickbay, when its sensors had read a single phaser discharge near the encampment border. Without even thinking, Choudhury had rushed to the transporter room, calling to the security officers on standby, and mounted the platform with them.

It wasn't until she was halfway down the slope that it occurred to Choudhury that she had beamed down unarmed, in violation of protocol. Fortunately, her uniform and her authoritative demeanor were enough to keep either side from escalating the situation any further. She approached Kadohata, standing midway between the two groups with a harsh-looking Selkie man wearing high rank insignia on his uniform breast. "Commander," she acknowledged the second officer, and then turned and offered a hand to the man. "Commandant. Lieutenant Jasminder Choudhury, *U.S.S. Enterprise.*"

"Finally," he said, giving her hand only the most perfunctory of squeezes. "You'll be removing this rabble at last, then?"

Choudhury forced herself to keep her expression impassive and nonthreatening. "We are here to alleviate the current situation and to ensure the safety and protection of all Federation citizens."

The Selkie commandant shrugged. "I just hope you're up to the task," he said, pointedly looking from Choudhury to Kadohata. He then turned to his troops. "Back to base."

The Selkies withdrew, except for one medic who stayed by the side of an injured human lying on the ground. Lieutenant Giudice went over to assess the situation, then he and the downed man disappeared in an emergency transport beam. Meanwhile, Choudhury adjusted her combadge for voice amplification and addressed the refugees: "Everyone, please return to the camp. We have further relief supplies on the way."

That proved incentive enough for those who were still gathered there, and the crowd rapidly evaporated away back over the rise. Choudhury reset her combadge and announced, "Choudhury to *Enterprise*. The armed confrontation has been ended. One potential casualty has beamed aboard."

"Excellent work, Lieutenant Choudhury," Commander Worf said. She could hear the proud smile in his tone.

"That was brilliant timing, too, Jasminder," said Kadohata once she'd ended transmission. "I don't know how I would have worked free of that spot."

"You shouldn't have had to be put in it in the first place," Choudhury said, looking her up and down. Her almond-shaped eyes were underscored with dark bags, her black hair hung limp around her oval face, and dried mud caked nearly every inch of her barely recognizable uniform. "How are you holding up?"

"Just tired, that's all, but never mind me," Kadohata said, fixing her with a deeply sympathetic look. "How are *you*?" The two women had not seen one another since their respective leaves following the *Enterprise*'s return to Earth spacedock, and Choudhury couldn't even recall having spoken to Kadohata at all in the hours following the loss of Deneva.

"I'm . . . I'm getting better. It's hard," Choudhury admitted for the first time of her own volition, "but I'll be all right."

"I'm sure you will, Jasminder," she said, reaching out and giving her arm a quick squeeze. "Well, I'm glad you're all right, and I'm glad you and the ship are here. There's a lot that needs to be done."

"Well, by all means, Commander," Choudhury said, gesturing for her away team to follow them, "Let's help these people out."

Both Acting President Barrile and Governor Tiernan had protested loudly all during the journey to Pacifica, up to and including their security-escorted walk from their VIP cabins to the transporter room. Captain Picard largely ignored their invective as he instructed Ensign Luptowski to put the three of them—plus their security escort—on top of the runabout, reasoning that would be a good vantage point for them to take in the entirety of the iy'Dewra'ni camp.

All the newcomers let the sights, sounds, and scents of thousands of homeless Federation citizens living in conditions closer to those of the fourteenth century than the twenty-fourth wash over them. "Mercy . . ." was all Tiernan could say, his earlier complaints dying in his throat as the enormity of the situation sank in. Barrile, for his part, was at long last struck mute by the grim reality before him.

"I hope you gentlemen now understand why I felt it so vital that you see this place with your own eyes," Picard told them in a low, even tone. "Because this is what's become of the Federation. That we can allow something like this camp to exist on one of our member worlds should shame us all."

"Hell," Barrile muttered, shaking his head as if unable to accept what his senses were telling him. "How could something like this be allowed to happen? Where are the Selkies? Why aren't—?"

"No!" Picard said sharply. "We cannot sit back and point the finger of blame at others, while we decide to close ourselves off and focus on our own problems to the exclusion of all else." Picard looked pointedly at both leaders. "These people are our fellow citizens. It is the responsibility of us all to do what needs be done in this time of crisis."

The two politicians did not disagree; they were still trying to recover from their shock and disbelief. Captain Picard, having seen many horrors in his career, especially over the last several weeks, was able to regain his bearing more quickly. In a way, he envied these men, who had not yet formed those emotional calluses. Still, he showed no pity for them.

"Come," he said, gesturing for the rest of the group to join him as he walked to the stern of the ship and lowered himself onto the column of footholds that ran down the rear hull, "let's get a closer look, shall we?"

"Computer," Ensign Gliv said as he stood up off his knees, "activate Emergency Medical Hologram."

The newly replaced holoprojectors around the infirmary powered up, and the form of a petite human woman appeared in the center of the ward. "Hello, how may I be of assistance?"

"She's alive! Alive!" Gliv exclaimed.

Crusher ignored his obscure joke and told the Mark IX EMH, "Hello, Nina. Please run a self-diagnostic."

A thoughtful look crossed the face of the thoroughly modern hologram, who then reported, "My available memory has been significantly curtailed, but otherwise, I am functioning at acceptable levels."

Crusher nodded, pleased. "Nina, your program has

been transferred to the infirmary of the iy'Dewra'ni Refugee Camp on Pacifica. Hopefully, your program won't be needed here, but just in case."

"What about the *Enterprise,* Doctor Crusher?" the hologram asked.

"We'll make do without an EHM for the time being." Crusher looked around at her surroundings. The *Enterprise* had beamed down or replicated the equipment for a state-of-the-art medical facility, but even with new biobeds, scanner arrays, monitors, and a surgical arch, there was no disguising the fact that they were in a plain, makeshift plastiform shelter. "This place is the very definition of emergency."

"Yes, Doctor," the EMH said, looking somewhat forlorn as Crusher ordered her deactivated and she faded into nonexistence.

"She didn't seem very happy about staying here," the Tellarite engineer noted.

Crusher nodded. "They're becoming more and more lifelike with each generation. Could we use one of the computer cores in the runabout to give her more memory?"

"If we still had any computer cores in the runabout," Gliv said. "Commander Kadohata had me move the library station into the administration building for the camp census data."

Crusher scowled, although she certainly couldn't fault Miranda for first having the same idea she did. As she tried to formulate an alternative option, Doctor th'Shelas approached. "Doctor

Crusher? Doctor Tropp just asked me to let you know that the infant, Matthew, has come out of surgery. He was able to repair all organ damage, and the patient is in stable condition."

Crusher felt as if the planet's gravity had suddenly been halved. "Oh, thank goodness," she said. She wasn't sure if she could have ever forgiven herself if, by grounding the runabout, she had put the child in greater danger.

"We have matters under control here now," the Andorian continued, considering her with one antenna crooked. "You should feel free to return to the ship any time you wish."

Crusher considered that, and then she turned to regard the patients still occupying the infirmary. They were not so ill as to need to be transferred to sickbay, but they still needed care. "Thank you, Shelas," she said as she picked up a padd, leaving her colleague to just stare at her back as she started doing rounds.

As powerful a blow as the initial sight of iy'Dewra'ni was, speaking with the individuals caught there was like a photon grenade blast between the eyes. Spouses separated from loved ones. Children separated from parents. People who had never in their lifetimes known want, afraid they might not get their next ration of food, or who broke out sobbing in the middle of their daily routines for reasons they couldn't quite articulate. But the worst were the ones who did not tell their stories, who only stared back mutely, their eyes glazed over and their minds barricaded behind defensive walls built up by their psyches.

The men eventually split up: Tiernan stopped to talk at length with a cluster of his fellow country-men and -women, and Barrile found himself frozen when a two-year-old child rushed up, grasped his shin, and shouted, "Pa-pa!" The boy realized his mistake when the governor looked down and gave him a direct look, and he ran off, frightened and miserable.

"Captain Picard!" He turned and saw Commander Kadohata approaching from behind him, with Lieutenant Choudhury right behind. "Oh, you're a sight for sore eyes, sir, if you don't mind my saying so."

"It's good to see you as well, Commander," Picard said warmly.

"I understand the *Enterprise* is the only ship we're to expect here for the foreseeable future," she said, exchanging a rueful look with Choudhury. "Is that right, sir?"

Picard sighed as he looked around and reflected on the scope of what surrounded them. "For the moment, yes, it's just us." The captain turned and started walking slowly back toward the runabout and the camp entrance.

"I was rather afraid of that," Kadohata said, falling in step beside him. "On the other hand, I'm quite thrilled that any relief has come." She held up a padd for the captain to see. "I've been prioritizing the needs of the camp and the people."

"We're already addressing many of the most basic concerns, such as medical care and food supplies," Choudhury interjected.

"Excellent," the captain said. "If the two of you would then coordinate with the appropriate department heads. We're here to do everything in our power for these people."

"That's good to hear you say, sir," Kadohata said, "because what these people really need is to be taken somewhere else."

Picard felt his entire body sag. There were close to eighty thousand people in this camp alone. There were more refugees, he knew, in other regions of the planet, and on scores of other worlds as well. The *Enterprise* could take a fraction of these people aboard and relocate them to Omicron Ceti or Typerias, but would that solve anything, or would it simply transfer the humanitarian crisis from one site to another?

". . . That way, we could get up to ten thousand of these people onto the *Enterprise*. That would greatly alleviate the burdens . . ."

"Ten thousand?" Picard said, suddenly aware that his second officer was still talking to him, and slightly embarrassed for tuning her out. "The *Sovereign*-class rescue profile gives a maximum figure of sixty-five hundred evacuees."

"It would be a tad uncomfortable, sir," Kadohata

said, "but it could be done . . . if we were deter-mined to do so."

Picard chose not to respond to the challenge in her tone just then. "Let's address the immediate concerns for the moment; we can discuss further options at a later time."

Kadohata nodded, showing slight disappoint-ment. "Aye, sir," she said.

Picard nodded back, and they reached the pre-fab building adjacent to the grounded runabout that housed the infirmary. As he moved toward the entryway, Kadohata added, "There is also a more personal matter I should like to discuss with you, sir, at a more opportune moment."

The captain turned back to regard his second officer, wondering at the curious tone she had used. Her face betrayed nothing, though, so he only nodded before walking into the camp infir-mary. As expected, he found Beverly still hard at work, checking on the condition of each of her remaining patients, even as her Andorian intern trailed behind her, quietly mentioning how unre-markable these remaining cases were and that he felt fully capable of taking charge of the ward. "Doctor Crusher," the captain called out, finally causing his wife to stop in her tracks and turn around.

"Captain Picard," she said, allowing herself only a hint of a smile. The infirmary was her domain, and she maintained complete professionalism.

"I've been expecting a report from you, Doctor."

"Of course, Captain. I . . . have a copy in the runabout. Doctor Shelas?"

The other doctor did not try to hide his amusement as she excused herself and led the captain to the ship. Kadohata and Choudhury were directing a small team of engineers to remove more matériel from the main part of the runabout, while Crusher and Picard wound their way forward to the cockpit. Once the door slid shut, and they were alone, Beverly's arms were around his neck, and they were locked together in a firm and ravenous kiss.

After lingering for several moments like that, reaccustoming themselves to this togetherness, Jean-Luc pulled himself gently away, looked deep into her eyes, and said, "You realize, I hope, that you had no real authority to ground and disassemble this vessel. Any recompense paid to the DPA will come out of your pocket."

"Excuse me?" she answered, giving him a mock-stern glare. "Is this the same man who kidnapped two Federation political leaders and brought them here against their wills, lecturing *me*?"

" 'Kidnapping' is such an inflammatory term . . ."

"But not exactly inapt," Beverly concluded his thought. "Jean-Luc, really, what were you thinking?"

"The same as I suspect you were," Picard answered. "That ordinary efforts would no longer suffice in the situation presented. That I could not simply refuse to do anything while the Federation as we've always known it crumbled around us." He gave a single dry chuckle and smiled humorlessly. "And to think, just days ago, I was absolutely euphoric at the thought of a universe without the Borg, and being free to become an explorer again."

Crusher gave him a more genuine smile back. "After all you've been through in your life, Jean-Luc, the fact that you've managed to hold on to that passion of yours . . ." She paused, and seemed to debate whether to mention whatever thought had just entered her mind. "You know, I've been thinking a lot about Jack over the last few days."

"Oh?" Picard said. Even though it had been nearly thirty years since his death, Picard still felt a sharp pang whenever his thoughts went back to his good friend, and his wife's first husband.

"Or, not Jack, specifically," Crusher amended, "but about . . . losing him, and how I lost myself afterwards. It's important to remember your passions, especially in times like this. We all have to hang on to as much as we have left, and as tightly as we can."

Before Picard could say anything to that, his combadge chirped, and Worf's voice said, "Enterprise *to Picard.*"

"Yes, Number One?"

"Sir, you have an incoming priority message from Admiral Akaar."

Picard's shoulders sagged. He was actually a bit surprised that it had been this long before the admiral had tried to contact him, but that made him no more eager to hear from him. He looked to Beverly for a bit of silent encouragement, and then tugged at his uniform and said, "Relay the message through the *Genesee*'s comm system." Crusher stepped back out of range as Picard sat in the forward pilot's seat and turned to face the screen to his left. "Admiral."

The centenarian Capellan stared daggers at him from across almost half the width of the Federation. *"Picard, explain to me what in the hell you think you're doing,"* he demanded.

"Sir, the *Enterprise* is responding to reports of an emergency situation on Pacifica—"

Akaar cut him off. *"Do you suppose there is currently any situation anywhere in the Federation that could not be classified as an emergency?"*

"I'd suspect very few, sir," he acknowledged.

"How did you determine the emergency situation on Pacifica was so dire that you had to abandon your assigned mission to Alpha Centauri III?"

"Doctor Crusher alerted me to the deteriorating situation—"

"So, it was your wife," the admiral practically sneered.

Picard bit his tongue. Akaar was a Starfleet traditionalist, who had vocally opposed Will Riker's decision to put his wife Deanna Troi in a key position aboard the *Titan* and who had also been none too happy when word of his and Beverly's recent nuptials had reached Starfleet Headquarters. "It was my chief medical officer," Picard told the admiral, "while on a mission for the head of the Displaced Persons Agency."

"And it wasn't some ethereal voice or mysterious psionic link that drove you to disregard orders?"

Picard bristled at the admiral's mocking tone. "No, sir," he said through a clenched jaw.

Akaar rubbed a hand across his tired-looking eyes and down his stubble-covered cheek. *"Picard, I think you'd agree that you were given extremely broad latitude in your current mission, yes?"*

"Yes, sir," Picard granted.

"And I should have hoped that, even given so much rope, you might have avoided hanging yourself, but no. They're screaming for your head on Alpha Centauri, and the Denevan councillor is no happier with you, either."

"Sir, if I could just—"

"Save it, Picard," the admiral snapped back. *"Whatever your excuses, this is no time for renegades. You are to leave Pacifica immedi—"*

And the screen went blank.

"Admiral?" Picard said, despite the clear evidence that the signal had been interrupted. He tried a series of controls on his panel, but the admiral was gone.

The cockpit door slid open behind him, and both he and Crusher turned to see Kadohata and Choudhury take a single step in. "Excuse us, sirs," the second officer said. "I'm sorry. We were salvaging the runabout communication relays for use in the camp. I didn't realize until too late that it was in use."

"Really?" Picard asked, arching one eyebrow

at her, and then at Choudhury. "That was rather careless. You cut off Admiral Akaar just as he was about to issue new orders for the *Enterprise*."

"Oh," Kadohata said, doing a serviceable job of looking surprised at learning that.

"Sorry, sir," Choudhury added. Far from looking contrite or shocked, she seemed to have at last regained much of the calm self-confidence Picard had come to expect from her.

"I suppose there's no real harm," Picard finally said. "He'll simply recontact us."

"I just checked with Commander La Forge," Choudhury then informed him. "The long-range transceiver was one of the systems we didn't get fully repaired before leaving McKinley, and it's posing intermittent problems. He can't guarantee we'll be able to receive any signals from Earth . . . for a while."

"Indeed?" Picard fixed both women with as stern a glare as he could muster. Then, he sighed. "Well. That being the case, I suppose the only thing to do is to carry on with what we're doing here, until we're able to reestablish contact with the admiral."

"Aye, aye, sir," agreed all three of his officers, including Crusher, who was no longer even trying to keep a straight face. Kadohata and Choudhury slipped out of the cockpit, and Picard turned to his wife. "You know, Beverly," he said, scowling as he rubbed the bridge of his nose, "we have had so many difficulties rebuilding this crew over the past year. Trying to replace Will and Data and Deanna and Christine . . . learning the hard way that we'll likely never recapture the chemistry we all had for so long. . . . Now, I have my operations officer and our chief of security colluding in a scheme to circumvent the chain of command . . ."

He then dropped his hand, lifted his head, and smiled at his beloved. "I think this new team is at last starting to come together."

14

"This is unacceptable!"

Worf considered the man on the viewscreen with the bland, impassive expression he had perfected over his four years as an ambassador. "To what, precisely, are you referring, Secretary Bemidji?"

The Selkie official expelled a hissing stream of air bubbles in exasperation. *"We called the Federation in to remove these . . . off-worlders from iy'Dewra'ni. What you're doing now is establishing a permanent colony!"*

Worf leaned back in the conference room chair and crossed his arms over his chest. "We are replacing the cloth shelters originally fabricated for the refugees with sturdier structures, but they are no more permanent—"

"If they're not permanent, then when are they coming down?" Bemidji demanded. *"When is Starfleet going to do what they were sent here to do, and give us our own planet back?"*

Just a few years earlier, Worf would have responded to this belligerent posturing in kind, baring his teeth and defending the honor of his fellow Starfleet officers in a throaty growl. What he said now was, "I can assure you that Starfleet and the Federation government are doing all they can to address your concerns." It was bland and, though perfectly true, largely meaningless. Yet, Worf could not see how this noisy *grishnar* was worthy of anything more from him.

"Do not insult me, Commander! It's bad enough that Captain Picard refuses to speak to me directly, making me deal through his underlings." Worf almost scoffed at the obvious attempt to rile him with the double insult. Bemidji knew full well Picard was right now in the middle of the iy'Dewra'ni camp looking for the very solutions he was agitating for; apparently he thought provoking an impolitic outburst from the Klingon officer would strengthen his negotiating position. *"I will take this directly to the Federation Council if I have to!"*

"That would be your right, sir," Worf said. "I for one would be fascinated to hear Pacifica stand up before the Council and announce they were unwilling to help those Federation citizens whose worlds have been destroyed. Given that so many of the planets razed were former Earth colonies, and that the plurality of refugees on Pacifica are humans, I am certain all of Paris will greet such an announcement with great interest."

The minister had no immediate rejoinder to that, and Worf took advantage of this, saying, "If you'll excuse me, Mister Secretary, I have other matters to attend to," and ending the transmission. This turned out to be true, as Worf noticed a waiting message from the bridge once the screen went blank. He stood up from his seat as he keyed open a new comm channel. "This is Commander Worf, *Enterprise.*"

On the wall screen appeared a human woman with a rounded face and a head of dark curly hair, sitting behind the desk of a small ready room. *"Commander Worf. It's been a while. I'm pleased to see you back in uniform."*

"Thank you, Captain Cukovich," Worf answered. Martina Cukovich had been commander of the *Litvyak* ten years earlier, during the Federation's brief war with the Klingon Empire. As strategic operations officer on DS9, Worf had had a number of interactions with Cukovich during that conflict, as well as during the war with the Dominion that followed. She was now the captain of the *Nansen,* which had been one of the ships that fought the Borg at Beta Rigel during the recent invasion. "What can I do for you, sir?"

"You can let me speak with Captain Picard," she said, dropping her earlier polite smile.

Worf had suspected as much. "I'm afraid he is not currently aboard," he said.

Cukovich blew out a gust of air in annoyance. *"Commander, I have been ordered by Admiral Akaar to intercept the* Enterprise, *relieve Captain Picard of command, and if necessary, place him under arrest on charges of kidnapping. Now, between you, me, and the bulkhead, I don't relish the idea of taking one of the captains who finally stopped the Borg and throwing him in chains. But I don't have a lot of options, not if you're going to continue to have all these 'communications issues.'"*

Worf clenched his teeth as he nodded. He had readily approved of Captain Picard's plan to bring Barrile to Pacifica, but the Klingon was becoming concerned that they had misjudged what the eventual result would be. The captain and his "guests" had been on the planet surface for just under six hours, and other than orders to beam down supplies and matériel from the captain, he'd heard nothing that indicated any progress. Not for the first time, Worf wondered if Will Riker had faced the same issues, or if the captain just enjoyed watching his Klingon first officer squirm. "I will convey your message to Captain Picard as soon as I am able," he said to Cukovich.

"Well, I hope that's within the next two and a half hours, because that's when we'll be making orbit," Cukovich said. *"Nansen out."*

Worf considered the black screen for several seconds after Cukovich signed off. Then he signaled the bridge. "Ensign Rosado, patch me through to the captain."

• • •

Picard leaned back in the runabout seat, frowning at the blank screen. The audacity of what he had done had not fully dawned on him until now; it was more in the character of the brash young ensign who'd helped Cory Zweller cheat a group of Nausicaans at dom-jot half a century ago than the man he'd since become. And yet, he didn't have any regret for what he had done. They'd improved living conditions at iy'Dewra'ni tenfold, and had gotten President Tiernan to offer an additional two hundred thousand non-Denevan refugees permanent settlement on Ingraham D. And if George Barrile could remain unmoved by what he had seen here, at least Picard could comfort himself knowing he'd done what he could. Though he knew that would be very weak comfort in the brig.

A scraping sound pulled Picard's attention to the runabout cockpit door. It was pulled open manually—the automatic servos had been salvaged for a piece of equipment in the infirmary—and Commander Kadohata entered. "Sir," she said, with a hopeful smile, "have you finished with the communications relay?"

"Hmm? Oh, yes, certainly . . ." the captain said, starting to stand to offer her his chair.

"No, sir, you're fine there," she said, reaching in front of him to reconfigure the setup. "Rather, I think you'll want to stay and listen." She tabbed a key and said, "Kadohata to Rosado. All set up there, Jill?"

"Standing by, Commander," the relief operations officer replied from aboard ship.

Picard looked up curiously at the younger
woman. "What is this?" he asked.

Kadohata answered with another grin. "We've
resolved our long-range communications problems,
sir," she told him, then tapped her combadge.
"Kadohata to Choudhury. Ready when you are."

Picard was still watching Kadohata when he
noted, from the corner of his eye, the comm screen
reactivating, and the image of George Barrile,
standing just outside the runabout, with the camp
behind him. He looked uncomfortable for someone
who, as a longtime politician, was surely used
to public speaking over subspace. After a brief
moment to gather himself, he looked up directly
through the screen and began to speak:

*"This is Governor George Barrile of Alpha Cen-
tauri, and I am speaking to you today from the
planet Pacifica. And this is the iy'Dewra'ni Refugee
Camp on Pacifica,"* he said, as the image moved
away from him and across the settlement behind
him, *"where about eighty thousand Federation
citizens forced from their homeworlds by the Borg
have been relocated. Until a few hours ago, these
people were living in tents, with only limited access
to adequate medical care, facing shortages of . . ."*

Barrile's voice trailed off, and the video sensor moved back to catch him looking at the scene
himself, his fist over his mouth, shaking his head.
"These images can't do justice." He slowly pulled

his eyes away and turned to face his audience. *"My words can't do justice. We've all been seeing images and hearing accounts like these on the news services over the last couple weeks, but . . . they're just not real to us. There's a camp not unlike this one just ten minutes' walk from my office in New Samarkand; I have not bothered visiting it. We humans eliminated scenes like this, scenes of poverty and disease and hunger, centuries ago. We've been so comfortable for so long in the Federation that we can't conceive of the idea that these evils can rise up again and overwhelm us. Worse, we can't even see it happening right under our noses."*

He paused. *"Citizens of Alpha Centauri . . . citizens of the Federation . . . it is happening right now.*

"Just days ago, I was sitting in my office resenting the way my comfortable existence had been disrupted, and in my self-absorption, I resolved to launch a campaign asking my fellow Centaurians to vote on whether we should secede from the Federation. Now, thanks to an utterly audacious act that has shaken me out of my complacency, I've resolved to add a second question to this plebiscite, asking whether we as Centaurians should reassert our commitment to the ideals set forth in the Articles of Federation. To renew the promises we made over two centuries ago to the peoples of Earth, Vulcan, Tellar, and Andor, and to all the peoples who have come after, to be a united society, dedicated to our mutual welfare and survival.

And I hope we will not be the only ones to reaffirm our commitment to those ideals at this crossroads in our history.

"I thank you for your time and your attention," he concluded, and then the screen went dark.

Picard looked up to Kadohata again, who was wearing a triumphant smile. Picard gave her a small nod and said, "Well done, Commander."

"The credit belongs to you, Captain," she said modestly. "You brought the governor here; I only guided him the last few meters."

Picard nodded again as she exited the cockpit, leaving the captain to consider the governor's address, and whether or not it might accomplish anything. It also occurred to him that with their communications "problems" now solved, he could expect to hear directly from Akaar, probably before the *Nansen* arrived.

"Let's hope his words do not fall on deaf ears," he said softly to himself.

Worf had gone to the transporter room to meet the captain. Picard's boots and pant cuffs were caked in mud, and a thin coat of sweat covered his head and face. "Number One," he greeted Worf as he stepped down from the platform. "Is Captain Cukovich still standing by?"

"Yes, sir," Worf said.

"Well, then by all means, let's not keep her waiting," he said to the ensign behind the control console. Picard stood beside Worf, his soiled uniform in marked contrast to Worf's immaculate clothing, making the Klingon feel strangely inadequate in comparison. "Energize."

The human woman materialized moments later, and stepped down as Picard said, "Captain Cukovich. Welcome aboard the *Enterprise*."

"Captain Picard. Commander Worf," she said, nodding to both. She was half a head shorter than Picard, but carried herself in a way that gave her the appearance of height. "I don't suppose you've reestablished communications with Admiral Akaar since Governor Barrile's address?"

"No, I've not heard from him," Picard said. They had hoped that what the Centaurian had said would have served to mitigate Akaar's ire and changed Cukovich's orders.

Unfortunately, this seemed not to be the case. "Neither have I, despite repeated attempts."

"A taste of my own medicine," Picard suggested.

The other captain shrugged. "Whatever the reason, my orders are now as they were." She surprisingly pulled herself up even straighter. "Captain Jean-Luc Picard." Picard likewise brought himself to full attention. "By order of Admiral Leonard James Akaar, Starfleet Command, I hereby relieve you of command of the *U.S.S. Enterprise,* pending a formal review."

Picard betrayed no emotion as he answered, "I stand relieved."

Cukovich then turned to Worf. "Commander Worf. I am putting you in temporary command of the *Enterprise*."

"Sir," he said, "with respect, I cannot take command."

Cukovich narrowed her eyes at him. "And why not, Commander?"

Worf shifted his weight from one foot to the other. "Because I supported Captain Picard's decisions, and because I believe it is essential that our current efforts here at Pacifica not be halted or suspended."

"Who asked you to halt or suspend anything?"

Worf and Picard both gave the *Nansen* captain looks of surprise, which generated an amused chortle from her. "Of course, Captain Picard is entitled to an expeditious hearing, but as long as he's in no hurry to get back to Earth . . ."

Picard looked at the woman askance, then said, "I'm willing to waive that particular right."

Cukovich said, turning back to Worf, "I would agree with your assessment, Commander, that the situation here is of a greater priority."

The Klingon considered Cukovich a moment longer, then allowed himself a small smile. "In that case, I accept command."

Cukovich nodded, then said, "Well, *Captain* Worf, I think the *Nansen* and the *Enterprise* should coordinate our efforts here. And if Captain Picard, having witnessed the situation on the ground, has suggestions . . ."

Worf shook his head. "Commander Kadohata and the other members of the DPA team have already made very thorough reports. I believe regulations state Captain Picard should at the least be confined to quarters."

Both captains stared at Worf agape. "Number One?" Picard said warningly.

Worf then turned to the transporter operator. "Contact Doctor Crusher and have her beam up immediately. I believe her unauthorized grounding of the *Genesee* warrants similar measures."

Cukovich hid a smile behind her hand as Picard's expression quickly shifted. "Ah. Yes, well . . . regulations are regulations," he said. Worf did not bother to hide his own smile.

It was impossible to look like a serious and respectable authority figure while wearing a hydration suit. At best, one could only hope to look not quite totally ridiculous.

Secretary Bemidji, fortunately, was too old, and too angry, to care about such things. Grimacing, he tugged the suit's hood over his gill crests as the aeroshuttle broke through the surface of the ocean into Pacifica's troposphere. He was at the age where he had now spent more than two-thirds of his life underwater, and the memories of his younger days living on the surface grew blurrier with each passing year. As the transport passed the apogee of its ascent, and then made its jarring landing at the edge of the iy'Dewra'ni encampment, he had difficulty even remembering the last time he'd set foot on dry land. He'd long ago reached the position where he could make air-breathing off-worlders come to him in hi'Leyi'a, and send younger subordinates to deal with matters needing attention above.

Once the shuttle was drained and repressurized, the hatch opened and Bemidji stepped out onto the surface of his planet. He used a polished worm-shell cane with pearl inlays to help make up for the lack of buoyancy he had in the air, again heedless of how it might be perceived, as he made his way to where Commandant Minha stood along with the human man, Dillingham. "Mister Secretary," the lawyer greeted him, while the commandant snapped to attention.

"Mister Dillingham. Commandant," Bemidji replied, his voice sounding alien as it passed through thin air to his eardrums. "What word of the injured man?"

"Mister Wheeler suffered a subdural hematoma and a mild concussion, along with lesser injuries. But he's now fully recuperated, thanks to the arrival of the *Enterprise*."

"Good news," Bemidji said, then turned to the commandant. "Minha, would you care to explain to me how this man was injured while within the area deemed a safe haven for the Borg refugees?"

"I failed in my responsibility, Mister Secretary."

Bemidji nodded, and at the edge of his vision,

he noted Dillingham nodding also. He of course knew the full story, and understood the impulses the men who attacked Mister Wheeler felt. But that excused nothing, neither in his mind nor, he was sure, in the minds of Dillingham and the Federation officials he was to report back to. "Thwa Minha, I've been obligated to inform you that you are relieved of your position in the iy'Dewra'ni Division."

Minha dipped his head again in an apparent show of remorse. In fact, Minha was nearing the end of his amphibious phase, and would have had to forfeit his position in a matter of months anyhow, when he was no long able to use his lung for breathing out of water. By letting himself suffer this little humiliation in front of the Federation observer, Minha lost little, while Pacifica, one hoped, regained some degree of respect from Paris. And after those images got out to the rest of the galaxy, Pacifica would need all the help it could get in that regard.

Dillingham smiled a large, toothy smile, and stepped forward with his right hand extended. "Secretary Bemidji, I appreciate your personal intervention in this matter. Thank you."

Bemidji let Dillingham pump his glove-encased hand. "You're welcome, Mister Dillingham. And," he added, as he started back toward his shuttle, "have a safe and speedy trip back to Earth."

• • •

Arandis was in a plain, sterile sickbay, breathing in air that smelled of absolutely nothing. She wore a loose-fitting medical gown that covered almost her entire body, from her neck to her wrists and ankles.

She had never felt so contented in her entire life.

The Risian listened to the steady rhythm of medical monitors chiming and beeping throughout the open ward, evocative of Algolian ceremonial music. She closed her eyes and let it soothe her, until she heard a set of footsteps approach. Opening one eye, she saw Doctor Tropp grinning down at her. "Hello, Arandis, and how are you feeling?"

"Better and better," she said with a grin of her own.

"Excellent," the Denobulan said as he looked up at her monitor. "We'll be coming around with lunch soon. Do you feel ready for solid foods?"

Arandis put a hand on her abdomen and realized that the discomfort she'd felt in her stomach and bowels over the last day and a half was now totally gone. She'd overheard Tropp telling another Starfleet officer how the *Enterprise* computer had found the genetic something-or-other easily, far faster than the runabout's computer could have, and led him to a more effective cure that would work on all cross-species mutations of the contagion. "Yes, please," she said, then asked, "but . . . could I still have the soft-food dessert? The . . . what is it called?"

"Cherry gelatin?" Arandis nodded, and the doctor gave her an indulgent smile. "I think that could be arranged." Arandis beamed back at him as he patted her hand and moved to the next bed. After a lifetime of tending to the wants and desires of others, it was nice to have others taking care of her, instead.

As she was finishing her pasta lunch and digging her spoon into the chilled, wriggling treat, another person approached. "Hey, darling, how are you doing?"

Arandis looked up at Don Wheeler, and smiled out of habit. "I'm fine. And how are you?"

"Good as new," he said, rubbing the underside of his now clean-shaven chin. If he had suffered an injury there, there was no scarring or any other sign of it. "They're moving me out of sickbay, into general quarters. I'll be sharing a cabin meant for two with eight others, but only until Starbase 18."

"And where from there?" Arandis asked.

His smile fell away then. "I don't really know yet. I've been thinking about Tellar, maybe."

"Good wines there?" she asked.

"No," Wheeler answered, making a sour face. "The Tellarite palate is like the human appendix."

Arandis didn't quite understand the analogy, but got the general meaning. "Why there, then?"

"It's doing something." He shrugged, then asked, "What about you?"

"I haven't thought much about it," she said. When she did, all she could think about was what she couldn't do: return to Risa. And without that option, what difference did it really make where she went? For now, she simply turned away, and spooned a cube of gelatin into her mouth.

This is like all moments: only temporary, she thought, as she savored the sweet dessert dissolving on her tongue. In the end, what happened next was up to the Givers. She would take pleasure in it for as long as it lasted, without concern for the moments to follow.

The children had been shooed off their soccer pitch, sent running back to their parents and caretakers. Taking their place on the field were one hundred eighty-four Kazarites, Cygneti, Dopterians, Pentamians, and others who had homes on nearby worlds to return to, but had been stranded on Pacifica during the crisis. They disappeared, six at a time, as they were beamed aboard the *Nansen*.

Miranda Kadohata watched from the sidelines, standing alongside that ship's captain. "Like trying to drain a lake with a teaspoon," Cukovich said just under her breath.

Kadohata nodded in acknowledgment, though she was feeling far more optimistic than the captain. *At least now we have a teaspoon, and there's hope we're not simply all going to drown.* Not only was the *Nansen* taking some five thousand refugees aboard, but there also were now two additional ships in orbit: transports out of Bre'el that had just returned home several hundred of their own evacuees, and upon hearing Governor Barrile's address, had headed for Pacifica. They were able to take aboard several hundred Trill authors and editors, who had been attending a literary convention at an Eden Beach hotel and had been stranded there during the invasion. Though they had been quite comfortable in comparison to those at the iy'Dewra'ni camp, they were more than happy to leave—and open up their rooms for several hundred iy'Dewra'ni transients who had, as yet, nowhere else to go.

"Still not enough," Cukovich grumbled as another half-dozen people dissipated into columns of light and energy. "Admirals and their half-assed—" she started, then stopped herself and turned to look at the woman next to her.

"I'm sorry, sir, I didn't hear you," Kadohata said in deadpan assurance.

Cukovich smirked, still slightly chagrined. "Thank you, Commander." She turned away again, back to the field.

A moment later, she said, supposedly still to herself, "I don't imagine Picard would be so shy about expressing his opinions of the admiralty, no matter how insubordinate, hmm? Seeing this, and knowing that all of them are just sitting there in San Francisco, celebrating the end of the war. Same damned thing that happened after the Dominion War. Betazed still hasn't one hundred percent recovered from their occupation during the war, did you know that?"

Kadohata decided that was a simple enough question that she could safely offer an answer. "Yes, sir. I was there just over a year ago." At Will Riker's and Deanna Troi's Betazoid wedding ceremony, Lwaxana Troi had complained to anyone who would listen about her ongoing struggles to bring more resources to her homeworld.

"And they're far from the worst off," Cukovich continued. "But instead of launching a concentrated rebuilding effort immediately after the war, we just did a little bit here, a little bit there, sometimes letting things go until they reached emergency status, like the damaged space elevator that nearly collapsed on that Tellarite colony. Criminal is what it was. And if they think we can dawdle like that for another four, five years this time . . ." Cukovich looked around at the camp, and blew out an exasperated breath. "I'm afraid we're going to find out we won the war against the Borg, only to lose the peace to our own complacency. And if we let that happen . . ."

Kadohata considered that possibility in silence. She couldn't imagine it coming to that; this war had been far more destructive and disruptive than the one with the Dominion, and undeniably called for a different response. At the same time, Kadohata had to admit the response she'd witnessed so far was not encouraging. "We all just have to do what we can," she said under her own breath.

Her combadge chirped, and Ensign Gliv's voice

reported, *"Commander, we've established your link to Cestus III."*

"Thank you, Gliv," she said, and then turned to Cukovich. "Excuse me, Captain."

The captain smiled at her. "Thanks for not listening."

Kadohata returned the smile. She then crossed the camp at a deliberate clip, and when she reached the *Genesee,* slipped into the cockpit and into the seat at the active communications console. She keyed the transmit key, and her smile widened as the image from home appeared on the screen. "Hello, Vicenzo. Hello, Aoki."

"Hi, Mummy!" her daughter, seated in her father's lap, shouted.

"Honey, the babies are sleeping," Vicenzo admonished her mildly.

"Hi, Mummy," Aoki repeated in a whisper. *"I miss you."*

"Oh, I miss you, too, darling, a whole lot. You too, love," she added to Vicenzo.

"Same, sweets," Vicenzo replied, half smiling. *"You're still on Pacifica, then?"*

"Yes," she said, nodding slowly. "It's still a right mooo horo; it'll bo moro than a whilc cleaning up."

"I saw the pictures," Vicenzo said, nodding. *"And the address Governor Barrile gave. It really looks dreadful."*

"It is," Miranda said simply.

Vicenzo continued to nod, then, after a mildly

awkward silence, took a hitching breath and said, *"Miranda, I'm sorry."*

"Sorry, love?" Kadohata asked, confused.

"I know what you do is important. And I really am—we *really are proud of you,"* he amended, squeezing Aoki tighter on his lap, eliciting a squirmy giggle from her, *"for doing what you do, even if it means some sacrifices."*

Miranda fought to hold back tears as she smiled into the face of this dear, sweet man who meant more to her than anything else in the universe. "I have some news, dear. Like I mentioned, it's going to be a time setting things to rights here. So . . . I've decided, when the *Enterprise* heads off . . . I'll be staying."

Vicenzo blinked. *"What's that, now?"* he asked.

"I've asked Captain Picard to allow me to remain on detached duty to the Displaced Persons Agency," she explained, "to continue to help with the refugee crisis here. It's a huge challenge—like being operations officer for a half-dozen starships—and it's such important work. Plus . . ." She smiled broadly then. "I'll be right here, set in one place."

Aoki seemed to catch the implications of this faster than her father did. *"How far 'way is Specifica?"* she asked excitedly.

"Pacifica, dear," Miranda corrected her kindly. "And it's only a few days by runabout."

"But, as busy as you'll be . . . ?" Vicenzo started to ask.

"I'm promised more help in the next week,"

Kadohata said, "and once things are in place, organized and up and running, I should have more flexibility in my schedule." She felt her entire face expand with her smile as she added, "So, we need to make plans for a big birthday party!"

Miranda Kadohata would forever treasure the looks of joy that blossomed on her family's faces.

15

———

Lieutenant Taurik had to admit to being impressed by the thought and planning that had gone into the *Enterprise*'s role in the evacuation of iy'Dewra'ni. Whereas the specifications for the *Sovereign*-class ship stated that it could transport a maximum of sixty-five hundred passengers in addition to a standard crew, every spare bit of space aboard was being utilized in order to relocate nine thousand eight hundred and seven from Pacifica to Ingraham B. In addition to filling the cargo bays, shuttlebays, laboratories, holodecks, the Happy Bottom Riding Club and other, smaller lounges with refugees, the regular crew was doubling and tripling up for the duration. The entire security team had given up their quarters, opting instead to "hotbunk" on cots in the corners of the armories and weapons control rooms. Captain Picard had said he was hard pressed to think of a time he had ever been more proud of his crew.

Unfortunately, the situation made the restricted areas of the ship more appealing to anyone wanting a little bit of privacy. And the Jefferies tube above the main shuttlebay observation deck had apparently been irresistible to one such person. Taurik inadvertently winced as he lowered himself to his hands and knees to open the hatch. He had not slept well in days, and the current accommodations were not helping in that regard. He also had not had the opportunity to meditate since leaving Pacifica, and the combination of these factors had inspired quite a few un–Vulcan-like thoughts about what he might do to whatever unauthorized person or persons he might find in the ship's restricted area.

He activated his tricorder and held it ahead of him with one hand as he crawled through the access tunnels. As it turned out, he didn't need it— after crawling just a few meters, he could hear crying up ahead. After a few more meters and a sharp left turn, he encountered T'Ryssa Chen, sitting with her legs folded to her chest and her forehead resting on her knees. Taurik froze, instinctively repelled by the naked display of emotion from this woman who, from all appearances, was no less Vulcan than himself. He watched her silently for several seconds, almost as if entranced, before saying, "Lieutenant Chen."

Her head snapped up sharply and turned. "Oh, hell, it's you," she said with a horrified look on her face. "Go away! Leave me alone!"

"You are not authorized to be in this area," the engineer told her.

"Here's your authorization," she said, and gave him a hand gesture that might have been a Vulcan salute minus three fingers. "I'm not hurting anything. I just want to be alone—need to be alone for ten damned minutes. Just let me be."

Taurik imagined himself whipping his hand out, grabbing hold of the histrionic woman's neck, and then dragging her unconscious form out of the Jefferies tubes, perhaps just dumping her in the corridor. He blinked those thoughts quickly away, disturbed by how he was letting Chen's undisguised emotions affect him. In an effort to counter these ideas, he lowered himself on his haunches and asked, "What is wrong?"

"What, like you care?" she shot back.

"It is often helpful to articulate one's thoughts coherently," Taurik said, paraphrasing one of Surak's teachings on emotional control for the half-human woman.

Chen glared at him, took a noisy breath through her nose, and said, "You wanna know? Okay. My mother, who I thought was alive, is dead. My father, who I used to consider dead, is alive. My grandparents, who I never knew existed, don't anymore. And the person who finally started to help me get over my mother-abandonment issues just left the ship herself without even saying good-bye!"

"You're referring to Commander Kadohata?"

Taurik asked. Given the chaos surrounding their departure from Pacifica, it was hardly logical to fault the commander for not saying individual farewells.

Chen laughed unkindly. "None of the rest of that even registered with you, did it? Mother. Father. Grandparents. They're just meaningless words to you, aren't they, you cold-blooded bastard?"

"Not meaningless!" Taurik snapped back. "Do not think, because of your mixed blood, that your losses are greater than mine!"

He instantly berated himself for his uncontrolled outburst. But now Chen was staring at him in wide-eyed amazement. "My blood has nothing to do with it," she said defensively. "You're the one acting like your wife and daughter being killed doesn't bother you."

Taurik stared back at her, unable to mask his disbelief. "What sentient being would not be bothered by such a thing? Surely, you know the power of Vulcan emotions."

"Well, it wasn't my human half that made me break down like a baby in the middle of breakfast," she mumbled.

"Then you must understand how powerfully I feel—"

"I don't understand jack about Vulcans. I mean, come on—you just told me it's better to articulate thoughts coherently. You didn't even go to the memorial; what is anyone else supposed to think?"

It was with no small shock that Taurik realized that Chen had made a valid point. She might even have put her finger on the problem that had been unsettling Taurik since the destruction of ShiKahr.

"I grieve," he said aloud. "I grieve for my mate. I grieve for my daughter. I grieve for all of ShiKahr, I grieve for all of Vulcan, I grieve . . ." He fell silent then, using all his strength to keep his expression of emotion limited to these simple words.

After a moment, Chen replied, "I grieve with you . . . uh, thee."

The two sat there in the Jefferies tube for an extended period of time together, silently.

While Ingraham B was an M-class planet, it was not a terribly hospitable or pleasant world. The original Earth colony established there in the early twenty-third century had a difficult time maintaining a subsistence living even before they were wiped out by the extraplanetary neural parasites that had later attacked Deneva. There had been a minor effort to reestablish the colony shortly thereafter, but most would-be pioneers at the time opted, at the Federation's urging, to settle the new worlds of the Taurus Reach instead. There had been occasional subsequent attempts at resettling the world, but they never attracted more than a handful of settlers, all of whom eventually left for greener pastures within a matter of years.

Now, the simple fact that this planet still had its atmosphere was enough to make it a desirable home. And with its huge new population and twenty-fourth-century technology to access the planet's largely untapped resources, it was hoped this time Ingraham B would flourish.

"But it's never going to be Deneva," Gar Tiernan lamented as he stared across the choppy gray waters of the planet's largest ocean. Jasminder Choudhury, standing beside him on the rocky shore, said nothing.

She had finally found the nerve to approach him during their visit to the Pacifican camp. She'd introduced herself as a fellow Denevan, which triggered his ingrained politician's response. "A pleasure, Lieutenant," he said, giving her a broad white smile and a firm, trustworthy handshake. "On behalf of the Denevan people, let me tell you how proud and grateful we are for your service, particularly in this time—"

Choudhury indulged him briefly, but then cut him off to ask, "Sir, what can you tell me about the evacuation of Mallarashtra?"

The man stopped in midsentence. "Is that where you were from?"

Choudhury nodded. "That was my home province. That's where my parents and family lived."

Tiernan's eyes softened in sympathy. "I should have guessed from the accent." He paused to formulate his answer, then said, "It was one of the only regions where there were no reports of violence or other problems during the evacuation. Unfortunately, that was because they almost all refused to go. Young children and their parents only. The rest of the community . . ." He shook his head in wonderment. "They only filled about half the seats on the transport that was sent for them. To see that kind of selflessness, in the face of . . . It was really remarkable."

"I see . . ." Choudhury said softly. Half a standard transport filled—which meant only three to four hundred evacuees. And tens of thousands of others, refusing to save themselves at the cost of another life. Knowing that her family had made a choice, that it wasn't something she did, or failed to do . . . well, it didn't take away the grief. But, hearing how they embraced their fates with eyes open, without fear, did ease her mind.

"I visited there once," Tiernan interrupted her thoughts. "Mallarashtra Province. With my ex. The Crescent Valley Retreat. Beautiful old place; you know it?"

"I worked at the Crescent Valley when I was a teenager," Choudhury said, grinning in spite of herself.

"This probably would have been before your time," he said, with a wink. "We loved the fountains that they had there, in the main courtyard. Every night after sunset, when they were lit up with all those multicolored lights, we would go out and stroll around them arm in arm . . ."

"That was where I had my first kiss," Choud-

hury admitted, smiling as she thought about Geeta
Jalal for the first time in twenty-five years.

They talked for hours, at iy'Dewra'ni and during the voyage to Ingraham B. Tiernan told his
story about watching Deneva's come-from-behind
victory over Bolarus in the 2338 Federation Cup,
and Choudhury told hers about the freak blizzard
that hit Mallarashtra when she was five. Both
exchanged memories of touring the *Libra* as school-
children, and of the Bicentennial World's Fair in
2361, and visits to the Summer Island Playhouse
and the Winston Memorial Art Gallery . . .

But since beaming down to Ingraham B, Tiernan
had been strangely withdrawn and quiet. Choudhury, acting as his personal guard and escort, walked
with him as he circled what would be the heart of
the new colony, considering it all distantly. Once he
completed his circuit, he muttered, just barely loud
enough for Choudhury to hear, "Little wonder this
planet's been abandoned for over a century."

He turned toward the nearby coast, and once
there, climbed up onto a large, weather-polished
boulder. He sat, knees up and together, staring at
the horizon. Choudhury scaled the big rock as well,
and stood back a few meters behind him.

"We're never going to rebuild all that we had,"
he said at length. "Not here. Not on Deneva—even
if we do rehabilitate the planet, it'll be a different
planet. There'll never be another Mallarashtra or
Lacon City. It won't be the same Summer Islands,
or the same Crescent Valley. . . . Deneva is gone."

"No." Choudhury stepped up to stand right beside the president. "The geography is gone, and the landmarks. But how can you say Deneva is gone, given all the time we've spent together, proving that it does still exist." She tapped her forehead, and then the center of her chest. "Here. And here."

Tiernan gave her a cynical look from out of the corner of his tear-filled eye. "Right. Lieutenant, I appreciate what you're trying to say, but *this*"—he pointed to his own chest—"is not what I'm talking about. I'm not interested in the metaphysical."

Choudhury was about to make a retort, but she held her tongue. Her beliefs were a personal thing, just as loss and grief were. Explaining that all physical things are impermanent, and that attachments to those things cause unhappiness, would not help him. Truth was, it was barely much help to her.

Sensing that the president wanted to be alone, she moved farther up from the shore, though still keeping him in sight. Behind her, she heard a heavy pair of treads moving toward her over the scrub grass. "Is anything wrong?" Worf asked.

Choudhury looked back at him over her shoulder and shrugged. "It'll just take time, that's all. When you lose so much, you just have to keep reminding yourself about how much you still have left," she said, at the same time reaching out and taking his hand in hers. Worf looked down in mild surprise, then looked up at her again, smiling.

• • •

As luck would have it, Chen's quarters were among the first to be emptied of refugees at Ingraham B. She now sat alone in the privacy of her cabin, as she had for nearly half an hour, staring at the blank monitor on her desk.

What are you so scared of? she asked herself. *There isn't anything he can do to you that he didn't already do twenty-five years ago.* And yet, it took an additional half hour, plus two servings of liquid courage, before she gathered enough nerve to hit the key on the base of her monitor.

Moments later, he was on the screen. He'd recuperated significantly since the last time she'd seen him. His hair had grown out some more, and the bandage that had covered most of the right side of his head was gone. Only a slight greenish discoloration indicated where new skin had been grafted on; in another couple of days, it would look completely natural. In contrast, his right eye had been replaced by a mechanical optical implant, identical to one of Geordi La Forge's. *Well, that's just going to creep me the hell out the next time I talk with him,* she thought.

"*Lieutenant Chen,*" the Vulcan said, dipping his head.

Chen took a breath, hesitated, then in a rush of air said, "Antigone is dead."

The Vulcan man paused. "*I see.*"

Oh, you see, Trys somehow kept herself from saying out loud. *Ah, well, great, I'm so glad I made the effort to let you know, considering what a pro-*

found effect the news is having on you. Even after her strange encounter with Taurik in the Jefferies tube, she still couldn't wrap her mind around this idea that what you saw of Vulcan emotions was not necessarily what you got. Of course, the fact that her mother was the supposed subject of his supposed emotions made a bit of a difference . . .

"I am sorry."

Trys thought her eyelids would tear at the corners, they had popped open so wide. "What?" she asked. "Don't you mean, 'I grieve with thee'?"

Sylix tilted his head. *"I thought the human sentiment to be more appropriate, considering."*

Trys shook her head. To think that she had almost believed he meant he felt actual sorrow. "So they're just empty ritual words to you, aren't they?"

"I am sorry," he repeated, making the words sound anything but empty. *"I do regret your mother's untimely death."* In fact, the words were full to overflowing.

A million questions went through Trys's head. *Really? Why? What do you feel for her now? Why didn't you feel it for her when you left? What do you feel for the daughter you made with her? What now?* But what she said, after a significant silence, was, "Well, you wanted to know, and now you do."

"Indeed."

"So . . ." Again, an uneasy silence grew between them. Trys thought she could see him contemplating a lot of the same questions she was. *What do you feel now for the father you never knew, T'Ryssa Chen?*

What now?

"I should be going," Trys said.

"Certainly." Sylix started to raise his split-fingered hand, but then seemed to think better of it, and awkwardly curled his fingers into his palm before dropping his hand in his lap. *"Good-bye, T'Ryssa Chen."*

And just like before, her hand hesitated just above the key she wanted to hit. "One more thing." The older man, who had already started to look away, jerked his head back around toward her. "If you ever get the urge to contact me again . . ." Trys said, looking him straight in both eyes, "I may not be completely averse to the idea."

The bastard still didn't smile before she ended the call, but Trys did get the impression that, deep down, he kind of wanted to. That was something, anyway.

It was the most productive chaos Picard had ever seen.

Nearly two hundred transports and smaller ships were in orbit of Ingraham B, most of them Denevan in origin, most on their fifth and sixth trips here. They were running to worlds like Aldebaran and Kreetassa, which like Pacifica were being overwhelmed by Borg escapees, and bringing back those willing to make this rough world their new home. In addition, two more Starfleet ships had come, technically in violation of their own orders, in order to assist in the refugee crisis.

"Commander Henderick's team thinks they can revive the old colony's water works," said Captain Zilssom of the *T'Pora*, referring to the leader of that ship's S.C.E. team. The *Saber*-class ship had initially been sent to survey for topaline in an uninhabited system nearby. "Most of it is terribly deteriorated, no surprise, but they believe they may be able to—"

"Yes, by all means," Picard said, nodding at him from across the *Enterprise* conference room table. Worf had magnanimously decided to allow him out of his quarters, although Beverly, after sleeping through the entire journey from Pacifica, had decided to continue taking advantage of her incarceration. Picard looked up from his padd to see the Tiburonian staring at him, nonplussed by his interruption. Picard gave him a half grin and said, "If a Corps engineer says it can be done, the explanation behind that judgment is usually superfluous."

"Just ask them not to make *this* planet disappear," joked Captain Mary Beth Sterling of the *Courage,* which was currently experiencing "a minor navigational malfunction" during their patrol of Sector 009.

"If you're going to rebuild the water system, you'll want to reintegrate all the old colony's plans into your survey maps," added Doctor Byxthar, who had taken a keen interest in witnessing the creation of this new Denevan homeworld, "and take it into account before breaking ground on any permanent structure. Otherwise, you'll have the same problems the Bajoran colonists on Golana did when they first discovered the old ruins—"

The doctor was cut off by a call from the bridge. *"Captain, we have another starship dropping out of warp and entering the system,"* said Ensign Balidemaj, who was manning tactical. *"It's the* Esquiline.*"*

"Uh-oh," Zilssom said. At the looks of the others, he explained, "Right now, every engineer on my ship is crowding at the windows, tongues hanging out, trying to get their first direct look at a *Vesta*-class ship."

Sterling snorted in amusement as Balidemaj added, *"They're hailing you by name, Captain Picard."*

"In here, Ensign," Picard said, moving to the wall-mounted screen at the far end of the room. At the press of a button, the *Esquiline* bridge appeared, and Picard recognized her captain, Parimon Dasht. But his attention was drawn first to the towering man standing to the captain's right. *"Captain Picard."*

"Admiral Akaar," Picard replied, straightening to attention.

"Prepare to receive me aboard."

"I stand ready."

The admiral looked past Picard. *"Sterling. Zils-*

som. It would be best if neither of you crossed my path."

"Yes, sir," both said as the screen went blank.

Picard made his farewells to the others in the room, and then stood and waited alone in the silent lounge for his superior officer to arrive. Even though he had been expecting the hammer to drop at any time, he was still surprised by the admiral's appearance. For the head of Starfleet to have come all the way from Earth, this was not likely to be a typical reprimand—perhaps he planned to personally keelhaul him.

Yet, Picard found himself remarkably calm, and when Akaar was escorted into the conference room, the captain stood, smiled warmly, and shook his hand, as if they'd run into each other at a holiday party. "Good day, Admiral," the captain said. "You made extraordinary time from Earth."

"The *Esquiline* has just been fitted with its new slipstream drive," Akaar said. "This trip had the primary purpose of testing the new engines."

"And the secondary purpose?" the captain asked.

The admiral glared down at him from his impressive height. "We have a problem, Picard," he said, starting to pace the room. "Do you understand the way the chain of command is supposed to work?"

"I believe so, sir," he answered, as politely as he could.

"The way the chain of command is supposed

to work," the admiral began, ignoring Picard's response, "is that we have the most experienced, most knowledgeable, and most intuitive people at the top, deciding what needs to be done, and giving orders to those under them to do it." Akaar gestured to the padds still strewn across the table in the center of the room. "Clearly, that is not what's happening here. Even relieved of command, you still manage to accomplish all this . . ."

Picard remained at attention as the admiral continued to pace and shake his head. "You were assigned to address a crisis on Alpha Centauri, and what you did was to abduct the governor and take him to the far edge of the Federation at the behest of your wife. No matter how influential Barrile's address was, or how loudly he's praising you now for helping him see past his own nose, kidnapping a government official goes beyond the pale, Picard."

"Aye, sir," Picard said, putting on his best poker face. He had resolved, when he first left Alpha Centauri, to face whatever consequences were levied for his actions. But still, he did sincerely hope that Barrile's advocacy would be given some weight once judgment was passed on him.

"And yet, there's no denying how out of place you are in the chain of command," Akaar continued, "so, we're going to have to promote you."

Had he been playing poker, Picard would have betrayed his hand at that point. "What?"

"We've lost Janeway, Ross, Jellico, plus Owen

Paris and dozens of others during the war," Akaar explained, his sorrow for his lost colleagues evident in his eyes. "We're facing an entirely reshaped and tenuously held together Federation, and frankly, it would be a lot easier to deal with a disagreeable equal than a disagreeable subordinate. You would be the primary director of our postwar rebuilding efforts, deciding how ships and personnel and matériel get allocated and moved around. It's going to be a vitally important role, Jean-Luc, and one in which I believe you will excel."

Picard recovered his composure and listened intently as the admiral further described this surprise promotion. When Akaar had finished, he responded, "I am deeply honored, Admiral. But, I must decline."

"Now, don't be rash, Jean-Luc."

Picard lifted an eyebrow, slightly amused by the fact that he and the admiral were apparently now on a first-name basis. "Forgive me, but it sounded as if I was being offered the position because of my tendency for rash decisions."

"For your *correct* decisions," Akaar countered. Picard was about to point out that his rash decisions were not deemed correct except in hindsight, but the admiral was continuing: "You've proven yourself. You've earned this. It's a chance for you to make a real difference."

Picard chuckled to himself. "A wise man once told me, 'Don't let them promote you, don't let them transfer you, don't let them do anything that takes you off the bridge of that ship. Because while you're there, that's where you can make a difference.' "

Akaar rolled his eyes. "And what fool told you that?"

"Admiral James T. Kirk."

Leonard James Akaar was, for the first time in Picard's experience, left speechless. The Capellan's life had been saved by the legendary Starfleet captain prior to his birth over a century earlier. His mother had given him his middle name, James, in honor of the man. And when Picard invoked his name, and repeated the advice Kirk had given his successor as the *Enterprise* captain in the last hours before his death on Veridian III, Akaar dropped his sneeringly contemptuous expression. "There's little point in arguing with that, then," he muttered.

The admiral turned away and started to pace the room, moving as if about to buckle under the weight he carried on his shoulders. The meeting had obviously not gone as he had anticipated—no doubt, very little over the past two months had gone as anticipated. Akaar's attention fell again on the collection of padds on the table, and he picked up one that displayed the planned layout of the new Ingraham B colony, supposed to support one and a half million displaced transplants. "There are a lot of differences needing to be made, Captain," he said, "and a lot of differences to be made in the way we approach them."

He turned, and held up the padd. "In a way,

we've been given a knock backwards to Kirk's era: our territory much smaller, millions of people heading for new worlds that will need our support for years before they become self-sufficient. . . . Maybe it is best to leave you here, Picard," he said, tossing the padd back onto the pile of others. "Maybe what we need more than another admiral is another James Kirk."

Now it was Picard's turn to be at a loss for words. The admiral gave him a slight smile and a nod, then turned to go, leaving Picard to consider his final comment.

And he could not shake the sense that the old Capellan admiral, in drawing his parallels between the two eras and the two *Enterprise* captains, had called down a curse upon his head.

EPILOGUE

Stardate 58357.1

Fromander IV wasn't such a bad little planet, after all.

Jean-Luc Picard stood atop a small rise and gazed out across a grassy plain that stretched all the way to the horizon. In the near distance, a herd of large, green-haired animals, somewhat akin to bison, grazed peacefully, ignoring the cadre of Starfleet science officers moving around them with tricorders in outstretched arms. The initial long-range surveys of the system done forty years earlier had identified this planet as being class-P— glaciated and incapable of sustaining humanoid life. More recent evidence, though, suggested those early determinations might have been inaccurate, so the *Enterprise* had been charged—following its latest supply run to Cestus III—with taking a second look. What they found was a world that, while apparently in the midst of an ice age and largely covered with glaciers and permafrost, featured a belt of land at the equator, about five thousand kilometers wide, rich with flora and fauna.

A stiff breeze sent the long grasses rippling like waves and cut through Picard's uniform jacket like a cold blade. He didn't mind, though; the thrill of discovering a new class-M world nobody expected to find, and being among the first to walk its surface, was enough to let him ignore the elements.

His thoughts as he admired the view were disturbed by the beep of his combadge. He gave it a responding tap and said, "Go ahead, *Enterprise*."

"Captain, you have an incoming message from Admiral DeSoto."

Picard smiled again. His old friend and the longtime captain of the *Hood* had been offered the promotion Picard had turned down. He had accepted and had been doing a superior job of directing Starfleet's recovery efforts. The captain made his way down the small hill to where his shuttle had landed and activated the small screen. "Hello, Admiral," he said as the white-haired man appeared on the screen.

DeSoto sighed and gave Picard a pained smile. He was still growing used to the title, and had asked Picard repeatedly to continue calling him Robert. This time, however, he skipped the collegial banter and said, *"Jean-Luc, we need you to pull your people off Fromander IV and back into Federation space proper."*

Picard was taken aback both by DeSoto's orders and by the dire tone he had used to deliver them. "What? Why? It is looking extremely promising as a new refugee colony—"

"Unfortunately, not from this perspective anymore," DeSoto said. *"Not that close to the Gorn border."*

"The Gorn?" Picard echoed in disbelief. The Gorn had not been seriously considered a threat since a faction called the Black Crest briefly overthrew the old leadership seven years earlier, and attacked several nearby Federation worlds. "Has there been another coup?"

DeSoto shook his head. *"No, not a coup. I'm sending you a secure data packet that'll give you all the gory details. I'm sure we'll be talking extensively about this in the days to come,"* he said, sighing. *"DeSoto out."*

Picard reviewed the report as the *Enterprise* headed to Starbase 120. He had to go over it a couple of times to assure himself he wasn't misreading it somehow, and even then, it wasn't until President Bacco gave her press conference the following day, formally breaking the news to the Federation, that he began to realize what it meant.

The Gorn, the Romulan Star Empire, the Tzenkethi, the Breen, the Tholians, and the Kinshaya had united in what they were calling the Typhon Pact, posing an external threat that could distract the Federation from its vital recovery work. The president stated that the rebuilding effort would continue to take priority—and perhaps, as far as the Palais was concerned, that was true. But Starfleet, as the Federation's first line of defense, could not define its priorities the same way.

"Jean-Luc," Beverly said softly as she tugged the padd free from his hands, "there's no point in brooding over it. Come to bed."

Picard let her take the padd, but made no move to get up from his seat on the sofa. Beverly instead lowered herself next to him. "Look on the bright side: Zalda's reaffirmed its commitment to the Federation and to helping the refugees."

Picard couldn't deny that, although that good news was tempered by the discovery that the Typhon Pact had manufactured the story about Zalda refusing to take in refugees in the first place. Still, they were now the fifteenth member that had chosen to follow Alpha Centauri's lead. The vote for Governor Barrile's plebiscite had gone pro-Federation by better than a four-to-one margin, and had proved a great boon in convincing people all across the Federation to rededicate themselves to its ideals.

"I received another report earlier today," Picard told his wife distractedly.

"Oh?"

Picard nodded. "The *Titan* has crossed into the Canis Major region."

From Beverly's reaction, she understood what

that indicated—Will Riker and his crew were again off into unknown territory, resuming their mission of exploration. And she of course recognized the small flicker of envy her husband felt toward his former first officer. "You do know, of course, that Will told Admiral Masc that he wanted the *Titan* to help in the recovery effort instead?"

"Yes, I know," Picard said with a self-effacing grin. "It's just . . . it seems I've been deluding myself these last few months. The Caeliar absorption of the Borg collective was such a . . . *transformative* experience. What I felt . . ." He trailed off, still unable to put it into words. And as the days passed, the intensity of the incident had faded, bit by bit, from his memory.

"But, the end of the Borg really wasn't the end of the struggle, at least not for us," he continued dejectedly. In fact, a nine-ship fleet was right now readying to head off to the Delta quadrant in an effort to look for the Caeliar, the admiralty having thoroughly rejected his assertions about their ultimate disposition. "We will always have our threats; there will always be other concerns and issues, even if we have to invent them ourselves. It was foolish of me to have hoped otherwise."

Beverly shook her head and smiled at him. "You're not a fool, Jean-Luc; you're a romantic. Big difference. You were ready to believe in a transformed world, in a better world. I think that you still do, that it is possible to help make a better world for the future."

"Indeed I do," he said, smiling back deep into her eyes and laying his hand on her ever-expanding stomach.

A few minutes later they were in bed, and Beverly was soon fast asleep. She was becoming more easily tired as her pregnancy progressed, though she of course refused to admit it, and continued to insist on working her regular schedule in addition to all the extra recovery work. Picard stared up at the bulkhead that arced over their bed as he listened to her soft snores, considering her thoughts about the true meaning of the Caeliar's effect on him, and about where, in this post-Borg universe, his destiny lay.

After a moment, he reached to the bedside stand and tapped the control pad on its surface. Above his head, the exterior viewport, which had been set to opaqueness for the night, turned back to its transparent setting. Picard dropped his head back onto his pillow and stared up at the billions of unexplored stars overhead.

And he dreamt.

ACKNOWLEDGMENTS

My thanks first go to my editor, Margaret Clark, for giving me the opportunity to write this story, and for pushing me to make it better.

Of course, I must acknowledge David Mack for his epic, galaxy-changing, and kick-ass *Star Trek: Destiny* trilogy. (It doesn't quite feel right to "thank" him for destroying half the Federation.)

I will, however, thank the other members of the "Mack's Mess" clean-up crew—Christopher L. Bennett (*Star Trek: Titan—Over a Torrent Sea*), Kirsten Beyer (*Star Trek: Voyager—Full Circle*), and Keith R.A. DeCandido (*Star Trek—A Singular Destiny*)— for their eagerness to make the post-*Destiny* books fit together as seamlessly as possible. Special thanks to Christopher, for his collaboration on the development of the Selkies, which he was concurrently building upon in his *Titan* novel as I was working on this one.

I must also thank the other authors of the pre-

ACKNOWLEDGMENTS

Destiny, post-*Nemesis TNG* books: Michael Jan Friedman (*Death in Winter*), J.M. Dillard (*Resistance*), Keith DeCandido, again (*Q & A*), Peter David (*Before Dishonor*), and Christopher Bennett, again (*Greater Than the Sum*). And needless to say, we all owe much to all the creative people behind the *Star Trek: The Next Generation* television series and its film sequels.

In creating the iy'Dewra'ni camp, I referred repeatedly to the "Anatomy of a Refugee Camp" feature created by the CBC, at http://www.cbc.ca/news/background/refugeecamp/. I do wish to stress, however, that my fictional twenty-fourth-century refugee camp does not and could not present the terrible realities that displaced persons live with in this century.

I also want to thank all the other wonderful and informative websites, wikis, and weblogs around the Internet that helped along the way, as well as the Hennepin County Library for their more traditional method of keeping and distributing information and for providing lovely quiet places to write.

Finally, thanks to everyone who said, "Congratulations!" or "That is so cool!" when they learned I was writing a *Star Trek* novel. Never underestimate the value of a good ego boost to the author who barricades himself in a room alone with his laptop night after lonely night.

ABOUT THE AUTHOR

WILLIAM LEISNER is a three-time winner of the late, lamented *Star Trek: Strange New Worlds* competition, and his first novel, *A Less Perfect Union*, was published in the collection *Star Trek: Myriad Universes: Infinity's Prism* in 2008. In between, he has written the *Star Trek: Starfleet Corps of Engineers* eBook *Out of the Cocoon* (the title story in the print compilation due out in 2010); the short story "Ambition" in *Constellations*, the *Star Trek* fortieth anniversary anthology; and the novella *The Insolence of Office*, part of the *Slings and Arrows* eBook miniseries celebrating *The Next Generation*'s twentieth anniversary. A few more credits, and he might convince himself that he actually is a real writer.

A native of Rochester, New York, he currently lives in Minneapolis.

STAR TREK

TITAN™

SYNTHESIS

by James Swallow

Coming in November 2009

1

———

Floating there, Melora Pazlar reached forward and carefully, delicately, put out the star with the cupping of her hand. The most gentle of radiances pushed back at her fingers, brushing lightly against her palm. She held it there for a moment, wondering about the shadow she was casting across a dozen worlds, the great darkness she had brought. If she wanted, she could have seen it for herself. A simple command, spoken aloud. A shift in viewpoint, down to the dusty surface of some nameless planetoid. Easy.

"The thing about this place is," said a voice, "you could let working in here go to your head."

Melora grinned and let the sun go, falling backward, dropping away. She made herself turn in midair, the spherical walls of *Titan*'s stellar cartography lab ranged out around her, and found Christine Vale looking up at her from the control podium. "It's been said," she noted. "Sometimes it is easy to lose yourself in the scale of things."

Vale brushed a stray thread of hair back over her ear, unconsciously straightening a recently added gunmetal-silver highlight amid the auburn bangs. She glanced around. "Like looking the universe in the eye, right?"

"That's why we're out here." Melora drifted gently down to the same level as the commander—it was a subtle thing, but she had always thought it bad form to look down on a senior officer—and she floated closer to the podium. The small catwalk and open operations pulpit were the only sections of the chamber given over to Earth-standard gravity. The rest of the room replicated the microgravity environment that Melora had known growing up on Gemworld. Her tolerance for the so-called standard-g setting deployed aboard most ships of the line was poor, and when she wasn't floating here, a restrictive contragravity suit was required to prevent the stresses overwhelming her body. The technology was leaps and bounds beyond the powered chair or exoframes she had used in the past but still not enough to tempt her outside the lab without due discomfort.

Holographic projection grids hidden inside the walls threw out scaled images of stars, nebulae, and all manner of other astral phenomena, filling the lab with its own tiny universe. It was a great improvement on the earlier versions of the imaging system installed on the old *Galaxy*-class ships, flatscreen renditions replaced by this interpretation of the interstellar deeps. She gave Vale a smile. "Want to step up?"

The other woman folded her arms. "Nah. I'll stick to solid ground for the moment." She refused with a half-grin, as if on some level she was hoping that Melora would try to convince her otherwise. But then the moment passed, and Vale *tap-tapped* on the console before her. "You've got something interesting for us?"

The ghostly pane of a control interface followed Melora as she moved, always staying within arm's reach, and now she reached for it, nodding. "I'm starting to think we might need a new scale of defining things, Commander. After all the stuff we've encountered out here so far, *interesting* sounds a bit . . . bland." The Elaysian tapped out a string of instructions on the virtual panel.

Vale nodded. "It does seem like we're using up all the good adjectives." Temporal discontinuities and ocean worlds, interstellar conduits and cosmozoans, new life and new civilizations around every corner. When the uncanny and the unknown became commonplace, there was a risk you could become jaded. "Okay, not *interesting*, then. Let's shoot for . . ." She paused, feeling for the right word. "*Beguiling.*"

"That'll do." Melora triggered a command, and the matrix of stars and worlds shifted abruptly, enough that Vale reached out a hand to steady herself on the podium. From her standpoint, it had to be like standing on the prow of a ship plunging headfirst through the void. By contrast, any sensation of vertigo was nonexistent for Melora, who had lived most of her life walking on air. She adjusted the scaling of the display and drew them deeper into the representation of the sector block that lay ahead of the *Starship Titan*. The viewpoint closed in on a relatively isolated binary system haloed by the indistinct shapes of a few planetary bodies. "Here we are."

"You got a cute name for this one?" Vale asked lightly.

"Just a string of location coordinates and a catalog number at the moment." She reached out and widened the interface panel, unfolding new windows that displayed real-time feeds from the Titan's long-range sensor pallet. "Here's what spiked my attention. Lieutenant Hsuuri pulled this out of a cursory automatic scan of the sector . . ." She highlighted a string of peaks in a sine-wave energy pattern. "Cyclic output on the extreme eichner bands, very tightly packed together."

"Natural phenomena." Vale raised an eyebrow.

"Not like this," Melora replied. "At least, not like anything I've seen before. It's too precise, too engineered."

"Artificial, then."

The Elaysian gave a slow pirouette. "And there's more. See here, and here?" She brought up a second data window, filled with a waterfall of text readouts. "That looks like some variation of a Cochrane-type distortion. Very faint but definitely there."

"Starships?"

"Starships." A note of wonder crept into Melora's voice. "Maybe."